I0598560

Sun Valley Mafia

REMAKING A MAN

AMY CRAIG

Remaking a Man
ISBN # 978-1-80250-509-2
©Copyright Amy Craig 2023
Cover Art by Erin Dameron-Hill ©Copyright January 2023
Interior text design by Claire Siemaszkiewicz
Totally Bound Publishing

REMAKING A MAN

Dedication

To Anya Pavelle, an early writing friend
and a Florida babe.

Chapter One

Standing on the marble front step of her family's Miami mansion, Gisella tapped her designer footwear, adjusted her sunglasses and blocked out the bright spring day. She breathed deeply and shuffled the bags hanging from her toned arms.

At the end of the driveway, her brother Antonio revved his red convertible's souped-up engine and pounded the dashboard in time to blaring rock music. Miami traffic streamed past the estate. People stared.

Why can't he just leave? She marveled at his arrogance, but she kept her expression neutral and her phone in her pocket. He was the youngest of her two siblings, and he had the stocky, tan physique her male family members prized. He also had a propensity to wear outlandish suits, a revolving door of girlfriends and a sophomoric sense of humor. If he caught her taking a selfie in front of the house, he would turn it into a meme, but her account depended on dance stills and teasing hints of glamour. The minute he left the estate, she would take the picture while her hair looked good.

Flexing her toes, she rifled through the bags on her arms. One duffle held her ballet kit, another tote functioned as a purse and the bags from her morning shopping spree hiked her credit card bill. Instead of feeling guilty for the extravagance, she admired her long, lean legs.

Her form allowed her to excel as a professional ballerina, but she worried she had the coltish naivety to match her legs. When would she work up the nerve to demand a driver's license and stop relying on Antonio for transportation? Every time she talked about her license, her father pouted and asked what more he could do to ensure her comfort.

If her mother had lived, Gisella's life might be so different.

A car horn honked. A woman blew kisses. "Antonio!"

He ignored the entreaty, let the engine rumble and scanned the beachside traffic. His muscled forearm hung over the door, and he tapped his fingers against the expensive paint job. Milky fingerprints marred the convertible's finish.

A second Miami driver slowed to gawk at the handsome, moneyed mobster. A trailing car smashed the vehicle's lights. Horns blared and doors flew open.

Releasing the engine's pent-up energy, Antonio took advantage of the distraction and roared across two lanes of traffic.

Gisella rolled her eyes and snapped the picture she needed, but she doubted her high-gloss smile was worth the price of the photograph.

Riding home with her brother from dance rehearsals and a shopping spree, she had stared out of the window and listened to him complain about women and their fickle ways. His problems never changed, but the consistency soothed her. If he spent more time listening to the women, he would have fewer problems with them.

For instance, she had wanted to close her eyes and rest, but Antonio couldn't take a hint. As soon as she made Principal Dancer, she could move out of her father's house and make rent, but she would have to stop shopping like a mafia princess.

Squaring her shoulders, she faced her father's front door. Most Miami residents painted their doors to ward off humidity's warping effects. *Papà* imported Cocobolo heartwood and exposed the precious wood to the elements. His house could grace the cover of *Architectural Digest*, but his acceptance in local society depended on discretion. Biscayne Bay would freeze over before he opened the mansion's doors to gawking strangers.

Every piece of furniture came with a decorator's commission, authenticity papers and a cataloged serial number. The insurance company knew the exact cost of her father's investment, and if the house burned, they'd be wise to pay up.

She appreciated the wealth, but its origins bothered her. Her sweet *Papà*, Gregorio Vitella, ran drugs from South America up the Eastern shoreline. She feared that enjoying the proceeds made her complicit in his crimes.

Pressed by a tipsy ballet friend, she'd admitted the concession that let her sleep at night. Her father's legitimate insurance company probably covered her bills, but how could a person separate good money from bad people — and where did that distinction place her?

Pushing open the door, she scanned the marble foyer and dropped her bags, but a green potted palm, a black concert piano and an excruciatingly expensive console table provided little company. The console table rested on acrobatic loops of brass. Beneath a glass top, python skin gleamed with a subtle sheen, and she wondered if the piece's black crystal pulls would make an interesting jewelry set. Opening a drawer, she checked for mail and flipped through the family correspondence. "*Come stai, Papà?*"

Her question echoed.

Raising her head, she set down the mail and waited.

A hidden white paneled door opened. Martin, the butler, emerged, wearing the formal black suit and crisp white shirt required for his service. He'd perfected the practiced, subservient gaze on his own. She'd grown to like him, but she wondered how long he would last in the household.

"*Signorina* Gisella, your father is in his study."

Keeping a bright smile on her face, she handed Martin her shopping bags and kept her purse on her shoulder. "Thanks. I'll freshen up and join him."

"Yes, *Signorina*."

The man couldn't speak ten words of Italian. As soon as staff members picked up a basic understanding of the language, her father fired them. Smart members played dumb. Gisella found her allies among them, but she'd learned to mind her comments, too.

Ducking into the gilt-papered bathroom off the foyer, she pinched her cheeks, added lipstick and prepared to act like a dutiful daughter. Her life revolved around the Miami Ballet Company, beachside runs and formal dinners, but in her father's house, she would forever be 'Gigi'.

Bracing her hands on the sink, she tilted her head. Her loving father owned Florida's biggest commercial real estate company, Cosmica Insurance Holdings, but he also ran the Florida branch of the Italian mob.

He wore a suit to school functions, but when business soured at home, he rolled up his shirtsleeves, and the gentlemanly look faded. When she had been ten, she'd witnessed the reality of his business dealings through a crack in the study door. She'd never seen his victim again, and she'd kept her observations to herself — but she listened.

When classmates at her parochial school asked what her father did for work, she parroted the company line. "CIH offers property insurance, casualty insurance and value-added insurance services across twenty southeastern states."

They looked impressed.

Why shouldn't they? Every new homeowner in Florida received a direct mailing touting CIH's low rates and friendly staff. The mailings glossed over the company's potential money laundering credentials, but who read the fine print?

Leaving the bathroom, she made her way to the back of the house and to her father's study. The caviar-black masculine room had views of the pool and heavy leather furniture. Despite a sparking oasis waiting beyond the windows, the room looked like a cave.

Last fall, her father's interior designer Lisette had joined the family before Sunday dinner. Wearing a pantsuit, she'd sipped a dirty martini and made vague references to former clients. *"I prefer to create a visual impact by mixing wood species and texture. That movie star I mentioned"* — she sipped her drink — *"had a thing for ebony."*

Gisella had wanted to like the woman, but her influence on the house's décor leaned toward gilt and Hollywood glamour. Having a thing for ebony shocked her as much as Lisette's cosmetic surgery bill. Once a woman immersed herself in wealth, keeping life entertaining required novelty and a steady flow of cash. *"How do you plan to tackle the study?"*

Lisette had wrinkled her surgically enhanced nose. *"The hospitality industry uses black to create glamour, drama and intimacy. Everyone's doing it."*

Gisella had sipped her wine and assumed Lisette was doing her father.

Walking across the room, Gisella admitted the study's black walls created drama, but if her father wanted to scare his minions into compliance, he could pull out the handgun he kept in the desk's top drawer. To keep her in line, he deployed guilt. *'What would your mother think?'*

She wrinkled her nose.

Walking around the polished walnut desk, she leaned down and pressed a kiss to his cheek. He smelled of black tea, Damascus rose, tobacco and leather. At sixty-five years old, he looked ten years younger. Faint silver streaks threaded his black hair. He could wear chinos and he would still smell like old manners and aged wine caves. *"Come è andato il lavoro, Papà?"*

"It is what it is." Continuing in Italian, he set aside his papers. "How was your shopping trip?"

She sat opposite him and crossed her legs. "Fruitful."

He laughed.

Pulling a stack of receipts from her purse, she slid them across the desk. "The rest will come by email."

Shrugging, he leaned back in his chair and left the crumpled slips on the table. "Gigi, you're old enough to drink and old enough to marry."

She picked at her nails. "Is that so?"

"More than old enough. In the home country..."

Looking up, she tilted her head. "We're not in the home country."

He held up a hand. "But if we were, you'd be a bride, and I'd be a grandpa."

"Ursula is older."

"Your sister wants to be a nun."

"So she says." Looking past his full head of hair, she regretted her outburst and second-guessed her decision to come home after rehearsal. If she'd stayed out and shared a drink with Antonio, she'd have to listen to his stories and give up her evening run. She couldn't hide from her father. He financed her life and provided patronage for her art. Looking at him, she softened her expression and recalled the sunlit days he'd spent with her and Ursula. "You're too young to be a grandpa."

"Hear me out," he said.

She exhaled. Drinks with Antonio sounded better. At least he planned to fuck up his own life instead of hers.

When her mother had drowned off the Amalfi Coast, *Papà* had whisked his three children to Miami and begun a new life on the Atlantic's eastern coast. Given how he'd lost his wife, one would think he would have chosen Oklahoma, but he knew how to make money along a coastline. Aunts and nannies had sopped up spilled milk, but when he'd come home at night, he'd kissed her cheek and left his old-world scent against her shoulder.

Some nights, remembering the smell of roses and leather, she recalled how much consistency mattered to children and old men. "Yes, *Papà*."

"I have a series of eligible young men lined up. You will give them each an evening and tell me which man suits you."

"What if I prefer women?"

"Gisella Santa Maria Vitella!" He slammed his palm against the desk.

A vase rattled but resisted gravity's lure.

She rolled her eyes and stood. The dates her father arranged would be insurance agents or mob hit men. She couldn't decide which option she found more appalling. "I can find my own dates, Daddy."

He gripped the leather armrests. "Sit down."

Lowering her frame, she kept her back straight and maintained eye contact. The company's Artistic Director scared her more than her father did, but his familiar expectations could surprise her. Cosseted and pampered, she enjoyed an easy life until she slammed into a glass wall keeping her from enjoying life's stunning vistas. Eventually, she found an exit, and her father acquiesced to her wishes.

He cleared his throat. "You're too old to prance around the stage in a tutu."

She wet her lips. "Too old to dance, and too young to procreate. What's a girl to do? Marriage is a contract, isn't it? Do I get a lawyer?"

He raised an eyebrow.

Outside the mansion's walls, ballet defined her life and gave her predictability. At fifteen, she'd enrolled in the company school and trained for three years. After graduation, she'd joined the ballet as a School Apprentice and spent two years in the trenches before joining the corps de ballet. Three years later, she'd made Soloist, then Principal Soloist. The lure of becoming Principal Dancer kept her focused.

The goal also kept her father off her back. It was like he'd made a deal with his six-year-old daughter, and he refused to back out of his agreement. For the last twenty years, he'd sponsored the company's performances, but rarely attended them.

Last month, she'd celebrated her twenty-fifth birthday. Most dancers stopped dancing professionally between thirty-five and forty years of age. She'd known her father wouldn't give her that much time and would propose an arranged marriage. She might have to accept it, but an IUD would buy her time to achieve her dreams. Crossing her arms, she settled back into the chair.

Sometimes, she lay awake at night and imagined defying her father, but he killed the men who disobeyed him, and she lacked a mother to intercede on her behalf. Caught between ideals and reality, she walked a narrow line and kept her gaze focused on the future. Sometimes, she dreamed of her mother, but she wondered how much time had reshaped the memories.

She remembered holding her breath under water to watch fish, but now she hated to swim. Her inability to trust her memories undermined her faith in herself, and her father's coddling approach undermined her achievements. She could dance across the stage playing a role, but striking out on her own meant vulnerability. Until she knew she could succeed, she would humor his demands. "I hear you, *Papà*. Who's the first victim?"

"You will love Marco."

Tilting her head to the side, she rubbed her scalp. "Doubtful, but tell me where to report."

"You're a good girl, and you'll make me proud. I've tried to raise you the old way, but your aunts can't

15

replace your mother. I'm getting old. You've had leeway to pursue your dancing, but tomorrow evening at eight, you and Marco will dine."

She shook her head. "Not tomorrow, *Papà*. I organized a beach cleanup."

"You hate the water. Find someone else to pick up trash…"

Holding up her hand, she interrupted his mandate. "CIH is sponsoring the event."

His forehead wrinkled.

Maybe he was getting old. "Perhaps Tuesday?" she offered.

His nostrils flared. "Tuesday."

Standing, she rounded the desk, pressed a kiss against his smooth cheek and let his scent calm her frustration. How many times had he threatened her dancing? How many times had he shipped her back to Italy to take in the old country? Here she remained. Marco and the remaining suitors would fizzle out, and she'd continue dancing. "*Ti amo, Papino.*"

He pulled back. "You will go on this date."

"Sure." Picking up the receipts, she dropped them in the trashcan. "I have plenty of new dresses to wear."

"Gigi…"

She winked. Walking out of the office, she let her clicking heels say everything she held back. The marble-backed rhythm sounded so final, like the sound of a bullet fired at close range. Violence hung over her family like a constant threat. If her father understood anything, he understood endings. Keeping him focused on new beginnings remained her job.

Opening the door to her room, she shucked the heels for soft slippers, settled into a stretch and let the music guide her.

Ursula opened the door connecting their rooms and pushed a shoe out of the way. "I thought dancers didn't wear high heels."

"They do when they want salespeople to take them seriously."

Dropping to the floor, Ursula lolled her head. "You'd think a black credit card and a bodyguard would be enough to get their attention."

"You'd think." Gisella deepened her stretch and puzzled through Ursula's recent transformation. Her sister's dark brown hair, olive skin and generous curves could rock a bikini, but lately she'd insisted on dressing like a martyr. If Ursula deviated from her prayers and walked into a boutique, the salespeople might press the panic button. Gisella suppressed a smile.

Her sister had always been serious, but her devotion had deepened in the last six months. After Sunday mass, Gisella had known why. No longer content to hide behind her hymnal, Ursula had stared at Father Pietro, the hot new priest. The man of the cloth must have given Ursula a bit of pious encouragement.

Gisella shrugged and laid her torso along her leg. If Ursula wanted to plan her life around vespers, God love her. "How was your day?"

"Good. Lots of praying, solemnity, hymns and stuff."

Gisella raised her head. "And stuff?"

Ursula swallowed. "Church stuff."

"Maybe you could put the stuff on hold and help me cleanup the beach tomorrow. Every set of hands helps."

"Sure." Ursula stood. "I have a few hours to spare."

Watching her sister slip into the next room, Gisella judged her sister's choices. Dancing made her feel alive. Why would any woman dedicate her life to an organization that spent so much time imagining what came after death?

* * * *

"I bet you can't speak for ten minutes," Ursula said.

Gisella gripped the handheld microphone and kept her back to the assembled crowd. A cool morning breeze blew off the ocean, and gulls circled overhead. Licking her lips, she tasted salt and stubborn determination. "What's the bet?"

"Ten minutes, and I'll do this year's Christmas cards."

"All of them?"

Ursula crossed her arms. "Three hundred max."

Nodding, Gisella stepped onto the plywood box erected for better publicity shots. She took a deep breath, let the ocean air fill her lungs and turned to face the crowd.

A toddler stuck out his tongue.

The petulant kid brought a legitimate smile to her face. Flipping on the microphone's switch, she imagined herself on the theater stage. Suntanned locals held trash bags and pronged grabbers. What was the worst thing that could happen? She started a timer on her watch.

"Thank you for joining us this morning. CIH cares passionately for the environment, and so do I. One day when I came to this beach for a run, and I realized I'd seen more plastic than the previous day. From that day forward, I knew I had to do more than admire the scenery, but hauling off a few handfuls of trash wouldn't be enough. In the following weeks, I spent more time picking up trash than running, and my smart watch let me know it."

The crowd laughed.

Ursula skewed her jaw.

Gisella wondered if pregnant pauses stopped the countdown. She cared about the beach, and she could use her father's money to hire beachcombers, but picking up trash meant more than wiring money. She wanted people to know the Vitella family had depth.

Okay, maybe depth was the wrong world. Antonio's muscle cars had the subtlety of a flashing neon sign. *Wide-ranging interests?*

She looked past the volunteers and media representatives recording her speech. Waves lapped the sand, and children built sandcastles. Plastic debris, broken glass and abandoned plywood shouldn't decorate their creations.

She cleared her throat. "Every morning, I run by the ocean, and I feel a strong connection to this beach. It's my sanctuary and the one place I feel free. The ocean's health is important for the planet's health, but it's important for your health, too. After digging for crabs, the kids behind you shouldn't need a tetanus shot."

Audience members turned their heads.

Checking her watch, Gisella wondered how she would fill five more minutes. "CIH offers property insurance, casualty insurance and value-added insurance services across twenty southeastern states..." She choked on the canned line and slapped her chest. How many times had she spouted that line without blinking?

A woman in the front row raised her phone.

Damned if she would end up a red-eyed, live-streamed mess, Gisella cleared her throat. "But Miami is our home. I care about the planet future generations will inherit."

The CIH employees in matching neon volunteer shirts fiddled with their phones.

From the front row, Ursula yawned.

Contained boredom would help her win the bet, but she didn't want to torture the volunteers. She wondered if Marco stood among them. Maybe a little torture wouldn't hurt. "With your support, we can do more than pick up trash. We can promote environmental policies and plastic ordinances to improve South Florida's beaches for people and animals alike. Our friends up the beach have a local ban on non-biodegradable containers. Why can't we do the same?"

Political activism would get her in trouble with *Papà*, but he stayed in bed until noon, and she could spin the event to her advantage. Feeling the pull of a performance, she raised the microphone. "If we operate plastic and foam free, we'll have less trash to pick up. Why stop there? We could band together and oppose new offshore drilling."

Antonio, as the lead CIH representative, walked toward the podium.

He had an associate's degree and an Italian sports car, but he also had a direct line to her father and the ability to upend her life.

Squaring her shoulders, she focused on the crowd. "I love this ocean, and you're here because you love it, too." Checking her watch, she realized she needed another minute. "The next time you spy a manta ray, a sea turtle" — rubbing her eyebrow, she made a show of her confusion — "a manatee, a shark, a dolphin..."

Antonio held out a hand.

She clutched the microphone and ignored his request. "Or a fish, think of what your inactivity says to those creatures." She checked her watch. Thirty seconds. "Thank you all for your support. I hope CIH continues to serve you as well as you're serving your community."

Her watch vibrated.

"Thanks again for coming out!" Grinning, she looked at Ursula.

Ursula offered her a slow clap.

The CIH representative lifted the microphone from Gisella's hand. "Isn't she lovely? Let's give Miss Vitella a round of applause."

The crowd complied.

A few cat calls earned harsh looks from the CIH crew, but most of the audience members looked bored out of their minds. So much for her rousing speech. Walking to Ursula, she picked up a trash bag and snapped open the sides. "I love volunteer events."

Ursula accepted the bag. "You know they're all here for community service hours?" The wind blew her dark brown hair across her face. "Nobody cares about the beach but you."

"Oh, shut up."

Antonio walked up. "Fancy speech, Gigi. All that time running on the beach, I thought you just wanted to keep your ass in shape."

"Shove it," she said. "You went overboard on the cologne, and it doesn't hide the cigarettes. No wonder the gulls hover. You smell like dead fish."

He frowned. "Is that any way to talk to your brother? I'm a leader in this family."

Two cousins snickered from the sidelines.

Turning on them, she pointed a long, delicate finger. "I see you, Luca. Antonio might be my brother, but you're like a third cousin once removed." She lowered her finger. "Then again, so are half of the CIH executive team, but I don't see them interrupting my speeches."

Palms up, Luca and her other cousin backed away.

She raised her chin and gave Antonio her haughtiest Sicilian Mafia Princess stare. "Don't you have something better to do than babysit your sisters?"

Stepping back, he inhaled and narrowed his eyes.

Instead of browbeating the man, she turned to pick up real trash, but she collided with a man's broad back. Stumbling backward, she gripped Ursula's arm for support. "Watch it!"

The man turned. "Excuse me?"

His deep, smooth voice raised the hair on the back of her neck. To shield herself from prying questions, she cultivated snobbery, and his jaded response matched her armaments. His size also dwarfed her. She stared at his chest and took a deep breath. "I didn't realize anyone stood behind me."

He cocked his head. "Perhaps you should have looked."

Standing this close to the man, he nearly blocked out the sun. His white button-down shirt and dark jeans looked entirely out of place amid the volunteers and CIH representatives, but she couldn't ignore him. She wore a loose sundress and sandals. As soon as possible, she would shuck the footwear and take her chances with broken glass. Barefoot, she could feel the sand between her toes. He'd have a harder time stripping off his socks and leather loafers. "Perhaps you should apologize for invading my personal space."

"Perhaps not."

Lifting her hand, she shaded her eyes and met his gaze. His light brown eyes bordered on hazel. Thick, dark lashes gave his expression a smoldering intensity. The dancers she knew spent big money to achieve his sultry look, but they couldn't buy his casual, arrogant irreverence.

Crow's feet revealed a paler complexion beneath his tan. His sun-streaked, wavy blond hair resisted the wind. Too bad his thick lips remained flatlined. God wasted beauty on this man. She looked away. "I have trash to pick up."

"You're Gregorio's daughter." He extended a hand. "People call me Dante. I believe I'm joining you for dinner this evening."

"I have a name."

"Gisella," he said.

The name's consonants sounded like an inappropriate invitation slipping across his full lips. Perhaps she should give her father more credit for his matchmaking skills. This blond angel could wine and dine her until her family dragged her home for curfew. She tipped up her chin. "Is that so?"

He left a hand extended.

Nestling her hand in his, she felt the strength of his grip. He didn't look like a violent man, but restrained violence could be sexier than brute force. "Pleased to meet you."

He released her hand. "A business meeting. Are you aware CIH is for sale?"

She dropped her jaw and her hand. "What?"

A flying disc sailed through the air and connected with her head.

Wincing, she squeezed shut her eyes and focused on the pain. "Fuck!"

"Gisella!" Antonio ran toward her. "Watch your language!"

A warm, steady hand supported her elbow. "Are you all right?"

Her brother's admonishment amplified the pain of his assault. Even though he gripped her elbow, and she leaned on his strength, she pulled free. "Antonio

23

Vitella, if you fucking touch me again, *Papà* will kill you" — swaying, she squeezed away the pain — "and I'll watch."

"Is that so?" Dante asked.

Blinking past the sunlight reflecting off the water, she realized Antonio was halfway down the beach, and the handsome stranger gripped her arm. She gasped. In her father's world, unwarranted contact could mean death, but Dante's heated grip felt secure. *What a way to go.* Unwilling to risk his life, she pulled free and rubbed away his touch. "You can't touch me. Nobody should touch me."

"Are you okay?" he asked.

His languid question compounded her headache. Most men would retreat from the threat of death. She raised her hand to her throbbing forehead and checked for blood. Her fingers came back clean, and she faced the innocent man. "Sorry. I thought my brother came to gloat."

Looking over her shoulder, he frowned. "That's how you talk to your brother?"

She gritted her teeth. "Unfortunately."

He rubbed his eyebrows. "What have I gotten myself into?"

"Welcome to the family." Catching the confusion on his stupid, beautiful face, she pitied him for showing up in South Florida without knowing the rules. Crystal chandeliers, glistening yachts and plastic surgery smiles had taught her power and persuasion. This man looked like he went to West Coast charity golf tournaments and took advantage of the open bars. Miami's cutthroat scene would eat him alive. "What are you doing here?"

"Buying a business."

Ursula coughed.

Turning, Gisella met Ursula's gaze. Her saintly sister looked unperturbed. "You knew about the sale?"

"I suspected it," Ursula said. "These days, the study door stays closed, and too many people come and go for business as usual."

Shaking her head, Gisella swiped a plastic straw from the sand and shoved it in the bag. If she hadn't immersed herself in rehearsals for her upcoming performance, she would have known about the impending sale, too. "Great. Welcome to the family, Dante."

He folded his arms across his chest. "Why does that greeting sound like a threat?"

She swiped her hair out of her eyes and adjusted her sunglasses. "Because it is." Turning her back, she walked toward the nearest cluster of volunteers and hoped the pressure building behind her eyes faded before dinner.

"Miss Vitella," Dante said, "meeting you was a pleasure."

Glancing over her shoulder, she thought about giving him the toddler treatment, but she settled for a more direct approach. "Go fuck yourself."

Returning her stare, he held his ground. "Noted. See you at dinner."

"I doubt it." Turning away, she let the wind carry off her response. If her father planned to divest himself of her, her sister and his holding company, he must have a reason for abandoning his life's work. She feared the reason boasted pristine beaches and unlimited coconut cocktails. He'd teased retiring to a private island, but she refused to relinquish her father to the tropics.

If Lisette had claimed his attention and spurred him into action, she would question the woman's motivations and undermine her claim. If Gregorio needed an easy lay, he could summon a call girl. At least then Gisella could ignore his companion.

And poor Dante had broken the news.

Shooting the messenger looked cheap, but she owed the man nothing. "He can shove his loafers up his bleached, West Coast asshole."

"What?" Ursula stared.

Smiling, she deflected her sister's confusion with a waved hand. Dante didn't merit her time. She had a show to perform and limited time to evict Lisette's influence from her father's life.

Chapter Two

Dante scanned the beach and wondered how agreeing to a community service event had thoroughly ruined his morning. Joggers thronged the side road and monitored their heart rates on tiny screens. Kids poked at gelatinous globs bobbing in the surf. CIH employees yawned while they supervised a motley gang of misfits. Why wasn't anyone smiling? He should have ordered an omelet, checked his portfolio and blasted through the hotel's gym.

His phone rang.

"Boss," he said.

"Dante."

Alessio's hard-edged voice reminded him why he worked for the asshole billionaire in the first place. ADC Industries owned several insurance companies, a boutique investment firm and a portfolio of casinos. Despite high-handed quirks and a penchant for hard-nosed decision-making, Alessio helmed the organization like a hard-assed, benevolent father.

"How's New York?" Dante asked.

"Fucking amazing," Alessio replied. "How's the CIH bid?"

Dante scanned the beach. The recent parolees, drug addicts and repeat offenders helping with the beach cleanup looked as cheerful as bus drivers. Picking up trash wouldn't reform their life, and it wouldn't do fuck for him, either. "Coming along."

"When you close this deal on my behalf, you'll make a significant profit."

"Noted," he said.

"I trust your instincts. Figure out the valuation."

Dante worked his jaw. "And if I'm wrong?"

Alessio let the question linger.

Rubbing his brow, Dante nodded. CIH looked good on paper, but the family running it waded balls-deep in illegal shit. He'd grown up in a drug-smuggling environment and knew the culture, but he'd fled from his father's empire to pursue corporate success.

"I knew I could trust you with these people," Alessio said.

Dante dropped the hand and flexed his fingers. Sometimes, his boss was a real asshole. He knew about Dante's background, and he'd thrown him into the Florida coliseum without fearing the lions.

Fair enough. Dante would navigate the local waters, complete the deal and get back on the corporate jet. Lining his bank account with another fat commission would confer the power and protection he craved, but it would also confirm his ability to thrive beyond his family's sinful past. "I'll take care of it."

"I have no doubt." Alessio ended the call.

Dante slid his sunglasses into place. He understood his opponents, but he didn't care about their rules.

A woman picked up a deflated blow-up dick and waved it around the beach.

So much for dignity. Shaking his head, he scooped up a six-pack ring and tossed it in the plastic collection bag. He'd modeled the CIH acquisition using robust data, but he didn't appreciate bagging trash to demonstrate his commitment to the company. He'd gone to school with the city's fucking mayor, Frantz, but the connection had little bearing on the impending acquisition. "And to think I went to Harvard."

"Use a glove," Antonio said.

He looked up. "People have given me that advice my entire life."

Antonio laughed. "You're not so bad. Later, I'll take you to my club."

"Sounds good." Dante hated clubs. He turned his back on the pumped-up wannabe club bouncer and exhaled. Back West, he knew a hundred men with Antonio's machismo pride, but he didn't have to schmooze them.

After he'd bought CIH on his boss's behalf and pocketed a portion of the proceeds, he would leave some efficient middle manager to run the company. Let that tool relocate to Miami, charm Antonio and give the market his love and attention. *God bless the fucker.*

"What kind of women do you love?" Antonio asked.

Dante inhaled. The last time he'd made love to a woman, he'd still had exam schedules. A few dancers, models and hookers had caught his attention and eased his frustration, but they'd never captured his heart. For the last ten years, he'd moved through Alessio's organization like an efficient machine. Sharing brews and bumping elbows didn't thrill him, but profits did. "Beautiful and complicated women."

Antonio whistled. "You came to the right place."

Shading his eyes, Dante scanned the female volunteers. The women looked like tanned versions of every other chick he'd seen in this town, but Gregorio Vitella's daughters moved through the crowd like ethereal beings. Ursula, the older one, stabbed excess trash with a piercing motion. He would watch his back around her. Gisella, the younger daughter, lifted each piece of trash like it was a treasure, considered its worth and begrudgingly slid it into her bag. The lithe sprite was into this gig, and he was into watching her moves.

Her white sundress and straw hat enhanced her angelic appeal, but her sass dissolved the illusion. He wondered what the upkeep on a woman like that would cost him. If ten thousand dollars disappeared up her nose every month, he couldn't afford her.

In another life, he could have. He'd grown up watching his male relatives direct drug traffic from California to Canada. Federally funded highways connected the Southwest and Pacific regions. If President Eisenhower had known that the Federal Aid Highway Act of 1956 would pave the way for black-market commerce, he might have shelved his pen and gone back to enjoying 1950s sitcoms.

Like most successful criminals, Dante's relatives paid taxes on modest, legal incomes and milked one hundred times the profit from illegal trade. Something had to pay for the sports cars, but the cover was a joke. If regulating commercial traffic paid as well as regulating narcotics, half the nation's workforce would sign up for the gig.

But these guys? Dante shook his head. The brazen Italians stalking the Miami Beach acted like they'd invented guns and gold, but they pissed the same way he did. The East Coast corridor followed I-95 from Florida to Maine. Just because their goods came by speedboat instead of container ship didn't make them the reigning gods of drug trafficking.

"You want a fresh bag?" Antonio asked.

Dante stared at the trash he collected. "No, man, I'm good. Thanks for the opportunity to" — he considered the dispersed volunteers and wondered what happened to Gregorio's daughters — "make a difference."

"Fuck you."

Laughing, Dante cinched close his bag and abandoned his token trash removal efforts.

Leaving the beach, he climbed into his car and sped toward his lunch meeting with Gregorio. Miami's high rises settled into the whitewashed, gilded, art deco splendor of South Beach. Pastel buildings appeared and faded from sight as he covered the sandy, sun-kissed miles.

Before arriving in the state, Dante had collected intelligence about Gregorio and planned his approach. The man had millions in his bank account and another three hundred million stashed in an offshore tax-haven account. Too bad he underpaid his accountant.

The accountant pocketed Dante's bribe, spilled the details of Gregorio's financial arrangements and packed his briefcase like a man eager to cut and run.

By the time Dante ended his discovery phase, he had enough gossip about Miami's elite to write a column for the *Miami Herald*. If the CIH deal fell through, he might publish the goods. For a city founded on basic principles and amnesty, the fuckers at the top liked to break the rules. Too bad their Colombian, Dominican, Mexican and Jamaican hookups let them.

Downshifting, he slowed for a historic mansion converted into a restaurant. A man wearing a white dinner jacket stepped out of the guard booth.

"Reservation?"

"Dante," he said.

The man's face remained impassive. "Yes, Mr. Dante."

Choking back a smile, he let the engine purr. Just 'Dante' would do.

Roaring into the courtyard beyond the guard gate, he aimed for the jacketed valet waiting to take his keys.

The man kept his gaze averted.

Dante wanted to slip him a bill and find out how long Gregorio had been on site, but Alessio had taught him a few things. If you're walking into the lion's den, sharpen your claws and be prepared to fight. Opening the car door, he stepped out, reached into the backseat and slipped on a jacket. Under the guise of adjusting his coat, he confirmed his gun rested in the jacket's built-in holster. Tossing the keys to the valet, he looked at the old house and squared his shoulders.

In the two days he'd been in town, he'd observed the hotel's pool parties from his suite's balcony. Below his viewpoint, scantily clad models slapped beach balls like they'd double-majored in bouncing cleavage. The women popped their asses to techno music so full of Latin influences that they might as well pay taxes to their southern neighbors. Finishing his work had required a monumental effort.

This place presumed it had class. In the 1930s, the mansion's architect had probably visited the Dominican Republic's Alcazar De Colon and copied the mansion's whitewashed aesthetic. Encircling the Miami building's ornate courtyard, an arched breezeway created shade, and three floors of windows projected quiet intimacy. Radiating from a large fountain, ornate stonework lightened the courtyard's solemnity. A slight breeze sent droplets through the air, and a bird alighted on the fountain. It stole a sip of water from the highest tier.

Dante walked toward the table set for two, then stopped.

Gregorio walked from the breezeway's shadows and presented a hand. "How do you like the place?"

"Fussy," Dante said.

Laughing, Gregorio gestured to a chair. "Take a seat. If you look down, you will notice the ground is original key lime coral. The house's interior designer left his mark on West Palm Beach."

"And the coral reefs," Dante said.

Gregorio settled in his chair across the table. "Art often results in casualties."

"In that case, the Metropolitan Museum of Art probably has catacombs."

"Too modern," Gregorio said.

Dante laughed and spread his legs. Gregorio had run the Miami drug trade for the last forty-five years. Pushing his late sixties, he looked good for a man who'd killed enough people to fill the damn catacombs. The courtyard's shadows almost hid the faint silver streaks in his black hair. Dante would bet the man spent more than a few hours at the hair salon.

His father's hair had gone white at fifty. One day, the man throwing a football to him looked like every other dad in San Diego. The next day, his hand shook and his bloodshot eyes looked cloudy. Years spent running a drug-smuggling ring could age a man. Before the year had ended, Dante had told his old man he wanted a different life.

A server brought out two bowls of cold soup, filled their wine glasses and retreated.

"You are enjoying your time in Miami?" Gregorio picked up his spoon.

Dante kept his opinion of the town to himself. He dipped his spoon into the smooth soup and nodded.

"The heat is good, yes?"

Florida's hyperactive playground branded itself as America's preeminent destination for escapism, but the last time he'd visited New Orleans, those creole motherfuckers had something to say about the title. Neither Dante nor national high-dollar party organizers cared about location. If sponsors added together booze, tension and beautiful people, the results exploded into a hedonistic caricature of adults gone wild.

Dante preferred whiskey, solitude and peace of mind. Until he amassed his fortune, he spent his days navigating Alessio's deals and bringing back results. His boss might have shacked up in his New York penthouse, but the rest of his associates had fortunes to amass. Lifting his spoon, he looked up. "I enjoy the climate's heat. It puts pressure on a man. Toughen up and thrive...or leave town."

"Well said."

Admittedly, the fennel-laced soup tasted good, and Dante needed to choke back his attitude. Miami wasn't all pool parties and mafia meltdowns. Walking the late-night streets, he'd seen transitioning neighborhoods, culinary adventures and a crop of new luxury hotels that offered architecturally dazzling art spaces near commuter rail connections. Judging by the lines outside the Pérez Art Museum Miami and the Miami Science Museum, the city's residents and visitors expected more than pool parties from their city.

"And the beach cleanup?" Gregorio asked.

"The media loved it," he said.

"Yes, the media matters more and more, don't they? Is your boss's company prepared to keep CIH a Florida company?"

Setting down his spoon, Dante cocked his head. "For the price you're asking, I could move it to outer space."

"I've had other offers." Gregorio lifted another spoonful of his soup.

Dante leaned forward and bounced his knee. Fuck the soup. He didn't have time for this shit. "You haven't. Nobody but ADC Industries will get their hands dirty untangling your books. You and I agreed to a fair price. As soon as you sign the paperwork, you can retire and sleep better."

"I'll never sleep again."

Stilling his knee, Dante exhaled. If he wanted to have a heart-to-heart with a mobster, he could return to San Diego and drop in on his family. "Not my problem."

"I knew your father. He was an interesting man."

Drawing a deep breath, Dante faced his past. "Sadistic, you mean."

Gregorio raised his wine glass to his lips. "I would sleep better at night knowing a family member helmed CIH."

"Then appoint one of your daughters to the board." He looked past Gregorio's shoulder and watched restaurant servers moving through the shadows. No matter how many courses the restaurant prepared to serve, it appeared over-staffed. Unless a pop star waited to climb into the fountain and conduct a strip tease, the servers assembled in the shadows had no excuse to linger.

"You've met Gisella," Gregorio said.

"Charming."

"Hard-headed."

Looking away from the congregated staff, Dante focused on his host. "Most women are stubborn as shit. The smartest ones hide their motivations."

"You'll do fine down here." Gregorio swirled his wine. "Pick Ursula."

"Pick her for what?" Dante asked.

"To marry. She'll give you children and leave you in peace." He waved a hand toward the breezy courtyard. "With her at your side, you can do as you wish. And if you decide to keep CIH's off-the-books profit streams intact" — he paused and wet his lips — "she'll give you the credibility you need."

Dante shook his head. "I'm not here to marry one of your daughters."

"I'll kick back ten million under the table. Keep it. Consider it a wedding present."

Inhaling, Dante leaned back in his chair and rubbed his jaw. With a ten-million-dollar dowry in his pocket, a man could marry a woman, leave her ass in Miami and move on. "I'll think about it."

Gregorio inclined his head. "Smart man."

"She'd have to agree. I'm not in the business of forcing women."

Waving a hand in the air, Gregorio sipped his wine. "Conduct your life as you see fit. I knew your father and he kept his word. I trust you're a good man, too."

Dante had his doubts.

A server ran into the courtyard, skidded to a halt near Gregorio and dropped to his knees. The man shook Gregorio's arm and released a string of Italian.

Dante knew how to order spaghetti, but the subtleties of the man's pleadings escaped him. He watched Gregorio's face for a reaction.

Gregorio narrowed his eyes and worked his jaw.

The longer the server spoke, the weaker his case. Some vocabulary crossed linguistic divides, and Dante had a feeling the server had fucked up a deal with a South American provider. He pitied the man.

Indomitable men ran illicit drugs across the Southwest border, and Dante knew better than to fuck with them. They used commercial trucks and private vehicles to smuggle cocaine, marijuana, methamphetamine and heroin through land points of entry. As soon as US Narcos caught on to their routes, the traffickers pivoted to rural supply chains and vast areas of desert and mountainous terrain. Last week, he'd heard about an underwater drone. The U.S. government could build walls, but it couldn't pivot fast enough to end drug trafficking.

Dante rubbed his temples. He could be wrong about the pleading server. Asian criminals, outlaw motorcycle gangs and Indo-Canadian drug traffickers transported significant quantities of high-potency marijuana and MDMA across the U.S.-Canada border, too. Mexican drivers had twenty-five entry points, but northern runners had one hundred backwoods options. Their all-terrain vehicles, single-engine aircraft, fishing vessels and burly buddies knew how to earn a buck...or a loonie.

"Please," the server whined.

Gregorio shook his head.

A gunshot echoed in the courtyard, and the pleading server fell backward onto the key lime coral. The bullet hole in his forehead ended his life and sent a spray of blood far from Gregorio's suit. Gregorio lifted his napkin and patted sweat from his forehead.

Dante exhaled at another loss of life, but he remained seated.

Two servers walked out of the shadows, hoisted the man and carried him away from the lunch table.

"Fifteen million," Dante said.

Lowering his napkin, Gregorio worked his jaw.

Dante would report the new sale price to Alessio. He didn't want to risk ending up in a boxing ring with his ruthless boss, but being a clever man, he could spin the decision as a strategic negotiation and keep a large portion of the proceeds. Clouds shifted across the sun. "And I get to pick the sister."

Gregorio smiled. "Done."

Chapter Three

After the beach cleanup, Gisella tossed her purse in the foyer's marble-clad corner.

Martin bowed. "Good afternoon, *Signorina* Gisella."

She blew past him and marched toward the study. *"Papà!"*

The black walls absorbed her outrage, but the room remained empty.

Approaching the desk, she rattled the drawers and hoped to find one open. For most of her teenage years, she'd sidled up to her sire and tried to apprentice in the family business. He'd sent her shopping, hired dance instructors and told her to get lost.

Dropping into his chair, she kicked up her legs and rested her sandals on the polished surface. Sand sprinkled his leather writing pad. She left it.

Ursula cracked open the door and leaned against the frame. "Did you run out of wildlife selfies?"

Lifting her middle ginger, Gisella tipped back her head and stared at the avant-garde light fixture recessed in the black, coffered ceiling. At night, LED stars blinked in time to the music. If she added a disco ball, she could host a rave in the study. Abandoning the night sky, she looked at Ursula. Her black leggings and loose tunic made her look more like a wraith than a saint. "Do you remember when I tried to teach you to dance?"

Toeing the carpet, Ursula looked up. "No."

"We had a little book about a dancing mouse, and I was so proud I knew the French terms. You read me the story, but for *rond de jambe*, you said 'jamba' like the ballet move was some frothy green drink we'd buy at a mall kiosk. I jumped up, pointed my toe and did a little round on the floor. You pretended to be impressed."

"Dance classes are boring," Ursula said.

"Dance classes take discipline."

"When's the last time you went to a public mall?"

Laughing, Gisella picked up her father's fountain pen. Ursula was right. Her father's wealth guaranteed early-morning shopping sprees and discrete boutique deliveries. "Why didn't *Papà* teach us to run the family business?"

Choosing a chair, Ursula flopped into it. "Maybe we're not cut out for it."

Her breasts bounced, and Gisella tried not to envy her sister's assets. In a leotard, those bouncing globes would be a nightmare. "I am."

She and her sister shared DNA, but their similarities ended at long, dark hair and olive skin. For the longest time, Gisella wondered if Ursula suffered from episodes. She went through such highs and lows that the staff charted her cycle.

Ursula loved deeply, but the simplicity of her convictions repelled Gisella. Every time she and her sister debated art, music and religion, Ursula laid down her beliefs. The certitude of her statements roiled

Gisella's stomach. She spent her days teasing out life's nuances, but her sister studied commandments. When would Ursula recognize the subtleties within the shadows?

"I mean, do you want to smuggle coke and negotiate arms deals?" Ursula asked.

"We sell insurance."

Ursula snorted. "Right, and the Pope's Catholic."

Frowning, Gisella pulled back her chin. "Wait! The Pope *is* Catholic." Church sat at the bottom of her priority list. "Did we have another schism?"

"You're hopeless," Ursula said.

"I'm not! And I've let all this shit swirl around me, but the blond asshole on the beach looked damned pleased about the CIH takeover. Why would *Papà* sell out to that man?"

"He's rich?"

Gisella narrowed her gaze. She shopped enough to recognize wealth. The boutiques she frequented would never stock Dante's loafers. Only painstaking hand work and exotic leathers earned their coveted shelf space. "Is he?"

"As far as I can tell, he's a senior associate with ADC Industries. The conglomerate owns several insurance companies, a boutique investment firm and a portfolio of casinos. Apparently they're interested in adding CIH to their portfolio."

"And the drugs and guns?"

"I thought we sold insurance." Ursula ran her fingers through her hair. "Shouldn't you be happy *Papà* is going legit?"

She tilted her head. "Trying to buy your way into the nunnery?"

Ursula laughed. "Cheaper than buying your way into a dance troupe."

Lowering her legs from the desk, Gisella straightened her back. "I earned my credentials."

"You were such a fortunate scholarship student."

Picking up a crystal ashtray, Gisella considered chucking it, but the flying disc had diminished her taste for projectiles. Rubbing fine grit from the ashtray's edge, she set aside the piece and wondered who actually smoked in this room. "You don't think he's losing his touch?"

Ursula stood and walked around the room's perimeter. Her black clothing let her fade into the shadows, but she held high her head. "Perhaps his priorities."

"Lisette?"

Meeting her gaze, Ursula nodded. "I never liked that woman."

"Me neither." Gisella tried a drawer and found it locked. "Remember the time she bought *Papà* a flamingo for his birthday present?"

"Poor bird!"

"Where did she expect him to keep it?" Kicking up her feet, Gisella imagined taking over her father's crime empire. She would fall for so many scams she'd be broke, or dead, within a year. Instead of intimidating scared mules, she focused on greedy interior designers. "The first time she came over, she probably left a pair of red panties in his jacket pocket."

"I'm sure they were leopard." Ursula toyed with the drapes.

Life felt heavy, but levity gave her respite. Instead of worrying about her problems, she focused on Lisette's sins. The woman had replaced her mother's imported decorating choices with gaudy, impersonal pieces. The interior designer over-indulged in plastic surgery, top-shelf martinis and gossip-based accounting. She fawned over Gregorio, but she showed little interest in the old country. "I wonder if Lisette's a law-abiding, licensed professional."

"Call girl?" Ursula asked.

"Interior designer." Pressing the call button to summon Martin, she lowered her legs and sat up in her father's chair.

Peering around the doorframe, Martin made eye contact and relaxed his shoulders. "*Signorina* Gisella."

His formal black suit and crisp white shirt looked pressed, but sweat glistened on his forehead. She wondered what exactly he'd been polishing. "Martin, who pays Lisette's invoices?"

He frowned. "I pay all the household expenses."

"And how much would you say we've paid Lisette?"

He loosened his collar. "In total?"

"In total," Ursula said.

Jerking back, he exhaled. "Sorry, *Signorina* Ursula. I didn't see you against the dark curtains."

"I can imagine." Walking around the desk, she put her hand on Gisella's shoulder and smiled. "The total, Martin."

"Um."

Gisella picked up the desk phone.

"Nearly a million," he said.

Looking up, Gisella exchanged a glance with her sister. "*Avida.*"

Ursula rolled her eyes.

Leaning forward, Gisella beckoned Martin closer. "I'm afraid Lisette's up to no good, and we should find out how much trouble we're in before the police beat us to the punch. Ask her for a copy of her insurance coverage. Check her licensing." She pushed the ashtray toward the desk's edge. It protruded over the edge.

Martin raced toward the desk.

Bumping the furniture, Gisella sent the ashtray crashing toward the floor.

Missing his chance to save the objet d'art, Martin watched it shatter on the floor and winced. He straightened and made eye contact. "I'll get a broom."

She stood, rounded the desk, and patted his arm. "Don't worry. I'll clean up the mess. *Papà* won't miss a stolen ashtray."

"Stolen?" Martin's face paled.

Escorting him to the study door, she made a soft clucking sound. "Stolen. Pity. Get the documentation."

He rushed toward the service corridor.

"Very theatrical," Ursula said.

She shrugged. "Where's the broom closet?"

"Fuck if I know." Ursula dropped into Gregorio's chair. "I'm not the cleaning lady. You broke the piece of shit. You clean it up."

Laughing, she pulled a sheet of paper from the trashcan, scooped up the crystal shards, and dropped them into the bin. "Lisette is going down."

Ursula chewed a thumbnail. "*Papà* might love her. She might love him. Stranger things have happened."

"I doubt it." She ran her hand over the floor to feel for missed shards. The smooth, polished wood felt lifeless. Drenched in sunshine, it should glow. Straightening, she examined the room. "I've been wrong about people, but I've never seen Lisette look at him like a woman in love."

"And how should that woman look?"

She considered the question. "Like the most valued thing in the room."

Ursula stared out of the window. "Wouldn't that be nice?"

* * * *

Paging through the eveningwear in her closet, Gisella skipped gowns in formal black, girlish pink and radiant red. Blue and green fabrics reminded her of the ocean. She rubbed her temple. Fingering the gold sequins of a sheath dress, she sighed and slid the garment along the hanging bar. The dress would shine at the opera but create a scene at dinner. She paged through additional dresses, but her fingers itched to reclaim the gold dress's drama. Pulling it out of the closet, she held the sequined sheath against her chest and looked in the mirror. Lisette would have a hard time stealing the show. She grinned.

Walking downstairs after she'd dressed, she watched dinner guests milling on the back patio and enjoying the *aperitivo* course. Servers circulated with champagne. Crystal dishes held an array of olives, nuts and hard cheeses. The men in tuxedos scooped up the savory offerings. The women in evening dress averted their gazes.

Her mother used to say, "*L'appetito vien mangiando.*" The appetite comes while you are eating. If the women on the patio didn't join the party, they'd have a hard time keeping up. Gisella turned back to the house for a glass of wine before joining the fray.

Inside, the house staff scurried back and forth between the kitchen and the dining room. Martin presided over the chaos with curt instructions and pointed fingers.

Instead of interrupting Martin's flow, she turned toward a hallway leading to the living room and the stocked bar. A fire door separated the foyer from the living room, but potted trees and a padded bench held court in the silence. Preoccupied with thoughts of her upcoming dance performance, she collided with a warm, solid mass. Examining the obstacle, she moaned. "Not again."

"Good evening, Gisella," Dante said.

His black-on-black tuxedo looked entirely too good on him. Without the beach and seagull effect, his easy good looks shone beneath the chandeliers and stole her breath. For a moment, she applauded her father's matchmaking skills, but reality's sour bite ruined that fantasy. As far as she cared, his sultry gaze and firm chin could go to hell. "Drinks are on the back patio."

"Noted."

In close proximity, he smelled like cedar woodchips, mandarin martinis and cut grass. She wrinkled her nose. "Why do you smell like a lawn service?"

He choked back a laugh. "I believe the term you're looking for is 'vetiver'."

She shook her head. "Cut grass."

"I'll take your preferences under advisement."

Pushing past him, she shook her head. "Don't bother."

He caught her arm.

Unease drifted through her body like a suppressed shiver. No longer surrounded by scores of volunteers and company members, she felt his size and looming, significant presence in the confined space. Her heartbeat and her shallow breaths echoed in her ears. Taking his measure, she inhaled deeply and considered her choices. The hallway insulated her from the chaos in the dining room. If she screamed, the staff would come running, and she lacked a reason to fear him. "Let go of me."

"I'd like us to be friends."

She stared at his hand. "I don't need more friends."

Uncurling his fingers one by one, he dropped his hand. "Allies."

Looking up, she examined the crow's feet near his eyes. Squinting on a yacht could have that effect, but his corporate allowance hardly left time for leisure sports. She'd seen the same etched wariness on a police officer's face. Scanning crowds for hidden threats could mark a man, too. Perhaps Dante would fit into the family mold better than she expected. "Are you afraid your bid for CIH won't be enough?"

He leaned forward. "ADC Industries has sufficient assets."

She stepped backward to gain footing, but his presence slowed her movements. Something about his scent and shadowed grin held her interest. Shaking off the impulse, she looked over her shoulder and focused on the hallway's end. Instead of curiosity, she needed breathing room and distance.

Her entire life, her father protected, her cousins hovered and she narrowed her childhood dreams to predefined expectations. She'd stolen kisses backstage, but local crushes took one look at her family and learned to keep their distance. Summer camps and trips to Italy gave her freedom to explore her sexuality, but as soon as the lights came up in Miami, she performed her roles. "I'm sure you do have assets, but they don't concern me." She faced him and raised her chin.

Pulling his phone from his pocket, he glanced at the screen and frowned.

Did he hear her? Caged next to a predator, she eased backward.

He grabbed her hand and held it fast.

"Do you have anxiety issues?" she asked.

Looking up from his phone, he cocked his head. "Excuse me?"

The man looked at her as if she belonged on a nature show. Remembering her golden sheath and pedigree, she stared at his grip. "You keep grabbing me. Are you afraid you'll drown?"

"You're certainly the most intriguing thing I've seen within a mile of the beach."

"Am I?" Raising her free hand, she traced his lapel and found the concealed weapon hidden beneath satin and wool. Jerking free, she shook her head.

"You don't like guns?"

She shifted away and rubbed her arms. "I would prefer to live without them."

"Then you would prefer to die." He straightened his coat.

Looking up, she considered his strong jaw and wondered how a corporate lackey ended up carrying a piece. "Is that the only way?"

"Many ways exist. Until I know where I stand, I carry the gun."

She shifted her weight. "In this house, you need it."

"I know."

The admission raised gooseflesh on her arms. She recognized the double-action pistol. Once upon a time, she'd held a piece at the firing range and known it wasn't for her.

He released her and rubbed his thumb along his finger. "You shouldn't be here. You should be outside amid the patio lights and lighthearted laughter."

"It's a veneer," she said.

"I know."

"Do you?" She stepped closer and searched for the source of his strength. Muscled men dotted Miami's beaches, but he held himself in check. The awareness garnered her attention, and she wondered if he felt exposed. Unwilling to add her burdens to his load, she dropped her hand.

"Gisella?" he asked.

She glanced at a pair of large potted trees halfway down the hallway. If she pulled him behind the screen, she could steal a kiss, test his assets and judge him. Considering the impatient way he had glanced at his phone, international machinations kept him from enjoying a beautiful woman in an evening dress, and she refused to be ornamentation. "Are you going to stand here all night, or are you going to the patio like a polite guest?"

He blinked. "And here I thought we were having a good time."

"This is a good time?"

Raising her hand, he kissed the back. "Do you want to have a good time?"

His lips felt softer than her satin thong, and her stomach dropped. A lingering kiss wouldn't satisfy this man. "Do you have a death wish?" she asked.

His eyes widened.

Pulling free her hand, she wished she had met him under familiar circumstances. "I'll see you at dinner."

Running his thumb along his jaw, he nodded and slipped his phone into his jacket pocket.

"CIH and I don't come as a package deal," she said.

He scanned her dress. "Pity."

She felt like an asset under evaluation.

He stepped forward.

Holding up her hand, she stepped back. "What are you doing back here, anyway?"

"Taking a call." He raised his phone. "Do you mind?"

His counter-questioned contained the slightest note of amusement, and she smiled. She preferred entertaining men on stage, but if he wanted to match wits in the hallway, she would sharpen her tongue.

"They call you Gigi?"

"No." She inhaled. "My mother and father called me Gigi, and she's dead. Don't pick up the nickname. You can't carry the load."

"Perhaps I can," he said.

Her heart skipped a beat, and she shook her head.

He slipped both hands into his pockets. "I should apologize. I've spent so much time researching your father's company that I feel like I know him and your family by proxy. We're strangers, aren't we?" He glanced at her chest. "Nice dress."

She snorted. "Well, aren't you the gentleman?"

"Hardly." He rocked back on his heels. "Is that the type you prefer?"

She wet her lips. "I don't have a type. I dance, I run, I pick up beach litter and I"—she wondered what his hair would feel like between her fingers—"obey my father. He set me up on a date next week. Marco? Perhaps you've met him."

Dante shrugged. "Can't say I have."

Before the evening ended, she had the distinct impression he would research Marco and his connection to the family. Instead of waiting for her future date to reveal his flaws, she could ask Dante and save herself the time, but she'd rather learn about the man standing in front of her. "Why do they call you Dante?"

Pulling up his jacket sleeve, he revealed a lifelike skull tattoo and black script spelling out *memento mori*.

She recognized the Latin phrase adorning ghoulish headstones and abstract paintings. "You have a thing for Dante's *Inferno*? Fallen angels and the like?"

He laughed. "Nobody escapes their fate, but what they do in their life matters."

"And what do *you* do?"

He rolled down his sleeve. "It's what I don't do. I don't give second chances."

"Ironic. We meet again."

Checking his watch, he shrugged. "Effective. When people know forgiveness is off the table, they stop asking for it."

"Well, I'll leave you to your call." She turned and headed toward the living room.

"Gisella?"

His question stretched her name into a dark tug. Slowing, she turned and tilted her head.

"Do you want me to be a gentleman?"

His thick, dark lashes and possessive, insolent gaze conveyed an alternative, and she wet her lips. To regain her composure before dinner, she needed fresh air and room to breathe. "Of course. I'll see you around."

"Why don't I believe you?"

Fear tinged the pleasure of finding herself alone with him. Most of her peers and female cousins held babies on their hips while their dried wedding bouquets crumbled in a closet. If her mother had lived, her father would have married her off at twenty-one, endowed her with a few million dollars and visited her for holidays.

The women in her family married safe, predicable threats to law and order. Dante held court in another world. Until she learned the rules, she needed to avoid his studied indifference and hooded promises. "Believe what you want. This is Miami, after all."

Closing the distance, he dropped his head close to her ear and traced the back of a hand along her upper arm. "The sun still sets, and women still moan."

Shivering, she jerked away and scanned the hallway. "You're playing with fire."

"I know."

"No, you don't." She dropped her voice to a whisper. She could deal with his heavy, immovable grips and testosterone-fueled bravado, but she couldn't please him.

Force didn't scare her but subtlety did. She spent hours perfecting her dance moves, but the effort exhausted her, and she limped home. The moment she stepped through her father's door, she resumed the subtle moves and manipulations her home life required. When she faltered, smiles and bright clothes filled the gaps.

In her father's house, his immoveable rules stood. Dante's touch, no matter how moneyed or flirtatious, could lead to his death, and he didn't seem to care for the consequences of his actions. "On the beach, I wasn't kidding. This family doesn't do casual flings. You're in or you're out."

"I'm in." He skimmed his hand along her lower back. "Your skin's so smooth and flawless."

She shivered. "You're not Italian."

His hand stilled.

"You're not *La Cosa Nostra* or *'Ndrangheta* or a member of any of the families my father respects."

He frowned. "Your father knew my father."

She sighed. "In my life, that doesn't qualify. He knows everyone. Everyone has a habit. You have to be part of *una famiglia*."

Pulling back, he straightened his bow tie. "You're kidding."

"Who kids about death?" Before he could answer, she put enough distance between them to emphasize her point. "Go back to your surfboards and vineyards,

Dante. Wire the money for CIH and read the quarterly reports. Nothing about this company will change under new ownership. Antonio and his peers are my father's vision of the future. They're the muscle behind the operation. You and I?" She shrugged. "We're nothing but entertaining footnotes."

He walked toward her.

His silent footsteps worried her.

Brushing his thumb along her lip, he smiled. "Thanks for the warning."

She exhaled and turned her head.

His fingers, rough to her delicate skin, rounded her chin, dipped along her throat and settled against her chest. The faint pressure compelled her heart to break free, but she held her stance.

Dropping her chin, he walked to the fire door and closed it.

"What are you doing?" she asked.

He sat on a bench, leaned back and unbuttoned his shirt.

Forbidden pleasure filled the hallway like a cloying smoke. Her mouth went dry, and an icy shiver ran across her skin. She watched him slowly reveal his smooth, sculpted chest and knew she should turn away. Desire and hesitation anchored her feet.

He spread his knees and rubbed his clean-shaven chin. "Are you in or out?"

She swallowed. "This isn't my game."

"Why not?"

Stealing a quick glance at the fire door, she struggled to find a reason anyone in the house would come down this hallway. Part of her wanted an excuse, and the other part of her wanted to live. She walked toward him, and her muscles ached for release. "If you say a word, I'll deny it."

"A word?" He raised an eyebrow.

She stepped between his legs. "Don't make a sound."

"Try me."

Pressing her finger against his lips, she trailed her other hand along his smooth cheek and gripped the hair at the nape of his neck. It felt as soft as silk, and she regretted not having time to savor it.

He let out a quiet, tense breath, and his hands skimmed up the backs of her thighs. "I didn't think you'd do it."

"Shut up." Spreading her legs, she let his hands rise higher and tease the empty ache between her legs. He skimmed her silk thong, and a shallow, ragged breath escaped her throat.

He gripped her ass cheeks.

She sank into his grip and let her dress ride high. Relieved of the gilded constraint, she spread her legs and straddled him on the bench.

Pulling one hand forward, he teased her clit, but left her thong in place. "Gisella."

Her name escaped his lips like a low growl. She rolled her hips forward and dropped her head to his shoulder. This man could handle her family's threats. "Fuck me, Dante, and don't say a word about it."

He slid his finger inside her wet folds and moved his fingers slowly.

The pressure built, and he increased his pace. She bucked her hips and ached for release. Burying her face against his shoulder, she ground her clit against his solid length and urged him to continue.

"This is what you want?" he asked.

She raised her head and looked at him. In the bright hallway, his eyes reflected the light, and his expression challenged her to claim more than shadows and liquid release. Wetting her lips, she stripped away the constraints and imagined him on the beach. "Dante…"

He ripped off her thong.

Cool air rushed against her skin. Inhaling, she dropped her hand and touched herself. The soft strokes fueled her desire, and she offered him a taste. "Is this what you want?"

Drawing her fingers into his mouth, he closed his eyes and sucked.

Restless heat and suppressed satisfaction rolled off his body. She could flee, but she wanted the tension and danger of the illicit encounter. Pulling her fingers from his mouth, she reached down, lifted his hand and placed it on her breast.

"Shit." He squeezed her through the sequins, but his other hand gripped her hips and pulled her forward. He rubbed the heel of his hand against her clit. "Good?"

She dropped back her head, moaned and rode the building pressure.

Sliding two fingers deep inside her, he pumped his hand and arched his fingers until she teetered on the edge of wanting something more than friction. Aching pressure filled her, and when his fingers no longer satisfied her desire, she reached for his belt.

He lifted his hips.

Releasing his erection, she stroked the hot, satin skin and lifted her hips.

"Condom." He choked out the word.

She blinked. Of all the reckless things she'd done in her life, sheathing herself on this man without protection would have been the worst. Before reality diminished her illicit high, he pulled a condom out of his wallet, ripped off the foil and cloaked himself. "Thank you."

Before she could say another word, he grabbed her hips, centered her over his erection and plunged her into bliss.

Pleasure and pressure forced her breath from her lips.

"Were you planning to fuck me, Gisella?" He thrust into her depths.

Her toes barely touched the floor. Suspended from his grip, she braced herself on his shoulders, buried her head in his heady scent and let him drive. "No." She breathed and shuddered in the same breath. "But I'm glad I am."

Thrusting and rolling her hips to meet him, he drove her climax until she arched in his grip. Each pulse filled the empty ache in her core, but she let herself go and rode him in a mindless, submissive, maddening frenzy. If her pleasure tarnished her reputation, she didn't care. "Dante, more."

He slapped her ass and pumped into her.

The mix of pain and pleasure sent her eyes rolling into the back of her head, but she held onto his strength. Dropping her hands from his shoulders, she slid them down his back and felt him bury his head between her breasts. Later, she would take off her dress and soak up the musty, clear scent he left behind, but now, she rode him until her thighs ached, and she only wanted release.

Arching her back, she pulled free of his hands and set the pace she needed. Each pump and thrust registered in her core. Every time his pelvis ground against hers, she chased the heat and friction she needed. A throaty moan escaped her lips, and when his hand rose between their bodies and took up the rhythm, she thrust against this touch and let herself go.

The orgasm sent shudders through her frame and sensitized every inch of her skin. When she came down, she felt him motionless inside her and exhaled.

Chest heaving, he buried her face against his shoulder, clenched her neck and groaned. "Fuck, I worried you wouldn't be quiet."

She raised her head from his exposed skin. So many clothes separated their bodies, but the points of contact had flashed into release and eclipsed the barriers. "You didn't think I could be quiet?"

"You're too tight to call yourself experienced. And the way you look" — he stroked her cheek — "you could unmake any man."

Her cheeks flamed. The assholes in her father's organization strutted around and reveled in their fraternal, 'made-man' hierarchy, but Dante came undone in her arms. He worried she would be the one to come unraveled? She felt his muscles quake and knew she tested his control, but faced with his memories of other women, she pulled back, and his assessment dimmed the aftermath of her release. She knew what drew her to him and tempted her into the liaison. He'd come and go from her life without leaving constraints. "Well, thanks for the ride."

"Who else fucks you?" he asked.

She shivered and straightened her dress. "Nobody."

Buttoning his shirt, he shook his head. "Liar."

He'd tasted like whiskey and poor decisions, but she doubted she would get a second taste. Smoothing her hair, she gave thanks he hadn't tried to kiss her and ruin her makeup. "Just you."

Hooking his arm around her middle, he pulled her close and pressed a kiss against her exposed navel. Before she could respond, he pulled down her dress and swatted her ass. "I'll see you at dinner, Gisella."

Free from his touch, she exhaled.

He looked up from the buttons. "Don't underestimate either of us."

"You're a businessman." The words scratched her throat.

"And you're a dancer."

She caught their reflection in a gilded mirror hanging on the wall. He stood close enough to kiss, and she weighed the risk. Death would mar his indifferent, brooding beauty, and she hated to waste something so perfect.

The next time she had an itch, she could ogle the pool boy and satisfy her desires. The pool boy would strip off his shirt and preen for her enjoyment, but she would never touch him. In her world, woman survived using strategy, not lust. She stepped back from Dante and smiled. "You're right. Dancing is what I do best."

Swallowing, she walked toward the living room and felt his gaze on her until she turned the corner and disappeared into the gilded room. Out of sight, she leaned against the wall, held her hand to her chest and sighed. The first time he'd said her name, every consonant had sounded like an inappropriate invitation. The first time he'd fucked her, she believed in happily ever after. "Idiot." Closing her eyes, she questioned to whom the term belonged.

Chapter Four

Fifteen minutes later, Martin rang the dinner bell.

Checking the hallway for guests, Gisella slipped into the foyer and smiled at the outside guests entering the house.

"Gisella!" Juniper waved.

Her father's sisters, Juniper and Julietta, walked arm-in-arm. The sequins on their gowns threw lights on the walls and matched their glittering jewels. She liked to think of them as Shrewd and Prude, but they remained family and told her stories about her childhood she vaguely remembered. Leaning forward, she accepted their kisses and switched to Italian. "I'm so glad you're here."

"Where else would we be?" Juniper asked.

"Bermuda," Julietta said.

Extending her elbows, Gisella offered each aunt an arm. "Ready for dinner?"

The women stared.

Juniper cleared her throat. "We have a full table tonight. Perhaps one of our guests will escort you to dinner."

Looking above her aunts' immaculate, dyed blowouts, Gisella scanned the dinner party. Ursula stood next to Antonio, and Lisette had her red nails wrapped around Gregorio's sleeve. Dante held court with two cousins responsible for CIH's sales centers and claims division. The remaining couple lived on the next estate and laundered her father's money for a healthy take. She almost felt sorry for Dante. A smarter envoy would have brought reinforcements. Perhaps he didn't need them?

Martin approached her father.

The two men exchanged words.

Clearing his throat, Gregorio grinned and faced the small crowd. "Friends and relatives, thank you for joining us this evening. We're delighted the rain held off, and we could mingle by the pool. Before the first course, would you humor me? I heard Ursula practicing this afternoon, and I'd be remiss not to let you hear her beautiful voice, too."

Ursula, wearing a black, beaded column gown, stood as still as a statue. Gisella raised her eyebrows. Unless her sister skipped lunch in favor of vocal exercises, no part of her afternoon had included a song.

Shrugging, Ursula cleared her throat and tapped a few keys on the piano. "You're so kind, *Papà*."

The crowd of twelve shifted and formed a semi-circle around her and the gleaming, black piano.

Ursula's throaty soprano voice carried the first longing verses of *Adagio.*

Gisella lost herself in the song's yearning melody. In an empty cathedral, Ursula could produce a three-octave range, but in the marble-clad foyer, she throttled her power. Gisella understood Ursula's constraint, but why couldn't her sister take the stage and let her voice soar?

Ursula sang of nights without love and no need to pray. In the final verse, she said only music remained, and her voice faltered.

Hearing the pain, Gisella understood that Ursula's fascination with the new priest had blossomed into unrequited love. Before Ursula tipped her hand with tears, Gisella stepped forward and clapped. "Beautiful! *Bravissima!*"

The dinner guests followed her lead, and their noise drowned out Ursula's gasp.

Her father cocked his head.

Gisella shifted to shield her sister, smiled and blinked.

Martin opened the doors to the dining room.

Crystal and silver gleamed in front of twelve place settings. Three low bouquets of fresh flowers in silver vases anchored the expansive table. Demure enough to allow conversation across the table, the arrangements created intimacy and interrupted the formal display.

Gregorio gestured to the doorway. "Shall we?"

Lisette smiled. "You're so kind."

The cutout on her silver dress looked appropriate for a twenty-year-old runway model, not a forty-year-old interior designer who never picked up the check at the client meetings Gisella attended.

Gregorio jerked his chin toward the sales and claims cousins.

Each man approached an aunt and offered his arm.

Antonio came for her.

She forced a smile.

The neighbors fell into line.

Ursula and Dante stared at each other.

In an instant, Gisella understood why her father set her up with Marco, but her predicament hardly mattered. If Dante chose Ursula, she would lose Fr. Pietro, and Dante's languid indifference would crush her. For what? Another broken arranged marriage to maintain pure Italian bloodlines?

Gisella questioned the conditions she accepted to enable her life and her art. Following Antonio into dinner, she moderated her pace and counted the floor tiles. Her father would listen. She would find the words she needed to free her sister.

Settling into her seat, she caught Ursula's eye across the table and tilted her head.

Ursula rubbed her throat and shrugged.

"What happened to free will?" she asked.

A server placed a tuna antipasto in front of her and another in front of Antonio.

He broke in half a breadstick. "You've got to be fucking kidding me."

She glanced at her brother. "What's wrong? You don't like tuna?"

He picked up his fork. "It's fine. I thought you said something."

Sipping her wine, she ignored the food on her plate. "I say plenty."

"That's your problem."

In a smaller setting, she might have thrown the wine in his face.

Gregorio stood and raised his glass. "I'm so pleased you were all able to join us tonight for a family meal. *La Cena* is the heart of the household. Tonight, as our honored guest, we have Daniel Johnson from ADC Industries. Please, treat him as one of the family."

She bit her lip. No wonder the man went by Dante. If she had such an insipid given name, she'd court a nickname, too. She hoped he understood the subtleties of her father's speech. If this had been a real family meal, her father would have conducted it in Italian, the neighbors would have peered through the hedge and Daniel 'Dante' Johnson wouldn't have made the cut. She held her smile.

"We have a saying in Italy. *Il sangue non e acqua.* Blood is not water. The ties that bind us hold us together during good times and bad. Breaking bread with you is an honor." He sipped his wine. "*Salute alla nostra salute.*"

Every guest turned to Dante.

Raising his glass, he inclined his head. "*Grazie.*"

Well, the man had balls. She smiled and sliced off the corner of her fish.

"How'd the beach cleanup go?" Luca asked.

"Great. We filled a few trucks. If I see another cigarette butt, bottle cap or piece of broken glass, it'll be too soon."

"What's wrong with cigarette butts? They're paper and grass."

She set down her fork. "And plastic."

Her cousin shrugged.

The server set down the *primi* of clear soup.

The rich, earthy smell of truffles rose from the broth. She looked at Ursula and Dante. Both parties conversed with their outside dinner partners. Their silhouettes looked like caricatures of a disengaged couple, and the arrangement had just begun.

"You get me a few tickets to your next dance recital? I got a date I want to impress," Luca said.

She nodded absentmindedly.

Dante leaned closer to Juniper.

The woman fanned herself and uttered a line.

The lines near Dante's eyes deepened with heartfelt laughter, and Gisella frowned. She wondered what Juniper had said to elicit his laugh, but more importantly, she wanted dinner to end so she could sort through her emotions.

Meeting him on the beach had left her tongue-tied and unbalanced, but his proximity in the hallway still warmed her skin. Speaking to him might be fraught, but looking in his direction required downcast lashes and a polite smile. Except for his size, he looked like a man who knew how to rig a sailboat, but he wouldn't salute. He'd be the captain. If he married Ursula to secure CIH, she'd have to spend the rest of her life covertly admiring her brother-in-law. She could think of worse fates.

As if he'd felt her observation, he glanced away from Juniper and looked at her. His curious stare raised the fine hairs on her skin. She shouldn't have been alone in the hallway with him. The memory would play on a loop, deep and suggestive, while Ursula bawled her eyes out and protested her intended fate.

To disguise her thoughts, Gisella held his gaze for a breathless second then looked at Lisette. If anyone deserved her ire and frustration, the woman playing hostess at the foot of the table earned it.

Feeling Dante's gaze, she looked at him, wet her lips and considered her choices.

Switching places with Ursula wouldn't upset Lisette's plans. To thwart the woman, she needed

Gregorio to retain CIH for another decade. Once she made principal and retired, she and Ursula would be too old to serve as bargaining chips. Gregorio could offload his responsibilities to whoever put up the funds.

She smiled. Let Gregorio's Sicilian brotherhood step into the insurance industry. Based on overheard cocktail conversations, they already had a hand in it. But God, the man glancing at her through the flower arrangements was handsome enough to inspire sinners. She considered switching places with Ursula to appease her curiosity about the man she'd fucked, but falling for the man would jeopardize her career. Dante didn't seem like a man who could execute a box step, much less appreciate a *pirouette*.

"You hear me?" Luca asked.

Discharging her thoughts, she looked up. "Sorry, what?"

"Eleanor. I want to take her to the ballet."

She frowned. "I thought Antonio was with Eleanor."

Luca's eyes widened. "What the fuck?" He stood, toppled his chair and threw down his napkin. "Are you fucking my girlfriend, Antonio?"

In the still room, a server's shoe squeaked on the hard floor, and classical music played in the background.

Blotting his mouth, Antonio stood. "I wasn't aware you were engaged."

Trapped between the men, Gisella closed her eyes and listened to the music. Rossini? Her father would make quick work of this squabble, and the meal could resume.

"I love her," Luca said.

"She's just a woman."

A powerful hand gripped her upper arm and hauled her to her feet.

Stumbling, she found herself pressed against Luca's chest. A pistol's cold steel pressed against her temple. Holding herself motionless, she focused on the music.

"Is Gisella just a woman? Are you fucking her, too?"

"Sit down!"

Gregorio's voice echoed in the room. She exhaled. Etiquette demanded white-picket-fence manners in public, but inside these walls, her father ruled.

"I love Eleanor," Luca said. "She should be here tonight."

She tried to remember how many drinks Luca had had. Without joining him on the patio, gauging his rationality seemed nearly impossible. The gun's cold weight felt steady enough. She looked down the table to access her father's reaction.

As if drawn by her attention, Luca shifted toward him, too. "If you'd give me permission to marry Eleanor, I wouldn't be losing her to this asswipe. Give me permission to fucking marry her, and I'll release Gisella."

"Watch your language." Gregorio remained seated.

The pregnant scene felt like the moment before the curtains closed, and dancers dropped their poses. Her heartbeat accelerated, and the longer Luca held her, the higher her fear climbed. If anyone on the street pulled this move, they'd be dead. For the first time in her life, she felt expendable.

"Release her, Luca."

Dante's voice overpowered the blood drumming in her ears. Low and smooth, it cut through her fear with precision and authority. If only his command mattered.

"Who the fuck are you?" Luca asked.

The gun barrel shook against her head. She focused on her *Papà* and waited for him to intervene.

"Your boss," Dante said. "Put down the gun."

Luca tightened his grip on her arm. "Fuck you!"

"She's just a broad," Antonio said.

Pivoting, Luca faced him. "If you ever fucking touch her again, I…"

A gunshot reverberated through the room. She froze, but Luca's blood splattered the table and her face. His hand fell away, and she stared at her wide-eyed cousin as he collapsed to the floor with a heavy thud. Blood trickled down her face, dripped past her chin and fell onto her dress, but for the moment, she breathed. As the echoing gunshot faded, the dinner party's cacophonous confusion flooded her sense.

Her aunts screamed, and chairs scraped as Lisette fainted into Martin's arms.

Antonio pulled Gisella into a chair. "I've got you."

She wrenched free her arm. "You almost got me killed!"

"Fucking idiot," Antonio said. "Over a woman."

Her remaining cousin, the one in charge of claims, held his gun pointed at Dante.

"Stand down," Gregorio said.

The man complied.

Raising her hand to her cheek, she pulled it away wet and looked at the heavy residue of Luca's life. Without the fight or flight impulse, numbness weighted down her limbs. The blood sprayed across the floor could have been hers. Raising her gaze, she looked at her liberator.

Dante laid his gun on the table.

She stared at the piece and swallowed. "Thank you."

He looked away.

Ursula came around the table, stepped over Luca's body, and claimed his seat. "Are you okay?"

"Serve the next course," Gregorio said.

Gisella pushed away her untouched soup bowl.

A server removed the dish and replaced it with the *secondi and contorni* dishes. Lobster served with a delicate cream sauce and a separate plate of asparagus would prime her father's appetite. Knowing the man, a meat dish would follow.

"Wine?" a second server asked.

She nodded and picked up her seafood fork.

As he filled her glass, his hand shook.

"Are you okay?" Ursula asked.

Gisella swallowed. "Later."

"Later? You have blood in your hair." Ursula's voice rose above the scrapes and adjustments of the seated diners.

"Girls," Gregorio said.

The subtle reprimand brought them back to their childhood, unexplained visitors in the middle of the night and countless friends and family members who came to holidays one year then disappeared the next. She put a forkful of lobster into her mouth and chewed the meaty seafood. Luca had scared the shit out of her, ruined her taste for lobster and upended her trust in her father.

Closing her eyes, she tried to savor the delicacy and find something beautiful about the evening. The music played, she breathed and Dante had saved her life. Opening her eyes, she found him talking to Juniper. The woman laughed like she had a box at the racetrack. Reaching under the table, Gisella found Ursula's hand and squeezed it. "You're not a bargaining chip."

"At least I'll be safe." Ursula picked up her fork with her left hand.

Gisella swallowed. "Is that enough?"

"You tell me," Ursula said.

Martin tossed a sheet over Luca and pulled the man's lifeless body from the dining room. His exertion muted his mumbled diatribe.

Gisella felt sure the man deserved a raise. Watching her cousin's exit in the reflection of a silver vase, she considered her sister's question. "I don't know."

Chapter Five

The tension in the formal dining room was thicker than the lobster's cream sauce. Dante itched to pick up his gun and slide it back into his jacket, but if any other mad Vitella family members wanted to act out, he preferred to be ready.

Sitting to his left, Juniper kept her eyes downcast, but she shook her head and picked at her dish. "He was a good boy."

Dante lowered his fork. "I'm sorry you lost him."

She turned and tilted her head. "I didn't think you had it in you."

"What?"

"*Il buonsenso.*"

He opened his mouth for a translation.

"Gumption. Grit. Common Sense. A man threatens something that belongs to you, you defend it," Juniper said.

"I get it." He ground out his response. "But I own nothing."

The woman leaned back in her chair and waved her hand over her dish.

A server appeared and whisked away the lobster.

She lit a cigarette, leaned back and crossed her ankles. "I had three husbands. Don't talk to me about ownership. The first one had me at a look." She smiled. "The third one paid for the privilege."

"What happened to them?" The Vitella family had frustrated him to the point that he wanted to yank the cigarette from the sixty-year-old woman's grip and burn it to the filter. He'd left San Diego to avoid meals and mistakes like this one, but fuck if they didn't find him.

Juniper exhaled. "Wouldn't you like to know?"

Snatching the cigarette from her sister, Julietta stubbed it out on a porcelain plate.

"Not at the table."

"Killjoy," Juniper said.

Julietta pushed back her chair and rose.

"Ladies." Gregorio lowered his cutlery.

Looking up, Dante examined the man seated at the head of the table. The threat of losing a daughter and the actualization of losing a nephew appeared to have no effect on the man's appetite, but a pair of bickering old women solicited a remark. Dante wondered if he'd bitten off more than he could chew.

The two black-haired prima donnas sitting across the table avoided his gaze like he had the plague, yet one of them would become his wife. The deal rubbed him the wrong way, but the dowry greased his uneasiness. If he asked them to pick, could he absolve himself of the choice? Divorcing the woman wasn't an option and would bring Gregorio's kin down on his head. Which sister preferred a life of abandonment?

The singer or the dancer? His dick twitched. He'd take the dancer's fire over the singer's somber control.

His father had made the same choice, and it'd landed him in his grave. Dante's mother, Isabella, could trace her lineage back to Christopher Columbus, but she whispered of the navigator's Portuguese past.

When Dante had challenged her European identity with four hundred years of Mexican residency, she dismissed her surroundings and the Aztec blood tainting her peers. A few years later, her husband floated a move, and she'd jumped on the idea.

Decamping to southern California had seemed like the natural, Caucasian progression to her elite ambitions, but cartel ties followed her. In the end, she had been right. Her peers' opioid-laced habits and her son's modern sensibilities had killed her and her blonde, blue-eyed husband.

Dante understood the flint-starved tinder created by big money and blood-bound brotherhood. Add a few tacos, regional grievances and Asian competition, and you had his childhood. As soon as he grew old enough to ask for the things he wanted, he had them and understood their cost. When he'd walked away from that life, he'd hoped an Ivy League education would reset his course, but it had only landed him back in the same testosterone-fueled shit show he'd tried to escape. Was anyone at this overly set table going to thank him for stopping Luca and ruining a perfectly good meal?

Gregorio met his gaze and raised his eyebrows.

Dante's mother, Isabella, had said her blood ran pure. She forgot to mention it simmered and smoldered with suppressed righteousness. Dante spent his entire life getting his impulses under control. He held Gregorio's stare like a man carrying the authority to invest billions of dollars in clean currency. Then he smiled like the entitled, greedy, possessive little shit he once was.

Gregorio nodded. Clearing his throat, he waited for the room's occupants to quiet. "Lisette and I are getting married in three months' time."

Every person in the room turned to stare at the empty chair at the foot of the table where Lisette had sat before she'd fainted and Martin had carried her from the room.

"As our family grows, I expect you to honor her as my wife. Whether people grow up in the Vitella family or marry in, once they're in, they're in."

Gisella and Ursula stared at each other.

Dante watched identical, cool masks settle over their beautiful faces. If the sisters knew of their father's upcoming nuptials, they hid it well. A second later, they looked at their father and smiled like obedient daughters.

"Well, that's wonderful news," Juniper said.

Dinner guests chatted with their neighbors.

Servers appeared with trays of champagne glasses.

Dante waited for Gisella or Ursula to respond to their father's news. The pair kept their gazes on their plates. Surely, a stepmother merited a vote of support.

The sisters remained quiet.

Narrowing his gaze, he wondered what sins Lisette had committed to keep the tanned Venuses from offering a hint of congratulations. Neither woman smiled. He exhaled and looked closer. Blood marred Gisella's hair, but as she raised her wine, her rigid backbone kept her hand steady. He expected a sip.

She gulped.

In that moment, he understood her fight for control. Whatever Lisette's sins, Gisella and her sister would weather them and fight their battles in private. The restraint impressed him, and he wanted to offer her a slow clap...or wipe the stain from her glossy hair.

At her side, Ursula picked at her nails like the announcement had little bearing on her life. She was a little aloof, but he found her curves attractive in a pin-up way. He could certainly consummate the marriage, but he'd rather not imagine Gregorio's staff jerking off to his Madonna.

If Luca had held Ursula hostage, would Dante have shot him as quickly? Looking back and forth between the sisters, he found himself staring at Gisella. He flexed his fingers and told himself the hallway encounter had primed his reflexes, but he couldn't claim the woman. She had to come to him.

"Thank you for your support." Gregorio sipped his champagne. "I hope our wedding is the first of many. I have two beautiful daughters, and a charming fiancée. What more could a man want?"

"Freedom," Dante whispered to himself.

Juniper elbowed him.

Gisella pushed back from the table. "Forgive me. I'm not feeling well."

"Stay seated," Gregorio said.

She had the nerve to glare at her father.

Dante smiled. Her long lines would look amazing on the stage, lounging in the bathtub or tangled between his sheets, but her long, black, mess of hair should be free of a tight-laced bun. If she wanted to dance, who was he to stop her?

Hemmed in by the hallway's walls, her sassy personality had suggested her creative freedom moved beyond tutus and lace, but she'd shied away from him and looked like a princess who liked to spend her father's money. She'd probably cost him millions in upkeep. He should have asked for twenty million, but if he wanted her over her busty songbird sister, he had to make her want him.

"I have to rehearse." Gisella crossed her arms. "My performance is in two days."

Gregorio shook his head. "Your ballet can wait."

The spoiled mischief of an eight-year-old boy coursed through his veins. "Aren't you a little old to be on stage?" he asked.

Gisella glared.

"I'm sure you'll prove me wrong. I can't wait to see the performance."

She frowned. "Only the women attend."

He cocked his head. "Really?"

Her tongue darted out, but she clamped her lips tight.

Feeling sure he could fold his six-foot-four frame into a theater seat for three hours, he toyed with his fork. "I'd like to attend. Unless you're embarrassed?"

"Ursula sings every Sunday at mass," Gregorio said. "Perhaps you'd rather join us in the family pew."

"Love to," Dante said, "but I think I'll sample both events."

"Sample?" She shook her head. "I doubt any tickets remain. The performance is in two days."

"And your father doesn't sponsor the event?"

"Platinum level." She stabbed at the food on her plate. "I'm sure you'll enjoy the show."

Gregorio cleared his throat. "Dante, why don't you move into the guest suite until we've finalized the deal?

I'm sure you'll find the house more hospitable than your hotel room."

"How generous." Alessio's penthouse apartment served as his hotel room. The unit's sleek opulence kept him comfortable, but it also reminded him of the gap between his achievements and those of his billionaire boss. "I'd love to stay here."

Gisella and Ursula looked at each other.

"Gregorio's fiancée will spend a fortune on the wedding," Julietta said. "She'll take over the entire house. Get out before the chaos begins."

"Probably." Dante glanced at Gisella. She kept her head down, but she and Ursula exchanged softly uttered comments. He'd lay down his credit card to know what every Vitella woman in the room thought of the evening. Judging by Gisella's gold sequined dress, the knowledge would cost him, but he'd faced tough situations and emerged unscathed. Rubbing his hand across his jaw, he met Gisella's stare and smiled. *This time might be different.*

Chapter Six

Slamming her bedroom door, Gisella stripped off the sheath dress and laid it over her dressing chair. She stood in front of the full-length mirror and admired her runway lingerie while her heels sank into the thick carpet. Thank God she lived. Her chin trembled. Perhaps she should have skipped the dress and paraded into the dining room in her silk and lace. At least the uproar would have spared Luca's life.

Dropping her shoulders, she unclasped her bra, kicked away her shoes and slid off her thong. She left the undergarments in a pile and headed for the shower. Safe beneath the hot spray, she let her tears fall and wondered who would tell Eleanor of Luca's death.

The pipes shuddered.

She screamed.

Pressing her hand over her mouth, she listened past the spraying water and heard Ursula singing at the top of her lungs. She and her sister shared bathroom plumbing, but their approaches to processing grief differed wildly.

Luca's cold gun barrel pressed against her temple and created a ghostly pressure. The memory couldn't erase their stolen beers and fraternal jokes, but if he'd pulled the trigger, she'd have died, and survival mattered more than family relations.

Dante had set down his gun as if he took a man's life every day of the week. Then he asked to attend her ballet performance. Luring him away from Ursula should thrill her, but she needed him to reject her father's Machiavellian manipulations, not move into the guest suite.

Turning off the water, she slipped on short silk pajamas, belted the matching robe and wrapped a towel around her hair. If she could convince her father to rescind his invitation, she could buy herself time to choreograph act two.

Jogging down the stairs, she gripped the handrail and pivoted on the first floor's cold, marble floors. *Papà* and her cousins had probably gathered in his study to address Luca's death. Dante would be well on his way to the hotel to pack his bags. If she could make her case, she could stop him from... She slammed into an unexpected body, and the impact expelled the air from her lungs. *Umf!*

The impact should have knocked her on her ass, but as she fell backward, Dante reached out and grabbed for her silk robe.

The robe's hastily tied knot gave way.

He lunged, wrapped an arm around her waist, cradled her head and rolled.

Instead of smacking her head against the cold marble, she found herself sprawled across a very warm and solid man. Her stomach and thighs tightened, and she traced the solid contours beneath his skin. Unable to stop exploration, she lowered her hand and gripped him hard. She couldn't stop thinking about the man. If fate wanted to plant her on top of him, half naked, she'd make the most of her opportunity. She rolled her hips.

"Shit," he said, "this isn't how things were supposed to go."

The note of censure permeated her lust. Scrambling off him, she stood and plucked her fallen towel from the floor. If the material held, she would have been fine, albeit embarrassed. It didn't, and she couldn't spend her life wallowing in the past or second-guessing her actions. "You can't stay here."

Bracing himself on his hands, he looked up. He curled his lips into a smile. "Why not? I enjoy the view."

Belting her robe, she scanned the hallway. "Well, the view's not part of the deal."

He narrowed his eyes. "It can be."

Shaking her head, she peered toward her father's study. "You don't know what you're doing. Ursula loves someone else. I'm a professional dancer, and you?" She lifted her chin. "Miami will eat you alive."

Standing, Dante brushed off his black pants. "Doubtful."

She'd meant to piss off the man, not give him breathing room to swipe the lint from his pants. If lust hadn't distracted her, she would have sent him packing. She needed him offended and pissed off enough to turn his attention toward someone else. If she had to bribe the maid to film a sex video with the guy, she'd do it. "Dante…"

Walking past her, he headed toward the front door.

His cold indifference hardened her reserve. Even as her cheeks burned, and her heartbeat raced from the impact, she knew her obligations. "Thank you for saving my life."

He paused. "You're welcome."

"I'll make sure you have tickets to the ballet, but don't sleep here. My family just lost Luca. You killed him, Dante. Give us some space."

Turning, he closed the distance and yanked her against his chest.

She inhaled the mix of woody and citrus scents she caught in the hallway, but time mellowed the cologne's intensity and added the subtle musk of subdued tension. Pressed against his chest, so close she could feel his heartbeat, she looked into his hazel eyes and felt his grip on her waist tighten.

"You should choose better allies." Releasing her, he stepped back and shook his head. "In my experience, a man who holds a gun to your head doesn't love you."

She covered her beating heart. "He was my cousin."

"And now the idiot's dead." Shaking his head, he turned his back on her. "And fuck the ballet. I'll find another way to make my mark."

Planting her hands on her hips, she watched him march toward the gleaming front door. "Excuse me?" Her question echoed.

He turned. "I said, fuck it. Ballet's not an institution."

His derision plucked the breath from her chest. He might as well have cocked his gun and pointed it. If the man could dismiss her art as quickly as he dismissed a server, he couldn't love her. The mistake served her right. In the course of a week, he'd surprised and delighted her, but she'd let her infatuation run wild.

The only times he'd flattered her, she was naked or spotlighted on the stage he despised.

"Choreographers revise ballets so often the original choreographers would barely recognize their pieces. Every dancer I know is a petulant child who goes by one name. Belinda. Coco. Lulu." He ticked off the names. "What piece are you dancing? *Romeo and Juliet? Swan Lake? Giselle?*"

She opened her mouth to correct him. The upcoming performance stripped off ballet's tragic romanticism and exposed the pain and misery of near-success.

"Who gets excited about gaunt women in pointe shoes, singing slaves, shameless Muslims, conniving Hindus? Fuck cancel culture, but your art form has an inclusivity problem. Coco was a fucking Black goddess, but she never landed the parts she wanted."

"Coco?" she asked. "You dated a dancer named Coco?"

He rubbed his jaw. "Flexible as fuck."

Gisella rolled her lips. "I didn't realize you were so...cultured."

He popped his collar. "Whatever. I'm here on business. Find me a ticket to the performance. You have two days."

Raising her chin, she smiled. "Why? You obviously won't enjoy it."

He narrowed his eyes. "Try me."

Martin walked into the foyer and opened the front door. "Will there be anything else, Mr. Johnson?"

Dante straightened his jacket and walked into the floodlit drive. His rental car idled, and a staff member stood at attention. "Probably not, but I'll let you know."

Waiting until Martin closed the door, she exhaled.

"Are you okay, Miss Vitella?" he asked.

Making eye contact, she swallowed. "Are you okay, Martin?"

He glanced toward the dining room.

Staff removed the remains of the meal. A woman unknown to her mopped the floor near her seat. She wanted to stop the progress and leave Luca's blood as testimony. He died, but she lived, and the razor's edge between their outcomes would stay with her for the rest of her life.

"I'm alive," Martin said.

"So am I." She cleared her throat. Finding allies among the staff helped her sneak in and out of the house, but she didn't plan to exchange life stories over espresso. "Where's Antonio?"

"Your father's study."

Resuming her path, she marched toward the back of the house, opened the door and found her *Papà* and her cousin sitting in front of the lit fireplace. "Am I expendable?"

The men looked at each other.

Marching up to Antonio, she examined the suppressed smile tugging at his lips. He'd used Eleanor to bait Luca, but he cared little for the woman. Gisella wouldn't fuck with the man. Despite family ties, he probably cared even less for her. Raising her hand, she slapped his face and waited for the chance to call out his barbarics.

He winced but remained seated.

She tired of waiting. "If you ever again put me in the middle of one of your testosterone-fueled pissing contests, I will call every asshole you've fucked and give them the codes to your apartment. I will dump my cell phone in the DA's lap. If you think…"

Antonio rose.

Standing, he had five inches on her.

She held her ground. "Eleanor and Luca deserved more than your over-indulged, asinine whims..."

"Sit down," Gregorio said.

Clearing his throat, Antonio complied.

"That's enough. Dante saved you." Swirling his drink, Gregorio sipped the amber liquid. "Move on and be grateful."

She faced down her father. "Why? So you can marry off Ursula, drop me with some idiot named Marco and let Lisette suck your cock until she drains you?"

"Gisella Santa Maria..."

She held up her hand. "No! You can't dispose of your daughters like anxious dogs. You want to spend your retirement in Tuscany? Go! Leave Ursula and I out of it. We'll be fine."

"Doubtful." Antonio raised his drink to his lips. "And he has Saint Vincent and the Grenadines in mind."

Pulling his glass from his hand, she hurled it toward the fire and let the alcohol bloom. Saint Vincent and the Grenadines was a Caribbean country located in the southeast Windward Islands of the Lesser Antilles. Her father registered his yacht and several questionable accounts with the island nation, but Antonio banked on Miami. "I don't care where he has in mind! I care about making the decisions that affect my life!"

Whiskey dribbled down Antonio's chin, and he narrowed his eyes. "Jesus, Gisella. What's gotten into you? One minute you're sweet, and the next minute you're like an old fish wife."

"I'm this close to achieving my dreams" — she held her fingers apart an inch — "and I won't let you derail my momentum with your bullshit." She turned and pointed at her father. "We had an implicit deal. I played nice, and you let me do what I wanted."

"Within reason," he said.

"You can't go back on the deal." She crossed her arms. "I won't let you."

"And you're in no position to make demands."

"You're in good health. Stay another decade, make another billion. Let Lisette build herself a castle," she said.

He sipped his drink. "She doesn't want to get caught in the crossfire."

Chest heaving, Gisella took slow, measured breaths. "I don't blame her."

Antonio cleared his throat. "It's a done deal, sis. Sit down."

Ignoring him, she focused on her father. "Pick, *Papà*. Am I in or am I out?"

He worked his jaw.

She switched to Italian. "You think firing a few maids will keep your secrets safe? I know how your empire works, and if I hadn't been so busy at rehearsal these last few weeks, I would have known about your CIH scam. Your company can't go legit. The minute you walk off, the back-office staff will disperse and transfer their allegiance to whichever boss starts handing out kickbacks." She stepped forward and dropped her voice. "CIH will crumble."

Their silence confirmed her fears.

"You don't care, do you?"

Ice clanked against glassware.

The urge to gag rose in her throat. Backing up, she shook her head and adjusted her worldview. The man preached about the old ways, loyalty and rewards. If he would cash out his reputation for a few million dollars, he'd cash out his paternal relationship, too. "Call off the deal."

"The deal will close," Gregorio said. "And you'll go back to obsessing over your shoes, picking up trash and living life like an entitled little girl. If you want to continue your lifestyle, you'll marry Marco, do your job and stop sticking your pert nose where it doesn't belong."

"And if I don't?" she asked.

Antonio rose, walked to the bar and refilled his glass. Leaning on the bar, he sipped his drink and waited.

She stared at her father.

"Go to bed, Gigi."

Turning her back on him, she slammed the study door and raced up the stairs to find her sister. Her robe tie slipped, and the panels flapped behind her as she climbed the stairs. "Ursula! Ursula, let's go! We're leaving."

She flung open her sister's door and stared.

Sitting in the middle of the floor, surrounded by lit candles, Ursula held a rosary and prayed.

Reaching past the ring of light, Gisella reached for her sister's hand. "Come on. We'll get a hotel room. You can pray there."

Ursula shook her head. "You don't understand, Gisella. I don't care what happens to me. I'll be fine." She lowered the rosary. "I love him."

Retracting her hand, Gisella struggled to understand the pronoun. Surely, her sister didn't love Dante. She loved God, but enough to weather an arranged marriage? She cleared her throat. "Who?"

"Pietro," Ursula said. "He's my rock, but he won't leave his vocation. Without him, I have nothing. I'd rather be dead."

Dropping to the floor, Gisella wrapped her arms around her knees, laid her head on her arms and stared. "Dead?"

Ursula nodded.

After the night's activities, the proximity of the term's significance overwhelmed her. Taking Ursula's place in the arranged marriage would jeopardize her dancing career. Ratting out her father would endanger her life. Fleeing into the night gained her nothing. "I hope it never comes to that conclusion. I'll convince Dante to call off the deal."

"How?" Ursula asked.

"I'll tell him the truth." She closed her eyes.

Picking up her prayer, Ursula prayed for atonement.

Gisella listened to the words. *Papà* was right. She was an entitled little girl. Her background afforded her every advantage and none of the stress plaguing the corps de ballet. Keeping out of the family business felt like enough distance. She didn't want to be the savior or the dealmaker. She wanted to dance. Letting Ursula's prayers guide her thoughts, she replayed her upcoming dance steps and let the music carry away her concerns.

Imagining the lifts and turns she'd execute with her partner, Jandro, she looked down to signal her descent. Instead of Jandro's disciplined frame, Dante held her firm. Sliding down his body, she cupped his jaw and wondered if she could dance with him.

Chapter Seven

"You must appear weightless and sylph-like," the Artistic Director said. "Float. Release your worries and let the music move you."

Holding a water bottle to her chest, Gisella accepted the director's notes. In her sweaty leggings and leotard, she could be any Miami woman recovering from an aerobics class, but those honed beauties wouldn't lose their careers if they flubbed a move.

In the stage's corner, Jandro spaced two chairs and supported his weight. As he used his body weight to deepen a stretch, his dark, wavy hair shone beneath the stage lights. Gisella looked away. The man had a wife and two kids. Lately, she had a thing for blonds.

Some of Jandro's stretches helped her. This morning, she followed his lead into an Upward Dog Pike. The quick stretch opened up her spine, strengthened her upper body and tightened her glutes. It also burned like hell. As soon as he'd ended the count, she sprang to her feet and begged off. If she didn't come up with an excuse to leave, he'd start doing *développés* from an arched handstand, and she'd fall flat on her ass. As long as he didn't drop her on stage, he could keep stretching and uploading content for his social media followers. They flattered him to his heart's content.

"Jandro, are you paying attention?" the Artistic Director asked.

He deepened his stretch. "Yes, Madam!"

"I still have your audition tapes from the Central Pennsylvania Ballet. If you don't nail your lifts, I'll send you back to the School of American Ballet to teach!"

"I love you and fear you, Señora!"

Gisella bit her lips to contain her laugh. After the dinner she'd shared with her family, she considered *Papà* and the Artistic Director formidable threats, but she preferred to deal with her problems by placating her aggressors.

"Go home, get some rest and come back for the evening rehearsal." The Artistic Director clapped her hands and dismissed the assembly.

The dancers dispersed.

Packing her bag, Gisella picked up her purse and traded cordialities. She headed for the back door. Antonio waited in the bright sunshine to take her home.

He leaned against the passenger door. "Good day?"

"Fuck off," she said.

Laughing, he walked around to the driver's side door and slipped behind the wheel.

The ride to her father's house took less than twenty minutes. By the time her mind stopped whirling with corrections and improvements, she stood in front of the imported hardwood doors, holding her dance bag and her purse.

Opening it, she stepped inside and listened. Her father and Dante stood in the hallway leading from the foyer. Dante's deep and indifferent voice overpowered her father's measured tones. A rush of awareness ran down the length of her spine, and she wished she had time to shower before confronting the pair.

"Martin will get you everything you need," Gregorio said.

"I'm obliged." Dante and her father walked into view.

"Trust me…the pleasure is mine."

She dropped her bags in the corner and crossed her arms. "Business is slow today?"

"Behave, Gisella." Gregorio headed for his study.

She turned toward the hallway leading to the kitchens.

Dante followed her but stayed two steps back.

The slow assault revved her senses. Stopping, she looked over her shoulder. "Are you lost?"

"Hungry."

"Call Martin."

Dante cocked his head. "You'll do."

"I didn't invite you to stay."

"Do you want me to go?" he asked.

She hesitated. "Make your own sandwiches." Pushing past the kitchen's sliding door, she waved to Tia. The family's cook was a welcome constant. Gisella opened the refrigerator and pulled out the high-protein lunch plate waiting for her. Setting the plate on the island counter, she sat on a bar stool and reached for the remote.

Tia circled the island and appraised Dante. "You're hungry? You eat in the dining room."

Gisella suppressed a smile.

"Gisella said I could make myself a sandwich."

"*Hmf.*" Tia opened a drawer, pulled out a butter knife and slapped it on the counter.

The woman spoke Italian like a native, but she only used it to intimidate the delivery drivers or cuss out the vegetables too stubborn to grow in the house's food garden. Tossing a handful of almonds into her mouth, Gisella hoped the matchup between Tia and Dante proved to be as entertaining as she expected.

"Shit." Dante picked up the remote and turned up the volume.

On screen, a tanker vessel burned off the coast of southern California.

"*Two hours ago, a fire erupted on a cargo ship named the Pressed Pearl. The vessel, which is carrying tons of chemicals and plastic pellets, is anchored near the port of San Diego.*"

Black smoke billowed from the ship, and the green shipping containers looked like a mess of melted and twisted candy-bars. Coast Guard vessels fought the fire, and marine tugs pumped gallons of seawater into the air. Despite their efforts, barrels littered the seas surrounding the burning ship, and helicopters transmitted the disaster to the news outlets. Gisella swallowed her almonds. Faced with an epic environmental disaster, her problems seemed petty. "They ought to tow it out to see and blow it up before the sea creatures mistake the plastic pellets for food."

"Have they said anything about casualties?" Dante asked.

"No." Tia waved to a delivery driver. "I'll be right back."

Alone in the kitchen with Dante, Gisella frowned and puzzled out his reaction.

Gripping the edge of the counter, he stood beside her and leaned forward.

Last night, he'd breezed into her life, invasive and rude, but his concern for the vessel's crew revealed unexpected sensitivity. At the same time, her pulse drummed in her ears. The nameless people on that ship mattered, but she couldn't mourn their loss in the marble-clad kitchen.

Looking away from the television, she admired how Dante's stance drew his dress shirt tight across his shoulders and shamed herself for the admiration while families lost their loved ones. Shaking off her reaction, she focused on the unfolding environmental tragedy. "Maybe this accident will lead to tighter regulations. I'm impressed you care, but it's not your problem."

He swatted her ass. "Shut up."

The brief pain summoned a rush of blood and annoyance. "Watch it."

"I'm trying."

His low, distracted words pulled her attention away from her warming ass. "The house has ten other televisions, Dante. Make your sandwich and savor your disaster voyeurism in another rom."

"My cousin works on that ship. He runs coke up the West Coast and unloads it alongside the plastics' feedstock."

"Oh." She processed the pieces of information. "Your family's in the trade?"

Turning his back to the television, he muted it and set down the remote. "They are. I'm not. Any more questions?"

She rubbed her butt. "Can you check on him?"

He tipped up her chin. "You care?"

Glaring, she held his stare. "I wouldn't want the seagulls to choke."

Dropping his grip, he spun her and slapped her ass harder.

The heat and pressure released something in her. Wondering what would override his control, she summoned a cheeky retort, but caught his furtive glance toward the television.

"He's a good man."

"I hope he's okay." She swallowed her curiosity. After a grueling morning, separating her response to the spanking from her response to Dante seemed like a fraught undertaking. Behind her, a man's possible death played out in a never-ending reel of flames, waves and black smoke. Beside her, Dante kept back his shoulders and accepted the outcome. She followed his profile and the luxurious sweep of his golden lashes. Her vision wavered, and she swayed.

Dante cupped her elbow and centered her on the bar stool. "Eat."

She picked up an apple. "The deal won't work."

Shifting, he looked away from the news coverage. "How so?"

She bit into the apple and chewed. "You can't replace my father. The minute he walks, CIH will crumble."

Dante smiled. "He's paying me fifteen million to marry you or your sister. Who will it be?"

She choked.

He slapped her back, and the apple piece flew from her mouth.

Carrying two cardboard boxes, Tia walked back into the kitchen and lowered them to the counter. "We're having veal."

Speechless, Gisella watched Dante's face to guide her reaction. Should she feel flattered? He looked toward the television set, and the lines near his eyes deepened. She couldn't pinpoint the cause. He seemed unfazed by CIH's impending collapse and the prospect of an arranged marriage. The man might be in so far over his head he'd drown them all.

Fifteen million. She pondered the amount and watched the ship burn. Saving Ursula mattered, but another opportunity appeared. If Dante collected the money, Gisella could dump him and get by on a tenth.

"Do you like veal?" Tia asked.

Dante turned away from the television set and nodded.

"You know it's baby cow?" Gisella asked.

He scratched the side of his mouth. "Is that so? I thought it was an endangered antelope." He raised his eyebrows.

Tia laughed and unpacked the box. "You'll fit in just fine."

"There's no 'fitting in'," Gisella said. "He's visiting, then he's going home to…"

"San Diego," Dante said.

She nodded as if his answer confirmed her stance on his imminent departure. San Diego and Miami shared a latitude, but as far as she cared, he could take his disruptive chest back to the West Coast.

Tia shook her head and walked into the pantry.

Dante leaned close. "You know I don't…"

She held up her hand. "Let's go back to the fifteen million."

Crossing his arms, he ran his tongue along his teeth and seemingly considered his words. "You want me to pick you."

"Hell, no. I want you to know how much Ursula will cost to maintain." The lie dug a hole, but she planned to use the embankment to her advantage.

He raised his eyebrows.

She kept her poker face. When Ursula refused to marry him, she'd offer herself on the condition he sign over a portion of his take. Given a choice between fifteen and zero, he'd settle for thirteen. Maybe twelve. She drew a salary from the company, but it seemed sufficient for lunch, not life.

Stepping closer, he leaned down. "I saved your life."

She swallowed. "You shot a man." His hand grazed her breast. She kept her breathing measured. "You're not the type of man I'd marry."

Pulling back, his expression hardened. "And why's that?"

"You're not Italian." She chewed her lips. "And you're blond, and poor and" —finding flaws with this man was harder than it appeared —"violent."

"Violent."

His dark tone warned her to step back. She focused on the television and pretended to ignore him, but she felt him lean close, and her heart skipped a beat.

"You're right, Gisella, I'm violent and possessive." He trailed his thumb across her collarbone. "I don't share, and when I want something, it's mine."

She held her breath.

Drawing the touch down the length of her arm, he lingered at her fingertips and pulled back.

Her skin tingled, but she refused to face him.

"You're a smart woman."

His observation felt too laden and dangerous for a compliment. A shiver ran down her spine. She wanted to be weak and so wrong about him that her knees shook.

"Throw your sister under the bus and run, little girl."

She absorbed the dark admonishment, closed her eyes and listened to him walk from the kitchen. His footfalls were so soft, she knew he could sneak into a woman's life and claim her heart. The second the door closed, she let her shoulders sag.

Tia walked out of the pantry. "You're playing with the devil, Gisella."

Exhaling, she looked at the cook. "I'm surrounded by devils."

"Better the devils you know than the devil you don't know," Tia said.

"What if he's not a devil?"

Tia shook her head. "Oh, Gigi, they're all devils. The sooner you harden your heart, the longer you'll live and the less you'll love."

She'd never considered loving a man. Lust, license and power made sense, but she barely understood love. It was a weakness threatening to cripple her ambitions. When her mother lived, the emotion made perfect sense, and Gisella absorbed waves of devotion. Now, she struggled to imagine loving a man so capable of taking care of himself that he pushed away other people. She loved her sister like a small, injured blackbird. She loved her father like a heavy, sovereign threat. But Dante? She only needed one thing from that man, and it wasn't love.

* * * *

Skidding down the stairs the morning before the performance, Gisella saw her sister floating in the pool. Her long, sheer black robe trailed behind her in the water like a dramatic cape, and the size of her sun hat made Gisella wonder if Ursula liked to swim or make a scene. Gisella opened the door to the patio and shaded her eyes against the sun. "What are you doing? I've seen wakes that look more entertaining."

Ursula trailed her fingers in the cool, blue water. "I'm praying."

"You're always praying."

"I'm praying for a miracle," Ursula said.

Gisella hesitated. If her sister couldn't have the priest, an arranged marriage might keep her out of a melancholy death spiral. At the very least, it would keep her off a bus to darkest Peru. "Shouldn't you be leading the choir?"

"We had a soloist. If you'd come to Mass, you'd have known."

Gisella cleared her throat. "I needed to run."

"Dante doesn't run, and he seems in fine shape."

Adjusting her bags, Gisella dodged the association and her interest in Dante. She subscribed to a minimalist religious approach, but if God had a plan for Dante and Ursula, Gisella would find another way to finance her dreams. "Good for him."

A car door slammed.

Peering through the French doors, Gisella saw Martin admit Dante into the foyer. The ADC representative wore black dress pants and a white short-sleeve shirt. His tired expression suggested he hadn't slept since leaving her father's house the prior night.

Antonio walked out of the hallway leading from the kitchen. Wearing ripped jeans and a black muscle shirt, he looked like a garage mechanic. She skewed her jaw. In another world, the men would give and take curt nods. They looked ready to exchange blows.

Her stomach twisted, and she broke out in a cold sweat. She couldn't afford to lose any more lousy relatives, and Dante meant…something. Abandoning Ursula in the pool, she marched into the house and faced the men with her hands on her hips. "What the hell do the two of you think you're doing?"

Dante held a stack of computer printouts in his hand. He shoved it hard against Antonio's chest. "You lied about the profit-and-loss sheets."

Her heart beat a mile a minute. Of course Antonio had lied. If Dante knew anything about her family's ethics, he'd second-guess and double-check every piece of documentation Antonio touched. Her cousin and her father took numerical rounding and unnamed accounting to an art form. Calling their documentation lies might be generous, but the Securities and Exchange Commission had either pocketed bribes or never caught on.

Taking the papers from Dante and dropping his arms to his side, Antonio shrugged. "You backing out? Figures." His fingers brushed the gun stashed in his waistband.

She stepped between the men.

Dante wrapped an arm around her waist, slid her to the side and leaned close to Antonio.

Before she had time to react to his touch, he slammed Antonio against the wall. A painting rattled.

"Get me the real numbers, or I'll get them myself."

Gisella heard the threat behind Dante's promise and shivered in the air-conditioned foyer. Being set aside like a child rankled, but she had to intervene. She flipped her hair over her shoulder.

Antonio turned his face away from Dante. "Good luck."

"You think you're the only man Eleanor likes to fuck?" Dante asked.

She and Antonio drew in simultaneous breaths.

Turning, Dante stared at her. "Is this how you spend your days? Traipsing around the house in tank tops and boy shorts? Put on a fucking shirt."

Popping her tank top strap, she exhaled and let the tension disseminate. "Or what?"

Brushing past her, Dante lowered his head. "Or you won't have a choice."

She tried to laugh off the threat, but the sound died in her throat.

He stopped, and his attention settled on her face. "Do you know anything about me?"

"You're Daniel Johnson, some trusted member of ADC Industries. Your cousin smuggles drugs out of San Diego, and you think you understand my world." She tried for nonchalance, but her voice shook.

A muscle in his jaw ticked. He turned toward the door.

"Did I forget anything?" The man seemed to do what he wanted, regardless of rules. She'd always worked within a rigid set of confines.

He paused, one hand on the doorknob.

"Dante?" she asked.

Turning, he let his slow gaze travel from her toes to her face.

She bore the inspection.

"I killed my father," Dante said. "Don't think you're special." Looking past her shoulder, he stared at Antonio. "Either of you."

Walking out of the house, he let the door slam.

Martin skidded into the room. "Did I miss something?"

She turned and yanked the papers out of Antonio's hands. "Could you find someone less lethal to torture? You think Ursula will marry him and lure him into the family business? You and *Papà* are out of your minds."

Antonio backhanded her. "Watch your fucking mouth."

The assault stung, but she knew his strength, and the blow barely registered. Tearing up the papers, she littered the floor with the remnants of his deal. "Give him the real numbers, Antonio. If he buys CIH and finds out you and *Papà* screwed him, you're as good as dead."

Scratching his neck, Antonio nodded. "I thought he'd wire the money and leave. By the time the company collapsed, I'd be on my way to Tuscany."

"With who? Eleanor?" She laughed. "That woman's fucking the gardener, too."

Antonio paled.

Slamming her dance bag and purse against his chest, she walked toward the front door, but heard her sister singing an old love song about wanting the thing you could never have. She turned.

Ursula leaned against the patio doors.

Water dripped down her legs and pooled on the marble. Her sheer robe hung to her ankles, but her swimsuit accentuated her breasts and her narrow waist. Gisella sighed. "You're late to the party."

Shrugging, Ursula ended the verse. "If God left you fools in charge, the party would never end. Was that my intended?"

Antonio nodded and rolled up her shirtsleeves.

"Give him my best." Ursula turned and walked back toward the pool. Her robe billowed behind her.

Gisella exhaled. She spent hours practicing leaps and turns, but her sister glided like a raven in flight. The thought of caging Ursula summoned her guilt. If she had access to her father's books, she could empower Dante and claim a kickback without marrying him. She could disappear into the witness protection program and start a new life. She could move to Thailand, but when the rice fields erased her identity, who would watch her dance?

* * * *

After the dress rehearsal, Gisella dispatched Antonio to pick up food, and she walked to the church where Ursula ran the choir.

Her sister and the priest stood shoulder to shoulder over a hymnal. In another life, he would be handsome, but his clerical collar stopped Gisella's appreciation. He might as well be a mannequin. Obviously, Ursula had no such compunctions.

Gisella wondered whether her sister consummated her lust or let smoldering glances light the church's candles. She'd rather have a brash, handsome husband who yelled and loved in equal measure. Solemnity and pining never made sense, but she understood passion. She cleared her throat.

Ursula glanced up and grinned. "Look what the cat dragged in!"

Gisella felt like yesterday's offering. The Artistic Director had pounced on every mistake, Jandro's strength had wavered and her thoughts had hovered outside her father's study. "I thought we could eat together. Antonio went to get food."

"He let you out of his sight?"

Gisella scratched her scalp. "Let's just say he's scrambling to stay in my good graces."

"Amen!" Ursula said.

Father Pietro winced, closed the hymnal and waved before he turned toward the vestry.

"Does he know how you feel?" Gisella asked.

Ursula claimed a pew. "I wouldn't put him in that position. Sometimes, we talk about moral dilemmas, but I haven't swiped the sacraments from the altar and thrown myself at the cloth."

"Could you throw yourself at Dante?"

Slipping down the polished wood, Ursula leaned her head against the backrest and closed her eyes. "For what? He's huge and abrupt. Can you imagine sharing breakfast with him each morning and discussing the news?"

Gisella sighed. She'd seen how intently Dante watched the news coverage of the burning cargo ship. If he cared about a cause, she believed he would dog it until he understood every nuance. "You're right. He's not exactly butter and marmalade."

Ursula licked her lips.

"But could you?"

Turning her head, Ursula stared. "Nobody can make me marry that man. My happiness depends on a spiritual connection. I don't need a thing in this world."

"I do," Gisella said. "If he marries one of us, *Papà* promised him fifteen million dollars. I need a portion of that cash."

"Take it." Ursula blinked.

"Are you sure? You don't want to be Mrs. Johnson?"

Turning to look at the fresco ceiling, Ursula smiled. "Truly, I could live my life on this pew listening to Fr. Pietro talk and singing my hymns."

"If you don't eat, it'll be a short life," Gisella said.

Ursula laughed. "You think *Papà* would let me starve?"

Weighing the question, Gisella imagined the lengths her father would pursue to get what he wanted. Luca lay buried in a cemetery, Lisette waited in the wings and Gisella and Ursula could produce a *bambino* to carry on his DNA. After they did their part, he'd shift his attention to the next generation. "He might let one of us go, but not both."

Linking arms, Ursula swung them like children on a playground. "When you're torturing Dante, try not to throw me under the bus."

"Who said I'm going to torture him?"

"I can hear your wheels spinning," Ursula said.

"That's my stomach rumbling."

"Oh." Ursula laughed. "Well, try not to get yourself killed in the crossfire. Those men play dirty games, and the only person who can redeem them died on a cross."

The admonishment hung between them, and dust motes floated in the air. "I'll do my best." She uttered the promise, but selfishness had gotten her into this mess. If she had a tenth of Dante's nerve, she wouldn't have killed her father, but she would have walked away from him a long time ago.

Chapter Eight

Behind the wheel of his convertible, Antonio approached the house.

Gisella puzzled at the gates standing open. As the driveway came into view, she gasped. Lines of parked cars waited, and uniformed attendants helped guests disembark. She turned to her cousin. "What is this?"

"An engagement party." Antonio loosened his collar.

"But I have a performance tomorrow. I'm supposed to sleep and"—she saw Dante alight from his car, and he looked deliciously good wearing a pale lavender shirt, a sports coat and navy loafers—"focus on my prep."

"Well, prep yourself a cocktail dress or face Gregorio's wrath."

"Why didn't he tell me?" she asked.

Antonio shrugged. "Dunno. The text from Lisette came in around ten."

She rubbed her temples. "Damn that woman and her fascination with spending money before *Papà* can do so much as blink. Take me around back."

"Sure you don't want to strut through the foyer in your stanky leotard and smashed hair?"

She punched his arm, and the outlet felt surprisingly good.

He glanced at the impact. "Suit yourself."

Slipping from the car, she rubbed her hands, let herself in the kitchen and came upon Lisette arguing with the catering staff. Tia stood in the corner sharpening knives.

"I wanted heirloom tomatoes!" Lisette said.

Gisella tried to sneak past the nightshade nightmare.

Lisette pivoted. "You! Why aren't you dressed?"

Replaying the question, Gisella searched for a hint of sensitivity. Finding none, she leaned on the island. "You're not mistress of this house. You think I care whether your party works out? Fuck you. If you cared about me, you'd have given me notice so I could honor your greedy little union."

"Your father told me not to bother you. He said you had to focus on your *performance*."

Lisette stretched out the noun as if Gisella strapped on her tap shoes and hustled tourists for tips in South Beach. Searching for parental concern behind the insensitivity, she could imagine *Papà* reining in his fiancée, but she couldn't imagine Lisette accepting the bit. Still, putting her pedicured foot in her mouth had to be one of Gisella's recently acquired talents. She took a deep, measured breath.

"She's lying," Tia said in Italian.

"What?" Gisella asked.

"Your dad gave his business associate her ticket to the ballet, and she called the caterer to fill her social calendar." Tia slid a chef's knife across the metal sharpener, and it made a metallic hiss. "She wouldn't know an heirloom tomato if it bit her on the ass."

Lisette stomped her foot. "Why does everyone in this house speak Italian?"

"Because we *are* Italian!" Multiple times in her life, Gisella felt like an outsider, but she didn't act like a spoiled brat to resolve her feelings. That skill came naturally, but Lisette had to understand family dynamics. "Every time I go back to Italy, I understand why *Papà* misses it. Italians understand nature's rhythms. The people in the cities and the countryside have different approaches to life, but they treasure family, food and hard work. When the world thinks of love stories, they think of Paolo and Francesca, Sigismondo and Isotta, Romeo and Juliet."

She swallowed. Romeo and Juliet might be overdoing it. The idiot teenagers had a lot to learn about weathering life's hiccups. If life beyond her sheltered bubble would be her new playground, she had a lot to learn, too. "If you're going to marry my father, figure out who you're inviting into your bed! He's *Italiano*." She enunciated the word incase Lisette failed to grasp it. "*Mafioso*. His roots are so deep, other plants wither. They don't" —she wrinkled her nose and looked at Lisette's flashy, bedazzled dress—"pretend he's someone he's not! I know who he is, and I love him. He's my father! You're…"

"What?" Lisette asked.

"His interior designer!"

Lisette laughed. "That's an insult? Well, aren't you special? You prance through the house like an entitled princess, but you do not know how many people suffer to produce your father's wealth. I'm trying to pull him away from narcotics. I'm trying to reform him."

Tia cleared her throat. "Good luck."

Before Lisette could turn on the cook, Gisella accepted the criticism. "You're right. I should have stepped out on my own, but I was too afraid to risk my comfort. You don't love my father. You love his money. Before you reform him, accept your motivations before you criticize mine."

"Brat," Lisette said.

"Gold-digger." Turning her back on the woman, she walked out of the kitchen and nearly collided with Martin in the hallway.

"*Signorina* Gisella…"

She held up her hand. "Martin, I need those papers we discussed."

He looked past her toward the kitchen. "*Si, Signorina.*"

"Your accent's terrible."

Swallowing, he pressed his back against the wall.

She closed her eyes and took a deep breath. "If you want to learn Italian, ditch the tapes and have Tia teach you, but don't let my father know what you're doing." She opened her eyes and flipped her hair over her shoulder. "In the meantime, get me dirt on Lisette."

He bowed his head.

Brushing past him, she climbed the stairs. The taste of power stirred her step, but she wanted Martin's loyalty, not his fear.

Striding into her room, she tried to ignore the frustration ulcerating her stomach. Gregorio had planned to leave Italy at his wife's request. In the 1980s, the maxi trials significantly weakened Sicily's *Cosa*

Nostra mafia families. The *'Ndrangheta* gained prominence, but Gregorio lacked influence in their power structure. His wife's desire to flee Italy saved his family, but she didn't live long enough to enjoy the escape. Fuck Lisette for reaping the rewards!

Stewing, Giselle chose a hot shower to purge the rehearsal's sweaty residue, but she had no time to blow out her hair or do more than slip on an iridescent green sheath dress. Lisette couldn't outmaneuver her.

Pinning her hair in a neat chignon, she added gold jewelry and lace-up sandals. She wagered she could make her rounds, slip off before ten and let noise-canceling headphones block out Lisette's dog and pony show.

Ursula stepped out of her room wearing a black maxi dress. "You look like a serpent. Wanna borrow my apple brooch?"

"Says the woman who looks like a wraith. Where's your scythe?"

Laughing, Ursula offered her arm.

Gisella caught of a glimpse of the dress's back and gave her sister props. Thin ties crisscrossed her sister's smooth skin. Sweet Ursula's dress had a built-in bra, but her side boob could tempt a saint...or a priest. "Did you invite Fr. Pietro?"

"Of course. When the real party starts, who will say last rites?"

"Ursula!"

"*Papà* invited him. Everyone reports to *Papà*."

Gisella swallowed. She could confront Lisette, but not her father. Throughout her life, she'd known of his professional activities, but they'd never touched her life. Lisette had been right about one thing. Gisella was a spoiled mafia princess. How long could she carry that title before that atrocity hit home? Hadn't losing Luca been enough of a wakeup call? She could leave. She missed a step and gripped the banister. "I know."

At the bottom of the stairs, Ursula released her arm and walked toward a bevy of female relatives and mob wives. "*Sorelle*."

Gisella stood alone in the foyer. Summer air flowed through the open house, music beckoned guests to the pool area and servers circulated holding champagne. Could she give up this life? Should she embrace it? If she gave up her dancing, every evening could end with bubbles and oblivious smiles. As long as she maintained her loyalty, thinking would never be an obligation.

Martin admitted a couple into the foyer.

She needed no introduction.

Miami's debonair mayor and his charming, gilded wife looked perfectly at home in the marble foyer. Big Tech and real estate investors believed Mayor Frantz' political promises. They poured cash into his campaign coffers and won him the election, but his dream for the city hadn't quite materialized.

Regardless, Mayor Frantz sent his high-school-age twin daughters to the best private schools, dined with Miami's influencers and promised results. *Papà* called him a press-hungry charlatan, but he acknowledged Frantz' political career might stretch past Miami's sun-kissed borders.

"Mayor Frantz." Gisella stepped forward and kissed his cheek. "I'm so glad you're here." His breath smelled suspiciously minty. Ignoring his heavy aftershave, she pulled back and looked at his wife, Cathy. "Look at that dress! Straight off the runway?" Cathy blushed, and Gisella held her smile.

"Well, I had to compete with you!" Gripping Gisella's elbows, Cathy kissed the air six inches from each cheek.

"Aren't you sweet? I can't wait to hear about your philanthropy. Cancer research? We should do lunch."

"Absolutely," Cathy said.

Gisella smiled. The mayor's wife built her platform on children's welfare, substance abuse and mental health resources. If she wasn't brave enough to correct Gisella's statement, she didn't care enough about her causes to earn *Papà's* money. "Drinks on the patio."

Mayor Frantz and Cathy strode toward the patio doors.

Her father stepped out of the dining room leading a heavyset man with an open-collared shirt and a thick, gold chain around his neck.

Bile crawled up her throat, but her father saw her, and she couldn't escape. She smiled. "*Buonasera, Papà.*" Leaning forward, she kissed his cheek. His familiar cologne comforted her, but the man standing next to him smelled of cigarettes and stale meat.

"Gisella, meet my friend, Marco Valachi."

She extended her hand. The man had the gall to press his wet lips against her skin. She struggled not to recoil. "It's a pleasure to meet you."

"Likewise," Marco said. "After your ballet performance, I look forward to taking you to dinner. Your father said I might want to see the show myself."

She blinked. "Oh, I'm sure it would bore you. The box office sold out to tittering old ladies, and Papà already gave his tickets to" — she smiled — "business associates."

Marco bobbed his head.

She smiled. With her father standing at her side, she struggled to escape the pattern of fake smiles and empty words that carried her unscathed through these engagements, but the stakes dug deeper.

"I'll leave you and Marco to get acquainted," Gregorio said.

She swallowed and watched him leave. In a house full of people, she felt abandoned to her fate. Turning to Marco, she weighed her options. "How do you know my father?"

"We met in Morocco."

She deepened her fake smile. Cannabis traveled from North Africa into Europe. She doubted Marco went to the country to drink mint tea. If her father fixed her up with a nice accountant, she might give the man a chance, but this portly idiot indulged in life's excesses, and she preferred to stay off his menu. "Would you care for something to drink?"

"Aren't you charming," Marco said.

"When I need to be," she muttered to herself.

"Come again?" he asked.

"I said, aren't you generous?"

He pulled back his shirtsleeve and flashed his watch. Street corner pimps sported more subdued timepieces. Trying to step back, Marco's hand settled on her lower back. She flinched and bile rose in her throat.

"Let's get that drink and find a nice corner to chat," he said.

She'd rather chat with a cobra. He stared at her dress's hemline like he couldn't wait to explore her assets. If she shrugged off his touch, would he complain to her father? Would her father care? Her heartbeat drummed in her ears. Trying to ease away, his hand landed on top of her ass, and she jumped. "Marco, I'd rather join the…"

He removed his hand.

Closing her eyes, she let relief wash over her.

"Who the fuck are you?" Dante asked.

Recognizing his curt, West Coast voice, she stepped back until she made contact. His heat anchored her unease. She hoped he would stay with her, and Marco would give up the dark corner he had in mind. She didn't need the oily wannabe, and he made her skin crawl. If she wanted to spend her life dodging drugs charges, murder, extortion, loan sharking and abuse of office, she had plenty of family members to support. Shuddering, she pressed into Dante's warmth.

"A guest," Marco said.

"Then go to the fucking patio and find a drink." Dante wrapped his arm around her waist. "I'm a houseguest, and she's with me."

"Does her father know?"

"Go!"

Dante's command rumbled through her core, and she bit her lips to suppress a grin.

Marco sized up his competition, adopted an oily smile and let bitterness creep into his gaze. "I'll see you at dinner, Gigi."

"My name's Gisella."

"Of course." Marco shook his head and headed for the pool.

"Nice guy." Dante dropped his arm from her waist. "Where'd you find him? Under a rock?"

She stepped free of his frame. "He found me." The panic she had pushed down welled in her throat, and she closed her eyes to moderate her breathing.

"Gisella?" Dante cupped her elbow.

Shaking her head, she held up a finger and breathed in his fresh, clean scent. "Just give me a minute."

"Take all the time you need."

He rubbed the soft skin above her elbow, and she relaxed into the touch. She appreciated his concern, but she needed to thank him for saving her from Marco's libido. Where Marco oozed grease and back-room deals, Dante offered light. His presence in the household had welcomed transparency, but then he had turned and pushed her away. The moment she had an angle on him, the odds shifted, and the imbalance formed a hole of uncertainty so deep it could swallow her life. She might be better off with a known threat.

"Gisella." He pulled her close.

She braced her forearms against his chest and shook her head. "We can't. My father…"

"Your father needs me."

He stroked her upper arm, but he gave her the space she needed to breathe. She stepped past him before she crumpled. "Excuse me."

He reached out and grabbed her hand.

Feeling his rough calluses, she resisted, but his strength compelled her toward the front door. Second-guessing her prior threat assessment, she planted her feet before he dragged her outside and gave the valets a family show. "What are you doing?" She sounded as breathless and uncertain as a lover questioning a betrayal.

He planted a hand above her head and pinned her to the front door. "Get me the real numbers, Gisella."

Anyone could walk in and find them in a compromising position. Dante would be millions of dollars poorer, and she'd find herself saddled with a man like Marco who disgusted her. She frowned. "I don't have access to his desk. He keeps it locked."

"Pick it."

Her breath left in a rush. "Right."

Footsteps sounded outside the door.

Dante pivoted and pulled her away from the hardwood barrier.

As Martin opened it from the drive, Dante stepped in front of her and glared at her father's newest guests. "Outside."

"That was Miami's mayor." She whispered the correction.

"Fuck if I care."

Rubbing her temples, she smiled and shook her head. She was right. This man would have a hard time making friends in Miami.

With the door open, Dante pulled her outside, past Martin and down the steps.

She made eye contact with the butler and shrugged like a woman caught up in a romantic assignation. If Martin had worked at the house a little longer, he would have recognized the act's absurdity, but she went with it.

Martin smiled. "*Ciao, Signorina.*"

Look at that! He'd learned an extra word.

Beyond the landscape lighting's warm glow, Gisella heard more guests arrive, but she couldn't see past the manicured foliage shielding her flight.

Dante released her hand and leaned against a stone-clad pillar. A second later, he lit a cigarette.

The lighter's orange flame cast his face in flickering shadows. "You smoke?"

Exhaling, he nodded. "Every man deserves a vice."

"And women?"

He smiled. "In my experience, women have many vices."

She wet her lips.

He jerked his chin toward the security cameras monitoring the drive. "Can they see us?"

Considering the blind spot, she dropped her shoulder and reached for the cigarette. "No."

Withholding it, he shook his head.

"Hypocrite," she said.

"Don't you have a performance tomorrow?"

She leaned against the pillar's adjacent side and glanced at the gray-blue evening sky. This close to Miami's light pollution, she rarely saw stars, but she remembered their sparkling show and believed they twinkled for her enjoyment. Dante wanted her business intelligence. "I told you, I can't get the numbers." She glanced at his face. He looked bitter, focused and intense. "Antonio's your best..."

Dante held up his hand. "Give me your best guess."

"Why?" she asked.

He peered around the corner.

The slow, deliberate motion looked more menacing than Marco's advance. Her heart stopped beating, and she considered retreating to the house, but Dante had saved her. She stepped away from the pillar. "I'm sure you and *Papà* can work out your differences."

Catching her hand, Dante spun her into his chest.

She braced her hand against his shoulder and caught herself. "Why is that?"

"You both come from...entrepreneurial backgrounds."

"I gave up that life," Dante said.

"Did you?" She pulled away.

Pulling the cigarette from his lips, he offered it. "Are you sure you want this? My lips sullied it."

"I wouldn't want to harm my health."

"Suit yourself." He made to drop it.

She snatched the glowing lure and drew a deep breath.

Since leaving high school for the dance academy, she'd immersed herself in her art and abandoned her girlish dreams of prom, stolen kisses and lighthearted contraband. Dressing for her father's parties and bantering with her cousins filled gaps, but the tension of sharing a cigarette with a handsome man eluded her. As the smoke filled her lungs, she held her breath and let the heady rush lighten her senses.

"I figured you'd choke," he said.

Handing back the cigarette, she exhaled. "A few of the dancers smoke on their breaks."

"Are they good?"

She shook her head. "Terrible."

He laughed and ground out the butt on the crushed gravel path. "Stick to the tutus. So far, you're a terrible spy."

A courtyard fountain glimmered, and she wondered what other skills she could perfect with a willing accomplice. The fallout's severity kept her hands glued to her side. "I'm not cut out to be a spy."

"But you like to dance. You're agile."

She turned and faced him. The cigarette's glow couldn't sharpen his cheekbones or guild his lashes. "The skills aren't interchangeable."

"Aren't they?"

She considered the question. Faced with a match like Marco, she would suffer the marriage, steal as much as she could and flee. Dante glittered like forbidden fruit, but taking a bite might banish her from the garden. Raising her hand, she fanned her fingers across his chest and felt his heartbeat. The heat scared her, and she pulled back her hand. The ensuing cold worried her more.

Capturing her hand, he placed it back where it belonged.

She sighed. "Dante, you can't take the millions. I can't marry you, and neither can Ursula. I'll help you value CIH, but you have to walk away from the easy cash. I'm sure you need the money, but no good will come of it. Let *Papà* and Lisette decamp. Let CIH prove its worth. My sister and I will figure out our paths. You should, too."

He raised her hand to his lips. "Gisella, I can't do that."

Satiny smooth lips slid across her knuckles.

"I want the cash."

She yanked back her hand. "Fuck you."

"Are you offering?"

She slapped him.

He absorbed the blow. "The apple doesn't fall far from the tree."

Turning, she marched toward the house and the party. Dante's comments were rude, short and demanding, but he roared into her life like a tsunami, left her reeling and threatened to recede before she could claim her bearing. Her body reacted to his proximity, but she blamed her awareness on the warm breeze caressing her skin.

"Gisella."

His rich command interrupted her retreat.

"Come here."

Turning, she looked over her shoulder. A single star shone in the sky. She waited for it to blip and sink like another satellite. It held its course. Lowering her gaze, she waited.

"I said, come here."

No longer indifferent, his beckoning command smoldered with intent. She raised her chin and stopped two feet away from him. Too wary to stand closer and too curious to flee, she held her breath.

He yanked her against his chest and linked his hands above the small of her back.

Her pulse skyrocketed, and the hot, spreading warmth of his grip stole her focus.

Dropping his head, he paused. "Who should I pick?"

Self-preservation stalled her heart.

He slid his hands to her waist and flexed his fingers.

He occupied the gray area between two lives, and loving him would strip away her power to decide her fate. Breaking free of his spell, she drew a breath. "Ursula, but she'll never love you."

He lit another cigarette.

Turning her back on him, she strode toward the house.

"Does it matter?" he asked.

His cool indifference startled her. He knew the answer, but he waited for her response. Instead of answering, she focused on his commanding arrogance and reminded herself why she needed to flee.

Chapter Nine

Dante replayed his encounters with Gisella. Spending time with her felt like a double-edged sword. He wanted to buy CIH, but he wanted Gisella in his bed. She walked a thin line, but if he harmed her family, he doubted she'd come to him on her own.

In another world, these games wouldn't matter. He understood Gregorio and his henchmen, but he hated the assholes for using civility to mask their violence. When he pulled a gun, he owned the reason and the fallout.

The party looked like it would end on a whimper, but part of him wanted to see a good old-fashioned fistfight. He doubted he would join in. Rolling up his sleeves might feel like the good, old times, but those times had almost killed him.

Lisette stepped backward, lost her balance and splashed into the pool.

Much better than a fistfight. Dante tried not to grin.

Gregorio and his butler fished the floundering woman out of the shallow end.

Dante watched the show for a moment then looked for Gisella, but he couldn't find the alluring siren. When she took the stage tomorrow, she would shine, but he wanted to know what kind of bouquet she preferred. Her old-school upbringing mandated flowers and chivalry, but he wasn't sure he carried that trait. If he chose incorrectly and she threw the bouquet in his face...well, he'd enjoy the show.

Gregorio led Ursula to his side. "Ursula graduated at the top of her class."

Dante cocked his head. "What did you study?"

"Women's/Gender Studies," she said.

He cleared his throat. "Ballsy."

"She means English Literature." Gregorio straightened his tie.

Ursula snorted.

"And who are your icons?" Dante asked.

Ursula plucked a glass of stemware from a passing server and ignored him.

After sampling Gisella's charms, chatting up the voluptuous beauty felt a little disingenuous, but Dante liked to maintain his options.

"I like art," Ursula said.

"What kind?"

Gregorio elbowed his daughter.

Ursula stared at a fly on the edge of her glass. "Abstract."

Dante thought the fly might try to drown itself. "I hear Miami has excellent museums."

Nodding, Gregorio turned his back and walked toward Lisette and her crowd of supporters.

Ursula looked up from her glass and smiled. "Finally." Turning, she decamped to whatever interested her more than Dante did.

He stood alone on the pool decking and shook off the loss. For all he knew about the woman, she might be mad.

Scanning the party's dregs, he worried about being mad for Gisella. The flowers were a fucking excuse. He couldn't get her smell out of his mind, and her body fit him like a glove.

Up to his neck in details of the CIH deal, he struggled to focus on anything but her pleasure-laced moans. Before she'd put herself together and disappeared into her domain, she'd been so wet for him that she'd forgotten discretion. What would she sound like uninhibited and released from her constraints? He wanted to rip her from her father's house, sequester her in the Sierra Nevada Mountains and find out how many ways he could satisfy her. Then what?

When he'd seen that asshat put his hands on her ass earlier in the evening, a burn had radiated in his chest and he'd had to stop himself from pistol-whipping the greaser. Then Gisella had told him to go after Ursula, and he'd tried to respect her wishes. Based on Ursula's fascination with the fly, he'd failed, and Dante had never been happier. Relishing the good faith effort, he let his thoughts refocus on Gisella.

The woman's strength surprised him, but a lifetime of managing the men in her life left a layer of deference he enjoyed. She listened and challenged him, but he wagered her obedience had a hard line. If he pushed her over that line, would she speak up, permit his stunt or attack him with another half-assed slap? He rubbed his cheek and grinned. Confessing to his father's murder hadn't shocked the Miami princess. What would?

The whole situation annoyed the fuck out of him. He came to Miami to do a job and found himself tangled up with the assets and sleeping in the fucking house.

A server walked by carrying a bucket of beers.

Lifting one from the ice, Dante twisted off the cap and downed the cold liquid. Wiping his mouth clean, he headed for the house before Gregorio could corner him and ask for a decision concerning his daughters.

Dante had a few questions of his own. Did the man know Antonio had siphoned off ten million dollars in revenue? Did he know the CIH claims adjustor denied hurricane claims from families too poor to sue? Florida's biggest commercial real estate company made money hand over fist, but it could make more.

Ursula leaned against the mansion's wall. "You're still here."

He pushed open his jacket and shoved his hands in his pockets. "Your father invited me to stay." Hearing laughter, he looked over his shoulder and found Antonio and Marco laughing on the opposite side of the pool. "Although his taste in people raises some questions."

"What'd he do to you?" she asked.

"Pissed off my delicate sensibilities." He sipped his beer. "What are you still doing up?"

"Waiting for my lover."

He cocked his head.

Father Pietro walked out of the house and looked around the pool. "Beautiful night for a party."

Linking arms with the man, Ursula grinned. "Let's get you home."

Frowning, Father Pietro hesitated. "You can't drive."

"No, but I can walk along the beach. Someone will come pick me up from the church." She pulled the priest inside the house, looked over her shoulder and winked at Dante.

He wondered if he'd ever had a choice of the women. Gregorio must have known of Ursula's infatuation with the priest. Maybe the fucker didn't care, but if he pushed Dante toward Ursula and expected the match to backfire, he was cagier than he let on. Men didn't accumulate billions playing dumb. Turning, Dante reconsidered the laughing assholes and finished his beer.

"Sir?" Martin asked.

Handing the man the empty bottle, Dante entered the house and climbed the stairs two at a time. He wanted another taste of Gisella's charms, and being marched to the altar suited him fine.

Prying open her bedroom door, he slipped inside and found her sprawled across the bed wearing a tank top and a pair of boy shorts. Her long legs lay tangled in the sheets, and one arm blocked the pool lights from her eyes. He itched to wake her, but the wireless headphones shielding her ears reminded him of her upcoming performance. Setting aside satisfaction, he walked toward the window and pulled shut the drapes.

"Dante?" Sitting in bed, she pulled off her headphones. "What's wrong?"

"Nothing, go back to sleep."

She yawned. "The party?"

"A bore." He reached for the door handle to leave the room.

"Stay."

"I can't, Princess." Sliding his hand beneath his shirt's placket, he rubbed an old ache from his chest. His father had shot him once, and Dante made sure the man could never shoot him again. "I have obligations. If you were awake, I thought we could play, but" — he shook his head — "go back to sleep."

He tried to pretend he could walk out and that her presence didn't fill the room, but his hand lingered on the doorknob. He watched every shift and flex of shadowed muscle as she swung her legs over the edge of the bed. The darkness saved her. If he could see her long lines and luxurious hair, he'd lose control and her dancing could go to hell.

"Dante."

"Shit." Walking across the room, he sat on the edge of her bed and cupped her chin. "What do you want?"

She traced the buttons down his shirt, and her nails ticked across his abs. Drawing a deep breath, he knew he should have stayed on the other side of the room, but she smelled like warm, filtered sunshine and soft, musky sleep.

If he stayed by her side until morning, would she roll over, kiss his lips and let her disheveled, luxurious hair trail across his chest? He swallowed. Giving her pleasure was one thing, but he had no right to be in her bedroom. Any other gentleman would leave. He wasn't a gentleman.

"You'll get in my way." She pulled back her hand.

He stood.

"I watched you tonight. You said all the right things and talked to all the right people. Who am I to keep you pinned to Miami?" She yawned. "Out there, you're intimidating, but here, you're soft and somber. What gives?"

"I'm soft?" He pushed her into the sheets and draped his leg over her thighs. His erection strained his pants, but he'd damn himself if he took her like a party girl a second time — let her feel him and know he held back. Sliding his hand beneath her tank top, he cupped her breast and squeezed the handful, but his weight kept her pinned to the mattress. "I think you're confused."

She smiled. "Which Dante is the show?"

Slipping his other hand beneath her back, he rolled and settled her against his chest. "I'm still answering that question."

She laughed and nuzzled into his warmth. "You're coming to the performance?"

He stroked her back. "Wouldn't miss it."

"And afterward?"

He drifted his hand to her ass and slipped his fingers beneath the waistband of her boy shorts. "And afterward, you tell me what you want."

"In bed?" She cupped him.

The heat and pressure felt so good he closed his eyes and exhaled. "For a start." Listening to her steady breaths, he lay immobilized beneath her hand. The little witch had him pinned.

Time stretched, and he thought about the analysis waiting in his room. Confident she slept, he rose and looked down at her. In the darkness, his eyes saw shadows, but his touch remembered her skin. Running his hand up her muscled leg, he stopped at her shorts' hem and marveled at her skin's softness. Releasing her, he rubbed his fingers together and felt the rough calluses. He was still a West Coast kid with sand between his toes. "Don't let wicked men into your bedroom."

She stirred. "Dante."

Leaning down, he pressed a kiss to her forehead and settled his palm between her breasts.

She quieted.

He left the room before he did something he'd regret. Millions of dollars to marry and dump a faceless woman meant one thing, but obsessing over a wife would derail his plans.

Opening the door to his guest room, he poured a whiskey, walked to his laptop and fired up the CIH model. Choosing the right price for ADC Industries would fatten his bank account, and marrying a Vitella woman would drain it. Shaking the ice in his glass, he drained the whiskey and imagined Gisella's legs wrapped around his waist. For the first time in a long time, he wasn't sure he cared about accumulating wealth.

* * * *

"You ready for this show?" Gregorio asked.

"Of course." Standing in the foyer with the man and his crew, Dante wondered if the party of six required a limo.

Lisette wore a white fringed dress and stood next to Gregorio like a sixty-year-old blushing bride.

Ursula yawned behind her hand and checked the time.

Antonio showed Marco something on his phone and snorted. Undoubtedly, the something lacked clothes.

Shaking his head, Dante adjusted his coat. He wanted to see Gisella dance, but he had two days to iron out the CIH deal before his boss brought in reinforcements. "We taking two cars?"

"How many can you fit?" Ursula asked.

He narrowed his gaze. "Two."

"I'll ride with you."

Martin opened the front door. A black chauffeured SUV idled in the driveway.

On the way to the theater, Dante tapped his fingers on the steering wheel. "Any luck with the priest?"

"Any luck with the books?"

He shook his head. Using a satellite link, he'd downloaded every government data source on the insurance company and modeled its profit-and-loss statements. At first, he'd thought Antonio had oversold the firm. If he'd built his models correctly, the company owed back taxes, but it generated wads of cash and could command a price higher than the one he and Gregorio had negotiated. Traps smelled sickly and sweet. He recognized the threat.

"Gisella has a good head for numbers." Ursula yawned. "All that rhythm and crap."

"I'll run my assumptions by her."

"Is that what they call it?" she asked.

He glanced at her. How close were these sisters?

"I see you watching her. You could do worse. Take the money, Dante. Don't let pride fuck up your chances."

He felt like a fly hovering at the edge of a lovely, velvet-clad Venus Fly Trap. Escaping a life of crime once before, he refused to fall into it a second time. "Noted."

Landscape lighting illuminated a white, three-story building that mimicked the tide's rolling waves. Ballet patrons climbed the steps to the auditorium, and valets whisked off cars. Stopping the vehicle he drove, Dante left the keys on the console, grabbed the bouquet and stepped out of the vehicle.

The ocean breeze played with his hair. He offered Ursula his arm.

Taking it, she smiled for the press.

Like a paid gigolo, he smiled. For enough money, he could play nice and escort Ursula, but his pulse remained steady and flat. If he married this woman, he would leave her to her arias.

The black SUV pulled up next.

Gregorio and his crew climbed from the vehicle.

Letting Gregorio lead, Dante and Ursula fell into line. He dropped his head. "Have you seen the rehearsals?"

She smiled. "Oh, you're in for a show."

After chatting with local notables and making his way to the box, Dante opened the program.

"In a new take on an old piece, Monsieur Provocateur illuminates the pain and passion of the corps de ballet. This ensemble piece highlights the parts dancers get, and most poignantly, the ones that went to someone else."

Fuck, the performance sounded like a French-laced version of *The Nutcracker*. If he wanted to watch a bunch of wannabes float through scenes from their favorite classical ballets, he could have stayed in San Diego. Leaning back in his chair, he crossed his arms.

The curtains opened on a scene of six dancers tightening the ribbons on their shoes and dusting their hands. The male dancers flexed and laughed while the ballerinas stretched. Gisella stood, raised her hands over her head and arched her back.

A second woman on stage shook her finger in admonishment.

Dante watched Gisella's choreographed movements. He'd slept through his ex-girlfriend's performances, but Coco took more pleasure from gracing magazine covers than perfecting techniques. Gisella danced like music flowed through her veins. Stranded in a box, he couldn't do anything but watch and yearn.

Lowering her hands, Gisella slipped to the edge of the stage and moved through a series of points and turns.

The bittersweet choreography captured his attention.

The audience remained silent.

As the music wavered, one by one the other dancers engaged Gisella with teasing swipes, tart rebukes and choreographed hugs.

She held her own.

Dante drank in her long, graceful lines.

The remaining dancer, a strong fucker with black hair, slipped behind Gisella and comforted her.

Sitting up straight, Dante leaned forward.

The duo moved across the stage with the practiced intimacy of longstanding partners.

"Jandro," Ursula said.

Dante ignored her.

As the music swelled, Jandro dipped Gisella over his arm, stroked her chest and pulled her into an obsessive pas de deux. His grip and intensity held her captive and kept her from rejoining the group.

"Mother fucker," Antonio said.

Wrapping her in his arms, Jandro claimed a kiss, and the stage went dark.

"Doesn't know his partner." Marco stood and straightened his pants. "Pretty boy's about to find out who he's mauling on stage."

Dante rolled his eyes.

"Sit down," Gregorio said. "The performance isn't over."

"Could be," Antonio said.

The lights came up.

Gisella stood amid the other ballerinas. They fluttered around her like sympathetic magpies. At first comforting, the attention ripped away her costume until she stood nearly naked in the middle of the stage, collapsed and curled into a fetal position.

Dante had to hand it to the woman. Nothing about her performance hinted at snowflakes and tulle.

Jandro strode onto the stage in a whirl of movement and energy.

Raising her head, Gisella's character watched his solo and slowly staggered to her feet. Mimicking his turns, she found herself in his arms for a second pas de deux. The dancer unfurled his arm, and she pirouetted toward the wing.

Dante frowned. Her moves, first hopeful then bittersweet, looked brittle and mechanical.

The stage lights dimmed, but a single spot kept Jandro illuminated in a feat of strength and balance while the rest of the stage went dark. The spot blinked off.

The audience jumped to their feet and applauded.

Dante slowly rose. Gisella's performance had captivated him, but it left behind the sour taste of regret. Tonight, when the mansion quieted, he would slip into her room and ask her to pick him for the last time.

Walking from the theater, he inhaled the sea air and closed his eyes. The bouquet in his grip was a fool's gesture. She deserved wine and roses, but he wondered how long the novelty would amuse her. Would it be long enough to kindle love?

Pulling out his cell phone, he scanned his emails and found a memo from his boss. He challenged Dante and his peers to manage their deals without involving him in the nitty-gritty details. If they produced profits with minimal oversight, they would earn a higher take. *Interesting.*

Dante stared toward the ocean and reconfigured the CIH deal in his head. His feelings for Gisella stood apart from it, but he had to provide for her. Clout and cash would keep the shitheads in her family from messing with either of them.

He scanned a second email from Alessio. Based on his boss's list of questions about the CIH acquisition, a week in bed with a woman named Nina hadn't diminished his micro-managing skills.

Stop being a dick. Are you in or are you out?

The question resonated. Dropping the phone in his pocket, he raised the bouquet and inhaled the heady floral scent. Gisella told him he smelled like grass, and damn if he didn't admire her resilience and shapely curves. But could she learn to love him?

Chapter Ten

"You were brilliant," Jandro said.

Wiping the makeup from her face, Gisella smiled. "Thank you."

"Join us for drinks?"

She shook her head. "You know I can't." She refused to wake up the next day too stiff to rise from bed. Many dancers used determination and painkillers to deal with soreness, but she'd perfected a cool down to help her body recover.

"Your loss." Jandro walked toward the back door and whistled for the other dancers.

Gisella released him and put an ice pack on her thigh. The group would walk to the nearest bar and settle in for a celebration. Low-intensity exercises like walking helped restore a dancer's heart rate to a resting level and prevented symptoms like nausea and lightheadedness.

"Go ahead." The newest dancer lay on the floor and elevated his feet against the wall. "My ankles are so swollen I'll look like an eighty-year-old woman."

The group laughed and offered him pointers.

"Amateurs." Jandro walked out of the back door.

Gisella laughed.

When the stage door opened, she heard Ursula's deep cackle and smiled. Turning in her chair, she prepared for her sister's critique. Ursula might have thought dance classes were boring, but she'd obviously paid attention.

Dante strode into the dressing room holding a bouquet of olive leaves and white peonies. The contrast between the elegant white flowers and the rustic, herbal leaves reminded him of Gisella's grit and poise. He offered them.

Pulling them to her chest, she let the ice pack fall and stood. "You brought me flowers?"

"Gave a guy a hundred bucks and yanked them from his hands."

Laughing, she buried her face in the fragrant, white blooms. "Nobody ever brings me flowers."

"You deserve them." Leaning close, he dropped his voice. "You were prefect."

His rough cheek grazed hers, and her cheeks warmed. A bouquet of tulips would have been enough. She didn't need such lavish expenditures. "Thank you."

"And if I come see you tonight? If I slip into your bedroom?"

His whispered questions raised the hairs on her skin, and her core clenched. "For what?"

"To show my appreciation." He kept his voice low and pulled back until they looked at each other.

Surrounded by other dancers, the conversation appeared as light and fawning as a fan's congratulations, but heat and desire smoldered in his eyes, and she wanted his praise. "Well, I look forward to it."

The idiot grinned like the fox in the henhouse.

She chewed her lip, picked up her ice pack and shoo'd him from the dressing room. "Now, get lost."

"I am." Hesitating for a second, he shook his head and walked out of the door.

* * * *

Gisella waited in her bedroom armchair like a love-struck teen. A single lamp cast shadows in the room. She'd made it to twenty-one before she'd seduced a gardener, but she'd walked away from the encounter and had never given him a second thought. Since that day, Tia consulted her on staffing decisions, and Gisella wondered how much the woman knew.

A minute before midnight, Dante slipped into her room.

"I thought you changed your mind," she said.

"Wait! This isn't Ursula's room?"

His joke upped the stakes, and she chucked a throw pillow at the door. "I'd rather fuck, but we should talk about my father's idiotic mandate."

"Let's get back to the fucking."

She stood. "Dante, you don't have to marry me."

He pulled her against his chest. "I won't give you the same leeway. In or out, Gisella?"

Exhaling, she searched for uneasiness in his grasp. She'd expected an arranged marriage, but she'd hoped her father would choose someone so focused on moving goods he wouldn't have time to pay attention to her personal life. Dante would ask all the questions. "Do we have to decide?"

"You have twenty-four hours."

She swallowed and eyed the bottle of champagne chilling on the side table. She didn't need the bubbles. After a few minutes near this man, she was drunk on his presence. Slipping from his grasp, she chewed her lip. "I'll give you my answer in twenty-four hours."

"You'd let me marry your sister?"

"Good fucking luck."

He laughed and leaned against the wall.

Lit by the single lamp, his features looked dark and beautiful. She wondered what atrocities carved his appraising expression. He'd said he killed his father, but she'd assumed he meant some avoidable tragedy or workaholic omission. Waiting for Dante's attention like frightened prey, she questioned her assumption. The man teased her senses, but she refused to go down as his first course. "Are you coming to bed?"

"I'm admiring the view."

His rough, restrained statement sent shivers across her skin. She popped the champagne cork, lifted the bottle to her lips and let the green glass obscure his heady stare.

He stepped closer. "You looked beautiful tonight."

She lowered the bottle. "That's my job."

Walking forward, he pried the bottle from her hand and raised it to his lips. "You outshone everyone on the stage."

She smiled. "Did you look at the other dancers?"

He lowered the bottle. "No."

Experienced granted her the tools to handle him cold, impassive and possessive, but he lightened up near her, and the power left her heady. No longer appearing indifferent, he walked toward her with an obvious, single-minded goal.

She stepped backward.

He stopped. "Second thoughts?"

"First." She swallowed. "You killed your father."

Raising the bottle, he drank deeply. "You want to ruin the night."

"I want to understand who's in my room." She reclaimed her chair and tucked her legs to the side.

He set the bottle down on the side table, walked toward the window and peered over the pool. "When I was in high school, he started running methamphetamine. The plant-based form came out of Japan around 1920. It increased alertness and impressed servicemen. Pharmaceutical companies co-opted the natural stimulant to make decongestants, and biker gangs developed a complicated, volatile alternative."

She wrinkled her nose.

"By the 1980s, the black market one-upped their competition and started mass-producing meth from decongestants. The biker variety fell out of favor. In the 1990s, my father imported something new. It eclipsed the ephedrine-based stimulants, and his supplier promised a continuous supply."

"You're against progress."

Turning, he exhaled. "I'm against lunacy."

"Isn't it subjective?"

Rubbing his lip, he nodded. "I'm entitled to my opinion."

Oh, the man acted entitled, all right—entitled to be rich, white and packing a gun. She gravitated to him like a moth to a flame, but she recognized the nearsighted danger of her attraction. "What did he do?"

Dante worked his jaw. "He linked up with a Mexican chemist who refined the biker gangs' recipe and isolated the byproduct that generates a high. With the refinement, nobody needed to raid drugstore shelves for decongestants. Cue the prime-time specials about mental illness and homelessness."

If Dante would shoot a man for importing potent drugs, he'd have a hard time making friends in Miami. She eyed the champagne bottle. She'd warned Antonio to find someone less lethal, but Dante's feral approach to life comforted her.

"The chemist creating my father's supply refused to quit adding more additives. My father passed on the product without understanding its effects. People started showing up dead in alleys, car crashes. Innocent bystanders living their noble lives ended up in the gutters. Fentanyl made it worse."

She stood and walked toward him. Cupping the back of his head, she spread her fingers through his hair. "You asked him to stop?"

Dropping his forehead to hers, he sighed. "I asked him to shut down the whole fucking operation. We had enough money. Most days, my mother was so high she couldn't remember my age. The conversation with my father came to blows, but he no longer had strength's advantage."

She thought of her father's empire and wondered how he viewed mortality.

"When I was nineteen and trying to figure out if I had the stomach for the family business, he found out a pair of truck drivers were about to turn on him in exchange for a plea deal with local authorities. He didn't blink, and I didn't ask questions."

"He killed them?" she asked.

"One." He stroked her cheek and dropped his hand. She wondered if this admission was goodbye.

"He drove us to the warehouse and walked straight up to the idling truck. It carried fifty-five million methamphetamine tablets and over two tons of crystal meth, but he shot a hole in the gas tank and lit it on fire."

The men came running.

She covered her mouth and pulled back.

He let her. "When I interceded on behalf of the drivers, he shot me in the shoulder and killed the first man. I watched him drop, and I looked at my father. His eyes were as dark as obsidian, and his mouth was grim, but he turned his gun on the second driver fleeing the confrontation. I pulled my gun, killed my father and peeled out of the warehouse lot."

She dropped her hand. "You went to the hospital?"

Shaking his head, he ran his hand through his hair. "I pried out the bullet and cried for hours. The next day, I left town."

She imagined him standing in the shower, shaking and needing confirmation he'd done the right thing. She wanted to believe the shock of killing his father cauterized his pain, but knowing he averted more deaths couldn't mitigate the pain of killing his father. "I'm surprised you waited."

"I wanted to tell my mother goodbye," he said. "I never understood how much she hated my father, but I felt her disappointment. Every one of us should have done better."

She swallowed. "You killed him in self-defense."

He withdrew his gun and set it on the side table. "The apple didn't fall far from the tree."

She considered the piece. "My father runs Columbian cocaine."

He rubbed his lip. "And you?"

"I dance."

"Then we're good."

She stared. Could they ever be good? "Maybe you should go. I don't condone my father's business, but I've profited from it. You're trying to profit from it, too. You think the millions he'll give you come from CIH's bottom line? It's blood money. Maybe it's hippie, plant-based blood money" — she stepped back — "but people still die from his business and their bad choices."

"You're right," he said.

In muted silence, she watched her bedroom's shadows swallow a glimpse of happiness. The allure of having the freedom and resources to dance without worries faded like a fairytale.

"Tell me what you know about CIH," he said.

"You want me to betray my father?"

"Honor your husband," he said. "Pick a side."

She swallowed. Women always made this choice. Nobody could force her to treat this man like a true husband, but the allure tempted her, and a strange discomfort curled in her chest. She blinked and tried to sort out her emotions. "You don't love me. You'd never be faithful."

The statement left a regretful aftertaste on her tongue.

He stared. "Would you be faithful?"

His deep, smooth question turned the tables on her. The men in her life considered strip clubs part of their jobs. Money and power corrupted them. Beautiful women fed their egos. She considered the handsome man risking his life to come to her room. Dante walked away from his black-market legacy. Miami might pull him back into it. "You're evading my question."

He backed her against the wall.

The cool paint sent a shiver down her spine. Trapped and pinned by a man who brought her pleasure and upended her future, she struggled to think clearly.

"Answer me."

"I can't trust you." The admission burned her throat, and she turned her head to the side. He came into her life like a tidal wave, and her fascination with him threatened to drown her. "Play your game with my father. Pick Ursula. Leave me out of his mess."

He stepped back and reached for the door.

She exhaled. His proximity could lure her deeper into hell.

"Last chance," he said.

His ominous reminder upped the stakes. He didn't give second chances, and as much as she craved his touch, she didn't know if she could continue saying no. She leaned against the wall and crossed her arms. "CIH says it finds safe, short-term assets to invest its premiums, but the money goes back into the drug trade. My father broke down the barriers between his private wealth and his public balance sheet. If he says he holds Treasury bonds, high-grade corporate bonds and interest-bearing cash equivalents, ask him to prove it."

Raising his hand, he stroked her cheek. "He says he'll cash out the securities."

Wanting to turn into his touch, she swallowed. "It's dirty money. If the feds come after you, you'll never untangle the mess."

He dropped his hand. "Why would you tell me that fact?"

She pulled up his sleeve and exposed his tattoo. "I won't be part of the lie."

Staring at the point where their skin touched, he ran his tongue across his teeth.

She jerked her head toward the door. "Go."

Stepping closer, he lifted the edge of her shirt. "Say goodbye."

His touch sent a rush of oxygen coursing through her system. She had to bite her lip to contain a whimper. To deny herself something then feel it pressed against her body... Her muscles contracted and flexed. She wanted more than a rushed hallway memory of Dante's touch. Lifting his hand, she pressed it against her breast. "After tonight, you're forbidden."

"What else is new?" He drew her close and dropped his head.

His kiss chased away her misgivings. If she ended up in a loveless marriage with an ass like Marco, she'd think of Dante every time her husband took her to bed. The thought tensed her, and she pulled back.

"I should go," he said.

She took his hand. The taste of his skin lingered on her lips. "Stay."

He lowered her to her bed and stripped off his shirt.

The backyard lights and single lamp cast shadows between his muscles. Raising a hand, she traced his tattoo. "Do you regret what you did?"

Bringing her hand to his lips, he kissed it. "Family isn't everything."

She grabbed the waistband of his slacks. "Do you have another condom?"

He groaned and lowered himself to the linen duvet. Dropping one knee on the bed, he pulled her nightshirt over her head and buried his face between her breasts. "I've never seen a woman tempt a man with such hidden curves."

Slapping his ass, she twisted out of his hold.

He caged her against the bed. "I never expected you to be beautiful and complicated, but you are, and I love it." Lowering his mouth to hers, he kissed her and covered her body.

He loved her personality, but he barely knew her. She closed her eyes and savored his weight. In the morning, he'd be a memory. Running her hands along his back, she slipped one hand beneath his slacks and palmed his ass. "You're wearing too many clothes."

"And you're impatient."

She raised her hips and pressed her body against his frame. "We have little time."

Settling her firmly between his legs, he lifted her leg and teased his erection against her heat. "I don't need time."

"Dante…" She lost her train of thought and savored his touch.

"Daniel." He whispered the correction, lowered his head and pulled her nipple into his mouth.

The delicate tension and scrape elicited a moan.

Teasing the rosy bud, he kept her leg pinned against his side and worked the angle's friction.

The contrast of pleasure and constraint escalated her frustration. Wiggling out of his hold, she braced her hands on the bed. "Get naked or get out."

Smiling, he rose and complied.

The scar on his shoulder drew her gaze, but she understood passion and loyalty. The rest of his body was too magnificent to ignore. She should have turned on every light in the house and memorized his form. "Much better."

His gaze glinted with dark promise.

Gripping his hand, she pulled him back to the bed. "Show me how much you'll miss me." He stroked her skin, and she savored his touch like the burn after a long workout. Even when she shied away from the heat, it strengthened her.

She matched his kisses. The possibility of letting him walk out of her life felt wicked and cruel. Breaking the kiss, she wiggled out of her underwear and braced herself on her elbows. "Condom?"

He pulled one from his wallet and tossed it on the bed. "You'd risk your future on a thin piece of latex?"

"I have an IUD." The admission slipped past her lips before she'd had time to think through what else she risked by indulging in her desire for him.

He pushed her onto the bed. "Good. I'm negative."

He tangled his legs with hers, and his rigid control seemingly checked his strength. As he traced her lines with his hands, he tested her contours and chased her satisfaction. If the sun rose, she'd find a million ways to say goodbye.

Cupping her sex, he slid his thumb between her lips. "You'll miss me."

She squeezed her eyes shut. The friction clenched her inner muscles, and her breath fled. Asking for more, she arched against his hand and buried her face against his neck. "You'll miss me, too."

He teased her clit and exhaled. "Fuck restraint. The night's young." He centered her hips and spread her legs until she reclined before him, glistening and exposed.

"Now, Daniel."

Holding her hips, he guided his erection into her body and stilled.

She stretched against him. "What's wrong?"

Closing his eyes, he exhaled. "Stay still, for fuck's sake. I haven't been with a woman like this in far too long."

She didn't want to be another woman. She moved against him and tested his control. "I need more." He grunted and withdrew, sliding into her heat. The movement grew as strong and glorious as a crescendo.

Shifting the angle of her hips, she matched his pace and absorbed every shuddering possession. The slide of skin against skin felt so mindful, and she arched to meld their heartbeats. When the pressure built in her core, she cried out, shuddered around him and met every stroke.

Losing control, he pumped into her sex and buried his face against her shoulder.

She felt her name on his lips. As he collapsed on her, she stroked his hair and let the echoes of his release ripple through her core.

He withdrew and rolled to the side.

Grabbing her nightshirt, she cleaned up the unrestrained, glorious mess.

"You're irreplaceable, Gisella, but I'll try."

She wanted to stroke his long lines and savor the afterglow. Instead, she wrapped her arms around her legs. "Good luck."

His dark laughter meant as much as his goodbye.

Slipping on his slacks, he reached for his shirt. "You're sure."

She buried the wistful doubts working their way past her reserves. "Go do your thing. I'll be fine."

Leaning down, he kissed her cheek. "You say that…"

She closed her eyes. Another man could never smell as good. She wanted to nuzzle her face against his neck and plan a future. The moment slowed, and the sound of her ragged breath filled the room. "Just" — she sighed — "go."

He ran his hand through his hair. "You can always come to me."

Gripping a pillow against her chest, she nodded. So many men had promised her protection, but the minute she stepped out of line, she feared their retraction. Dante's indifferent gaze had sharpened into the honed perfection of a man who kept his word. If he said she could come to him, she could. "Thank you."

Her phone's screen glowed.

She picked up the device. It was a text from her Artistic Director.

Someone beat the shit out of Jandro. Broke both legs and tore his Achilles tendon. He may never dance again.

Gisella gasped and covered her mouth.

Three dots signaled an incoming text. The dots disappeared. The recriminations taunted her, and she threw the pillow from the bed. "Of all the petty, asinine things."

She slipped past him, but Dante gripped her arm. "What's wrong?"

Seeing red, she let the fury course through her veins, but Antonio deserved her wrath. Dante offered comfort. "Antonio beat the shit out of Jandro, my dance partner. The stage kiss meant nothing." She looked at the unfastened buttons on Dante's shirt and watched the steady rise and fall of his chest. Her breathing slowed. Anger wouldn't rehabilitate Jandro's career. "My cousins never understood the arts."

"You want to go to the hospital?" he asked.

She shook her head. She could imagine the snapping and ricocheting pain Jandro endured. During bouts of frustration, he fell into his native Spanish. Strangers might have ignored his pleas. While her asinine cousin pummeled him, he endured the pain, begged for his life and wondered if his career as a professional dancer had ended. It probably had. "No, I'm going to my father's study."

After pulling open drawers, she shrugged into loose pants and a sweatshirt.

"Gisella, you don't know Antonio was the aggressor."

She paused. "You don't know this community. The heritage and history matter. My father safeguards everything. His rule is law. If Antonio beat the shit out of my dance partner, my father allowed it. If he didn't" — she shook her head and swallowed — "he's losing control, and we're all fucked."

Dante tightened his belt. "Okay."

"What?"

"I said okay. You want to charge into your father's study with swollen lips and beard burn on your cheeks? I'm right behind you."

She raised her hand to her cheek. "Thank you."

He opened the door. "You will marry me."

Striding past him, she headed for the stairs. "Fuck you."

"That's the idea."

Furious over Jandro's pain, she ignored Dante's jest and raced down the steps to her father's study. Ignoring her family's business had worked for many years, but it never hurt the people she cared about. Tonight it had, and she refused to bear this pain and regret again.

Chapter Eleven

"*Papà*, how could you?" Gisella asked.

Antonio pointed toward the door. "Leave, Dante."

The man's arrogant command fell flat. Dante crossed his arms and leaned against the black wall. Antonio's presumption piqued his interest, but Gisella held his heart, and he wouldn't let her cousin toy with her. "I think I'll stay."

Gregorio smiled.

Gisella launched into an Italian tirade.

Dante rubbed his ear. Gisella, his sweet-natured firebird, had volume. Standing at the room's perimeter, he listened to her unleash a storm of Italian. His Spanish was good, but the romance language only got him so far. Gisella's waving arms and staccato reprimands made one thing clear. The woman he would claim looked pissed.

Without putting a ring on her finger, he had no right to intercede on her behalf. How the hell would he get her to marry him? Biding his time, he considered the room's black paint and masculine furniture. During the day, the modern combination gave off a hotel library vibe. Without pool views, the room felt like a mortuary, and he loosened his collar. The last time he'd occupied the office, the CIH deal had held his attention, but his feelings for Gisella raised the stakes.

He'd heard rumors of *Cosa Nostra* induction ceremonies. Led by a trusted member, new recruits presented themselves to the family's leadership, spilled drops of blood on a saint's prayer card, watched the card burn and repeated a loyalty oath. If the newly made man messed up, he'd end up as windblown as the card's ashes.

Gisella leaned over Gregorio's desk and jabbed against the wood.

Ogling her ass wasn't Dante's best move. He'd reorganize his life to incorporate her sass, long lines and thick black hair, but moving drugs remained out of the question. Still, she held his loyalty as if he'd pricked his finger on a melodramatic saint card and watched the blood pool. In San Diego, his family trusted people until they messed up. If they wanted drama, they went to the theater.

Jandro was lucky Antonio hadn't killed him. If a stage kiss set off the Vitella family's protective instincts, Dante should check the locks on Gisella's bedroom. How could Gregorio have invited him to stay at the house? He considered the cagey mobster and wondered if he issued the invitation in good faith or laid out a lure that would pave the way to hell.

Juniper and Julietta burst into the study arm-in-arm.

Their matching house dresses looked like floral tributes to the 1960s. Dante preferred Gisella's white satin.

"How am I supposed to think with all this racket?" Juniper threw a hand over her eyes. "The noise is relentless."

He bit back a smile and gave thanks for English. The two opinionated, aged women crowded the study, but he welcomed reinforcements. Gregorio and Antonio claimed the space behind the desk, Gisella commanded the center of the room, and he searched for his place in the room's shifting crowd.

Julietta put her hands on her hips. "Seriously, Gregorio, what have you done now?"

He shrugged. "Me? Nothing?"

Antonio picked his teeth.

Dante raised his eyebrows.

Gisella pointed her finger at her cousin. "He destroyed a man's career. Jandro kissed me onstage, and Antonio broke both his legs. The man's sadistic."

"Jandro?" Juniper covered her mouth. "But he has a wife and two children."

Gisella threaded her fingers through her hair. The long, black strands covered her face. When she parted the curtain, tears glistened in her eyes. "I know."

Dante stepped forward.

Julietta stilled his progress.

"Gregorio." Juniper started and cleared her throat. "Say you've wanted to train a new butler."

Dante stared at the woman.

Gisella closed her eyes. "*Zia*, we're not talking about staff."

Juniper waved off the comment and walked closer to Gregorio's desk. She sat on the desk's edge and wrinkled her nose. "This room stinks."

Dante bit back a laugh. Antonio reeked of weed, but nobody called out his usage. Did his violence wax and wane, or did he habitually close out his evening with a toke? Most people used inhalers. *Neanderthal*.

"Imagine you want one," Juniper said. "But you tell everyone you want a maid."

"We're not getting new staff," Gisella said. "Martin's fine!"

Julietta made a circular motion near her temple. "*Pazza*, I know."

"But you're making such a fuss about wanting a maid that nobody shows you a butler. Then the maid arrives" — she flung wide her hands — "and nobody knows what the fuck to do with her. She can't do her job. The household collapses!"

Dante shook his head. *The women in this family…*

"*Papà*, make this right," Gisella said. "Take care of Jandro! Pay his medical bills, apologize and make him whole."

"Not going to fucking happen," Antonio said. "He crossed a fucking line."

"On stage!"

Gregorio raised his hand. "And if I really wanted a butler?"

Juniper smiled.

Dante and everyone else in the room stared.

"Stop telling people you want a dim-witted, thieving maid!" Juniper dropped into a gray leather club chair studded with nail heads. "*Pazzo*."

Antonio scratched his head.

Drawing a deep breath, Gregorio nodded and turned to his right-hand man. "Juniper's right. You're rash and power hungry. The minute I unload CIH's protective shell, you'll have an army of back-room lieutenants looking for guidance. You can't beat them to teach them discipline and boundaries. That's not how our family works."

"Of course that's how it works," Antonio said. "People step out of line, and you make them disappear."

"And if I did that to you?" Gregorio asked. "How many times have you fucked up a deal?"

Antonio exhaled.

"Jandro," Gisella said.

Gregorio turned. "Your friend isn't part of this family. He has a wife and daughters. He knows I'm your father. You think my reputation serves me? It serves you. Jandro should have known better than to lay his hands on you. He's on his own."

She opened her mouth. "What? You just said Antonio made a mistake."

"Let him fix it."

"We're talking about a man's livelihood! You can't strip away his art and his family's income to appease some asinine definition of family honor. If you think I'm some principled virgin..."

Dante cleared his throat.

The room's occupants faced him.

He'd left his gun upstairs, but if Antonio pulled his piece, he could escape the room before the dazed motherfucker ticked off a shot. "Focus on the theater assault."

Gisella rounded the desk and faced her father. "You have hundreds of millions of dollars in an offshore tax-haven. You're willing to offload your daughter for ten million."

"Fifteen," Dante said.

Juniper cleared her throat.

"Take responsibility for this assault!" Gisella slapped the desk.

Gregorio held his ground. "How do you know these things?"

She threw up her arms. "I leave my bags everywhere. It's not my fault you and your friends can't sweep a room. With Active Listen, my phone acts like a microphone and streams your conversations straight to my headphones. Why do you think I spend so much time lounging by the pool? It's not to listen to the radio. When you and Antonio review accounts and logistics, I can hear your conversations like I'm sitting in the room."

Rubbing his chin, Gregorio inhaled. "Maybe I should have given you a chance to lead."

"I don't want to run drugs for a living." She enunciated every work. "I want to dance."

Antonio sneered. "Then stop making a scene and go back to your fantasy land."

Gisella walked up to her cousin.

Antonio pulled back his hand.

Striding across the room, Dante moved to protect her.

She laughed in the face of her cousin's threat. "I know your secrets, too. You complain to me about women?" She shook her hair away from her face. "You can't get it up, you chauvinistic asshole. All the bravado and posturing is a joke. You're afraid to admit who you are, and the lie will haunt you. You won't last a minute in *Papà's* shoes."

Antonio lowered his hand and sneered. "Bitch, you'll pay for this insult."

"*Fermare!*" Gregorio's shout echoed.

The study door opened, and Ursula walked into the room. Seaweed protruded from her hair. "What's going on?"

Dante could only imagine how the plants ended up tangled in her locks.

Looking at each person in the room, Gisella shook her head and fled.

Dante weighed the CIH deal's value and looked at Gregorio. "You'll pay outstanding claims, deposit three years of premiums in a commercial bank account and turn over the company's legitimate balance sheet. The minute I read the profit-and-loss statement, I'll burn it. If I find out you screwed me, I'll come after you. You knew my father. Now you know me."

Gregorio scratched his chin. "Interesting."

Narrowing his gaze, Dante stripped away emotions and focused on the bottom line. Price to tangible book valuation stripped out goodwill and other intangible assets. If CIH closed shop, the approach clarified the company's remaining net valuation. "ADC Industries will pay you the value of the deposited premiums and nothing more."

"That's a scam!" Antonio jammed his hand into his mouth.

Dante glanced at the man but focused on Gregorio. "It's the ultimate form of money laundering."

"And my other offer?" Gregorio folded his hands over his chest and leaned back in the chair.

"You owe me fifteen million dollars." Walking out of the study, he followed Gisella. He sought the power and protection money afforded him, but he would do anything to claim her. Striding through the marbled foyer, his footsteps echoed. This house, or one like it, could have been his, but he refused to leverage his family to amass his wealth. If Gisella accepted him, he would do everything in his power to make her happy, but he wouldn't let her family destroy her heart.

Chapter Twelve

Tia dumped kitchen scraps into the black plastic compost bin. "People think one good deed erases their misadventures, but you haven't saved yourself until you've turned over a heaping pile of garbage and looked at what's underneath it all."

Pausing in the shadows, Gisella weighed her options. She could vault the perimeter wall and flee, or she could run to her room and regroup. Seeking refuge among her childhood awards and dance accolades felt too easy, but once she hit the streets, she'd fear returning home. "Maybe it's all garbage."

Turning beneath a spotlight, Tia laughed. "Maybe you're right." She slammed shut the compost lid. "But we'll keep trying to make something of it."

"My mother" — Gisella exhaled — "she wouldn't let me pull this shit."

Tia laughed and picked up the wide stainless-steel bowl she used to ferry out scraps from the kitchen. "Your mother recognized rot. When she drowned, your father blamed himself for leaving her unattended. He had one foot in the church and one foot in the grave. Why do you think she wanted to come to America?"

"For a fresh start?"

Tia shook her head. "She wanted freedom. Your grandfather would have ruled her life until he drew his last breath. Every chance she had, she escaped to the sea or took you and your siblings into the country."

"You couldn't know that," Gisella said. "You never met her."

Propping the bowl on her hip, Tia walked toward the kitchen. "Who do you think keeps Juniper and Julietta company when you're away? Those biddies talk, and your mother sounds just like you. The aunties said she drove you to your first ballet lessons. She could have been a professional dancer."

"But she died," Gisella said, "and I'm the dancer."

Tia nodded.

"Is it worth it?"

"Gigi, I've seen every person in this household stop to watch you dance across the patio. Don't apologize for your passion."

Rubbing her arms, Gisella nodded.

"That doesn't mean you're free to come and go as you please."

Gisella smiled. "Back to the compost."

Tia nodded. "Everyone needs to deal with their shit."

Wrinkling her nose, Gisella gave thanks that Miami's municipal services took care of some responsibilities, but she understood Tia's advice.

"Come back to me, Gigi. Give Tia a call and share an espresso."

"But you hate espresso."

Tia leaned in close. "But I love you."

Full, heavy warmth crept into Gisella's limbs. She could stay at the house and reason with her father. Antonio and Marco — she shuddered — didn't have to govern her life. To secure her freedom, she'd turn over every piece of information she had, but first, she'd try to reason with the men.

Dante's silhouette appeared at the back doors.

She couldn't pull him into the life he'd escaped. He belonged on private jets and video conferences. Her life in Miami would shrink to endless rehearsals, aching feet and nail-biting reviews. She would love it. Even as the shopping stopped, she would find happiness in a simpler life. Every time she flipped through a fashion magazine and admired the costumes, she would think about the what-ifs, but she would maintain her resolve.

Dante would crack. Sheltered in her father's house, he slipped into her dreams and risked his life for minor pleasures. No matter how hard she ignored her longings or hid the magazine, he would catch her wistful look and second-guess his decision to stay clean. Eventually, he would succumb to an asshole cousin's easy lure, and the skull tattoo's mournful admonishment would mark his grave.

"I have to go." She kissed Tia's soft cheek. "I can't think straight in this house."

Tia snorted and waved her toward the garden. "The gate's unlocked."

Gisella blinked. How long had the gate stood open?

She shook off her inertia and walked out of her father's house. A night on the beach wouldn't kill her, and in the morning, she would walk to the ballet studio and ask for help. Her performances might not win her an award this season, but she collected a paycheck, and leveraging her art would cover her base needs.

Crossing the busy road, she felt the cool sand between her toes and sighed. Running along the beach had always been her freedom. No matter how far she strayed, the lapping waves always waited for her.

"You won't get far without shoes," Dante said.

His curt observation brought a smile to her face, but logistics hardly mattered. Somewhere in the city, Jandro moaned in a hospital bed, and she bore a measure of responsibility. Her male family members never came to the performances. When the choreographer suggested the kiss, she could have said no. She shrugged.

"What are you going to do? Bunk down with the turtles?"

She crossed her arms and turned her side to the onshore wind. Streetlights lit the road, and downtown's glow obliterated the stars. She'd have to wander pretty far to forget her past. "Couch surf."

He took her hand. "My hotel room has a couch."

His warm grip tempted her, but she looked out to sea. "And when you go back to ADC Industries? When your boss stops paying the bill?" She shrugged. "I'll be right back to couch surfing."

Turning over her palm, he traced her lifelines. "What if I stayed?"

She blinked. "For how long?"

"Forever, Gisella."

Turning away from the faceless sea, she considered his lamp-lit profile. The light blue and lavender shirts he wore picked up the green in his eyes. When he found something funny, his high smoldering intensity lightened into a smirk. She thought him indifferent, but she was wrong. His flatlined expressions shielded an aching heart. He couldn't forgive himself for killing his father, and she refused to be his curse. "I don't want you to give up your life for me."

"Why? A man needs a wife."

Yanking free her hand, she stared. "We've known each other a week."

"And fucked twice."

She blinked and looked away. "Thanks for the reminder."

He turned her chin. "Twice wasn't enough."

Staring, she waited for him to backtrack.

"Gisella…"

His persistence gave her reason to pause. "You don't know me. Why on earth would you want to marry me? I don't need a protector. My father"—she glanced toward the mansion—"would never hurt me."

"Your father is leaving."

The truth of his statement raised her awareness and prickled skin. "Fine. I have assets. I can leave, too. Dancing is a career."

"Which requires a stage." He stroked her cheek. "To thrive, you need an audience. To survive, you need anonymity. Which will it be?"

His astute observation pained her, and she exhaled. "You don't even like me."

"I do," he said.

His simple statement stole her breath. "Why?"

"You're beautiful and graceful, but you shine. No matter how many times your family pushes you into the shadows, you emerge, and I need that light. I need that optimism. Admit you like me."

"Hardly."

He snorted. "I look forward to changing your mind."

"You have a thing for dancers." She pulled out of his grip and paced the sand. "Belinda. Coco. What was the last one called?"

"Lulu," he said. "Trust me, the woman was delusional."

She smiled. "Maybe it comes with the territory."

He ran his hair through his hair. "Maybe it does."

Free of his influence, she paced the sand. "You're right about some things. The shadows of my family's sins haunt me. I thought I could walk a line and keep myself removed from the family business, but I was wrong. Bad family members and good people can't coexist."

"True."

He swallowed like the truth lodged in his throat. She understood that scraping, breathless sensation. She'd exercised her privilege, handled her father and used art to absolve her guilt, but she'd also matured. Jandro's loss summoned recollections of his family. Every missing person left behind a lover. Yet, despite Dante's past and his actions, she sensed his goodness, and she dared fate to prove her wrong. "I love my family, but I don't love what they do. I won't pull you into that world."

Reaching down to the sand, he picked up a shell and chucked it back to the sea. "You can't pull me anywhere."

"Dante, I'm about to be poor as shit. We'll have to live on ramen."

"Have you ever eaten ramen?"

She kicked the sand. "That's not the point!"

He laughed.

"And I live in Miami." She glanced at the glittering skyline. "What are you going to do in Miami?"

"Run CIH," he said.

Turning her head back to him, she stared.

"CIH offers property insurance, casualty insurance and value-added insurance services across twenty southeastern states. If I can't make money off the brand, I'm a shitty businessman."

"You buy companies and walk away from them."

He hurled another shell into the waves. "Now I'll run one. My boss isn't a complete asshole." He smiled. "As long as I meet my deliverables, he'll cash his dividend checks and leave me to admire endless sunsets and my hot new wife."

"The local dating scene sucks."

He captured her hand and yanked her against his side. "Good point. Marry me."

Wiggling out of his grip wasn't an option. Pinned against his solid warmth, she closed her eyes. "No."

"Well, I'll add kidnapping to my resume. I know a few men — Antonio, Marco."

She snorted.

"For a few million, they'll get me what I need."

She rolled her eyes. "Be real."

He turned her and gripped her hips. "Gisella, I am being real. I need you, your grace, and your cavalier enjoyment of life. I'm glad you shop and find beauty in everyday goods. I need you to look at me the same way you did tonight. You think I'm worth saving. I'm not, but I need you to believe I am."

Raising her hand, she stroked his cheek. "Daniel…"

He smiled.

"Diablo would be better," she said.

Laughing, he lowered his head.

She raised her hand and stopped his kiss. "Give me the fifteen million."

He frowned. "Who said anything about money?"

"I did."

He pulled back, but kept his grip on her hips. "All of it?"

"Yeah." She swallowed. "All of it."

Drawing a deep breath, he nodded and yanked her against his hips. "I'd marry you for free. Hell, I'd write the check for fifteen million."

She laughed and nuzzled against his neck. "You don't have fifteen million."

"Hmm." Sweeping her hair over her shoulder, he picked up her ass and pulled her close. "What are you going to do with the money?"

She wrapped her legs around his waist. "Give it to Jandro."

"Lucky bastard."

"Dante, he can't dance. Antonio took everything from him."

Striding toward the road, Dante stole a kiss and loosened his grip. "Not everything. He has his family. I've heard that can be enough."

She slid down his frame.

He held his fist between their bodies. "I grew up in a drug-smuggling world, but I left and tried to replace the power and protection with corporate success. If your father took everything from you, would you still dance?"

She nodded.

"I never found that passion, but being with you makes me think it's possible. You understand where I came from and where I want to go." He turned his wrist and took a deep breath. "You understand me."

In the shadows, his gesture felt like a child's game, but she understood the stakes. If she married him, he would hold her fast, and she would treasure every second she spent helping him find his passion. Miami, for all its palm trees and gleaming charms, wasn't his home, but it could be a place where they built a future.

He opened his hand.

A polished, opaque piece of green glass rested on his palm. "Marry me, Gisella. Make a home with me. We both have pasts, but we also have the capacity for passion. I won't stop you from dancing. I'll be at every opening night. And when you come home, we'll navigate the world together."

She looked at the small, wave-washed gem. The beach was the one place she felt free, but choosing Dante as a running partner would remake her entire experience. In his arms, she experienced windswept freedom and endless possibilities, but she feared losing her footing. The cool sand grounded her to her obligations, and she narrowed her gaze. "You're still handing over the dowry."

He smiled. "I know."

Snatching the glass, she threw her arms around his shoulders. "When we met, I thought you were too good to be true."

"I am." He buried his head in her hair. "I leave wet towels on the floor."

"I told Ursula you could shove your loafers up your bleached West Coast asshole."

He pulled back and shook his head. "Well, that's unfortunate. She'll never forget that image."

Laughing, she nodded. Arranged marriages might be par for the course in her family, but she and Ursula would chart alternative courses. In the next few weeks, she hoped Fr. Pietro would resign for personal reasons, and Ursula would have more than seaweed to decorate her hair. In the meantime, she and Dante would eke out a new life. "I might have pegged you for someone who enjoys charity golf tournaments."

He pulled back and swatted her ass.

The tingling reprimand smarted, but his wide palm cupped the same cheek, and she leaned into the grip. He strode into her life like another muscled idiot following orders, but his scars and independence set him apart. Gripping the sea glass in her palm, she raised her free hand and toyed with his sun-streaked, wavy blond hair. "I didn't know you. I can't make up for the past, but I can help you build a future."

"That's a yes." He cupped the other ass cheek.

"It won't be easy. People like Antonio"—she frowned—"people like my cousin will try to stop us. I can't leave Miami, but I'm afraid of what happens when we stay."

"Gisella." He raised his hands and kneaded the tight muscles in her lower back. "I could be down to my last dime, lame and half-blind, and I'd still protect you from your family and anyone else who tries to hurt you. If you're worried about Antonio, Marco and the rest of the buffoons, call the police. Give Jandro his day in court."

She closed her eyes. "I can't."

His stands stilled. "Leaving hurts. Complicity can be worse."

"Dante…" She pulled back.

He tightened his hold. "I'm not telling you how to run your life. Antonio will get what he deserves."

"I hope so." She stroked his hidden tattoo. For so much of her career, she'd raced toward center stage, but

Dante compelled her to linger on a moonlit beach. As the wind whipped her hair and pushed her deeper into his arms, she savored the moment, pulled down his head and claimed his lips. Their warmth emboldened her.

Pulling back before she found herself with a ticket for indecent exposure, she looked at the smooth piece of glass she held. It promised her that she could enjoy her freedom without lingering in the past, and Dante would be by her side. He imbued it with that power, and the act rendered it priceless. She looked up. "That's a yes."

He smiled and linked his hand with hers. "You want to go back to your father's house?"

"Absolutely not. Are you crazy?"

He laughed and pulled out his phone. "Okay, I'll call a ride."

She scanned the traffic flow and looked toward her father's estate. In an upstairs window, a figure looked over the beach. She recognized that window and wondered what her father thought about her choices. So many issues concerning her family remained unsolved, but she resolved to enjoy this moment. "Dante, one day soon we'll have to face my father. I don't want him to disappear from my life." She thought of Tia and her family. "I don't want to lose the people I love."

"We won't. Only death is final." He rubbed his shoulder.

She wanted to take away his pain.

A black sedan stopped at the curb, and a driver opened the door.

Looking at the vehicle, she tilted her head. "Is this how all taxis look? I thought they were yellow."

Laughing, he pulled her hand to his lips. "Well, you have a lot to learn."

She climbed into the car and settled into the soft leather. Dante draped an arm over her shoulders, and she leaned into his heat. Looking out of the window, she spied a forgotten sandcastle draped in moonlit shadows and smiled. Sometimes dreams came true, but sometimes a woman chose the most promising path. Dante would protect her, please her and support her art. What else could a woman demand?

Chapter Thirteen

Dante watched the streetlights flicker over Gisella's features. She gazed out of the window like a lost soul, but he'd promised her protection, and he refused to be the looming asshole who snuffed out her light. Picking up her hand, he stroked her palm and traced the subtle lines that might reveal her fate. "Having second thoughts?"

She turned and bit her lip. "No."

"You're sure?" He raised her hand to his lips.

"Dante?"

Drawing her thumb into his mouth, he sucked and held her gaze.

"Dante."

The slow, sensual act eroded her pensive expression, and her forehead relaxed. Satisfied, he released her thumb and trailed his teeth along the lush pad. "What?"

"How do you do that? One minute, I'm pensive" — she frowned—"or infuriated, and the next minute, I only have eyes for you."

"Sex." He whispered his answer. "You like sex."

She swatted his chest. "Can you be serious?"

"Sometimes." Drawing back, he gave her space. Looking at her shadowed expression, he waited to see joy but doubted it would come until she felt secure with her decision. Once she had accepted her complicity and faced her family's sins, she'd felt their weight. He understood the burden. Nobody had expected him to make anything of himself, but he had. Now a beautiful woman blinked in the moonlight, and he understood her doubts. The unexpected responsibility of caring for another person's feelings eroded a decade of decisiveness.

He'd never owned so much as a cat, and now he had a beautiful, temperamental woman on his hands. Letting her sink into sadness would ruin whatever fresh start fate owed them. "Do you want to go for a run?"

"At night?" She turned and chewed her bottom lip.

The city's lights gilded her hair. He wanted to touch it. Any other night, he would raise his hand and run the silken strands though his fingertips, but responsibility stilled his hand. "I'll keep you safe."

She sighed. "I don't have my shoes, and I'm not in the mood."

"Okay." He looked away and drummed his fingers on the door panel. Chocolate chips and whipped cream wouldn't get him out of his mess. *Then again, whipped cream…* He shook his head.

The driver pulled the car up to the building housing Alessio's penthouse. Before Dante moved into the Vitella mansion, the apartment had served as his corporate hotel room. Twenty flights above him, sleek opulence had kept him comfortable, but it had also reminded him how much he had yet to achieve. CIH, in whatever form it came to him, would have to be his next steppingstone to wealth. Fifteen million would have been a hell of a down payment on a place of his own.

"This is a hotel?" Gisella asked.

The doorman approached her side of the vehicle.

Dante reached for the door handle. "My boss keeps a space on the twentieth floor. He lets his associates use it when we're in town."

She nodded. "Practical."

Stepping out of the car, he stood beneath the glaring yellow lights and watched the doorman tail Gisella toward the brass doors. She moved like a queen, but she accepted the marriage out of practicality. Why should he expect more?

She looked over her should. "Are you coming?"

He inhaled. "Yes."

The doorman examined her loose pants and sweatshirt.

Dante glared at the asshole until he backed up.

Riding up in the private elevator, Dante kept his hands pressed to his sides. In close proximity, her familiar scent beckoned him, but uncertainty paralyzed his muscles. Hours ago, she'd wrapped her legs around him in her father's house. Would she accept him in the real world? Their stolen trysts lit a fire in his veins, but the building's blasting AC cooled his ardor. "Do you need anything tonight?"

She tilted her head. "A toothbrush?"

"Right. How about a fucking bottle of brut and a rose-petal turndown service?"

Laughing, she yawned. "That would be nice, too."

The elevator doors opened.

Striding past her, he punched the code into Alessio's front door and stepped aside. She strode into the penthouse like a fucking queen, and he followed. The floor boasted a privileged view over Millionaire's Row, but the local vernacular struggled to keep up. These days, a man needed a billion dollars to count.

For the time being, he had a billionaire's view. Sixteen-foot ceilings and floor-to-ceiling windows led to an outdoor terrace and a wrap-around deck. A hot and cold plunge pool glowed and beckoned visitors for a midnight swim. Inside the penthouse, a top-of-the-line kitchen and acres of soft beige carpet invited guests to linger in intimate seating areas, sit at the wide dining table or approach the built-in bar. "A drink?"

She sank onto the nearest couch. "No, I think I'll just sleep."

"Here?" he settled beside her. "You can have your own room."

Rubbing her face, she nodded. "I don't need my own room. I want to be with you, Dante. I just need a little" — she sighed — "time to process things."

If he gave her too much time, she'd regret her decision and kowtow to her family's expectations. He knew how much separation hurt. After his father had rejected him, he had killed the man and extinguished the threat. His actions left him with misgivings, but his throbbing shoulder reminded him how much obedience hurt. He pulled his gun from his ankle holster, opened a safe and slid the piece into the secure vault.

"Don't you sleep with it under your pillow?" she asked.

"You're safe tonight."

"And tomorrow?"

"I'll always keep you safe." Standing, he walked to the bar and poured himself a whiskey. He raised the bottle.

She shook her head.

"Champagne?"

She summoned a smile. "I wouldn't want to get you into trouble with the boss."

Rattling the whiskey, he raised it and took a deep, fortifying sip. "Alessio won't give a fuck." Her laughter fortified him, and he smiled. "I'll replace it."

"I don't want to cause you problems," she said. "I'm fine."

"You don't look fine." He sat on the coffee table. "You look like you're about to break."

She frowned.

Setting aside his glass, he reached for her hand. He knew her impossibly smooth skin, but he needed her matching smile. Despite her upbringing, she viewed the world with a soft-filtered optimism that fueled her dance and added meaning to humanity's inevitable tragedies.

In his experience, difficulties brought out the best and the worst in people. Gisella had lost her mother, but she appreciated life and her hodgepodge family of lithe dancers, taciturn staff and eccentric relatives. Her compassion, altruism and purpose created a worldview that accepted vice, but funneled energy into creativity. One day, his strength would run dry, and he would need her optimism. Until their roles flipped, he would protect her weakness and stay strong. "Relax. I'll take care of you."

"How? My family..." She shuddered. "You don't know them."

He considered his answer. Profit had brought him to Miami, but she compelled him to stay. Dropping to his knees on the soft carpet, he knelt between her legs, moved his hand to the edge of her sweatshirt, and slid his calloused skin against her bare stomach. Words might fail him, but he could fall back on the pleasure that had brought them together. Skimming a hand up her slender ribcage, he stroked her nipple. It pebbled beneath his touch, and the involuntary reaction gave him hope. She might shield her emotions, but her body couldn't lie. Looking up, he met her gaze. "Should I stop?"

She shook her head, raised her arms over her head, and removed the sweatshirt. Naked from the waist up, she raised her chin. "Keep going."

Leaning forward, he trailed gentle kisses along her jawline and retraced her ribcage. Dipping his fingers into the waistband of her sweatpants, he tugged on the loose material. "Are you sure?"

She raised her hips. "Dante?"

He ignored the question on her lips. Pulling off the sweatpants, he gave thanks haste had compelled her to skip underwear. Even though he knew the feel of her wrapped around his cock, the freedom to admire her pulsed like a heady aphrodisiac. "You're so beautiful."

Lowering her shoulders, she reached toward him.

"Let me take care of you." He batted away her hand before it obscured his view.

She curled up one leg.

Her silent request fueled his exploration. He skimmed his palm along her bare upper thigh. His dick throbbed, and her scent thrilled him, but every muscle in his back went taut as he was. He stilled his hand inches from where he wanted to bury his face and feel her come against his skin. "You should sleep."

Leaning forward, she pressed a kiss against his neck and shuddered. "I can sleep later."

He ached for her, but her uneven breathing worried him. "We have all the time in the world."

"Is that true?"

He stroked her cheek. "I will protect you."

Resting her forehead against his, she sighed. "Dante, you're only human."

In her arms, he felt divine. Gripping her ass, he pulled her forward on the couch and spread her legs. "You've never been shy with me."

"Why should I be?"

He lowered his head and claimed her mouth. His demanding kiss challenged her to keep pace, and he tugged on her lower lip. When she opened her mouth, he slid his tongue over hers and captured her breathless moan. Her taste and smell invaded him, and he chased the aching needed, asking for more. Pushing her down to the plush couch held merit, but he moved his thumb along her thigh's soft crease and lifted his mouth from her lips' warm allure.

She shifted against his touch. "Dante?"

Trailing kisses down the side of her neck, he lingered over her pulse and scraped his teeth past her pulse point, along her collarbone and toward her breast.

She moaned. "You're torturing me."

He stilled and pulled back.

She opened her eyes. "What's wrong?"

Her question threatened to derail his intentions and the heavy-lidded pleasure in her gaze. He stroked her cheek. Whisking her from her father's house had triggered a heavy dose of testosterone, but the moment they stood on the sand, the risk-seeking euphoria had ebbed, and her eyes had reflected the moonlit uncertainty behind her decision to leave her family. He refused to orphan her from the people she loved, even if they were a bunch of jacked-up assholes. "Are you sure you want to be here?"

She brushed her hair out of her eyes and tilted her head. "The couch?"

If dropping her on the guest room's king-sized bed would solve his problems, he would set a land-speed record, but he meant the men who had perfected praising the old country, flouting laws and laundering millions "For starters."

Looking around the penthouse, she shrugged. "It's nice."

"It's not mine."

Licking her lips, she tugged at his shirt. "I don't care. You're more than enough."

He could give her pleasure, but he wanted to understand her needs. Running his hand between her beautiful breasts, he spread his fingers over her abdomen. Hidden strength flexed beneath his palm, and he smiled. "You sound lazy and content."

She laughed.

The soft, self-aware puff kindled his smile. He kissed her collarbone. "I like hearing your happiness. I wish I heard the sound more."

"Well, stop being such a tease, and you'll hear plenty."

He nipped her shoulder.

She swatted his back.

He understood playfulness, but he wanted more than tenuous affection and wave-washed glass.

Moving lower, he pressed kisses along her curves and scraped his chin over her breasts.

She sighed and gripped his biceps.

The swells tempted him, and he detoured from his intentions. Licking her peaked nipples, he blew softly and watched them pucker. "Does that feel good?"

"They're sensitive."

Cupping her breast, he drew a nipple into his mouth and sucked.

She lifted her hips.

Catching them, he held her fast, released her nipple and looked up.

Opening her eyes, she smiled. "You've never been this languid and lazy."

He could bend her over the couch and fuck her, but understanding her subtle preferences mattered. If she could trust him in the bedroom, she could trust him in life. Well, in this case, they would start in the living room. He smiled. "Nobody's going to interrupt us."

She glanced toward the front door and frowned.

Shaking his head, he lowered her hips and changed his plan. Licking her until she screamed his name would satisfy his ego, but it gave her none of the power and confidence she needed to get through the coming days. "Look at me, Gisella."

Turning her head, she complied.

"I want to know what you like."

She ran her fingers through his hair. "I like you."

"Good." He gripped her knees and pulled her forward. Pressing kisses along her abdomen, he skirted her bellybutton and kissed each hipbone. Her soft, musky sent teased him, but he planned to spend a lifetime savoring her.

"Daniel."

Her voice wavered, and he looked up. "You can call me whatever you like."

She laughed. "You must have a preference."

He lifted his head and met her gaze. "I prefer you."

She sighed. "Good."

Moving his thumb along her inner thigh in slow, wide circles, he spent his time teasing her breasts and honed strength while he waited for her to spread her legs.

Sliding her hand down his arm, she covered his hand and intertwined their fingers.

He stilled his lazy, glancing explorations. Despite keeping his hands free of her warmth, he felt the dampness gathering between her thighs and her shifting impatience. Lifting his head, he stared up. "What do you want from me, Gisella?"

She sighed and moved his hand toward her heat.

"Show me," he said. "Show me how to please you."

Her hand stilled over his.

He held his breath.

Placing his thumb over her clit, she traced small circles.

He held her gaze and teased the bundle of nerves. "Is that enough?" Intensifying the pressure, he rolled her soft flesh and watched for the rhythm that stole her focus. When she lowered her lids, he wanted to grin, but he suppressed his smile. "Tell me what you need. Show me."

Cupping her fingers around his hand, she pressed his finger against her softness.

Feeling her heat and wetness, his dick twitched, and he wanted to abandon his game. Instead, he parted her flesh and slowly sank his finger into her warmth. She watched his movements, and her fascination steeled his resolve. Twisting his wrist, he found a rhythm that let him rub her clit and slide into her warmth.

Her hand kept him pressed against her heat. The subtle control encouraged him. Changing the angle, he curled his finger and stroked.

Her hips twitched off the couch.

"Now we're getting somewhere," he said.

She laughed, but the sound ended with a sigh. "Maybe." She pressed a second finger into her heat.

Drawing a breath, he held it and savored her clenching muscles. "I wasted too many chances to heighten your pleasure. I should have wined and dined you." He slid his fingers in and out of her warmth, raised his gaze and inhaled. "I should have courted you."

"I wouldn't have given you the time of day. You're not Italian."

Curving up to the spot she liked, he stroked her heat.

"Fuck, Dante." She closed her eyes and gripped his wrist.

"Italian?" She felt like silk and a candle's simmering heat. If he had to learn to make lasagna, he'd turn the recipe into a fucking art form. "Are you sure?"

"Fuck the Italians."

"Don't lie to me." He rose on his knees and dragged his teeth along her earlobe. "Keep fucking my hand," he whispered as she ground against his hand. "I can feel your muscles clenching my fingers. I can see your chest rising and falling. You're close, aren't you?"

She dropped her head to the couch and closed her eyes, but her hips matched his thrusts and twisted against his penetrating hold.

He wanted to abandon his deft exploration, free his cock and slide into her heat, but he refused to prioritize his pleasure. She looked so lost in the sensation that he could spend hours feeding her need. If the tension building and coiling in her core demanded release, he would provide it. Kissing her lips, he plumbed her mouth and eased off.

She pressed his hand back into place. "Don't you dare stop."

Grinning, he let her set the pace and eased to the side to give her room to move. In minutes, her wet thrusts matched her panting breaths, and he doubted he would finish this game without blowing his load in his pants. The woman was fucking glorious.

Her back arched. She pressed his palm flat against her clit and ground against him. "Dante!"

Savoring her cry of release, he trailed soft kisses along her shoulder, held her fast and reveled in the pleasure pouring through her pulsing body. When her hand fell away from his wrist and her hips dropped, he eased his fingers from her warmth, lifted his mouth and made eye contact. "Again."

She laughed and rolled her head to the side. "Impossible."

Trailing two fingers against her swollen labia, he raised his fingers to his mouth and sucked her juices from his fingers. She tasted like decadence, and he craved an indulgence. "Is it? Now that I know what you like, I'll be ruthless. And here I thought my beautiful dick was the only thing that could make you come."

She yawned. "While I had your fingers inside me, I thought about your dick."

Restraint seemed overrated. Standing, he braced his arms on either side and loomed. "Did you?"

She grinned.

Scooping her into his arms, he strode toward the bedroom. Lamplight spilled from the room and pooled in the hallway. Beyond the door, the guest room he occupied while in town had a desk, and couch and a small seating area designed for breakfast. If he could make it down the hallway, he could take advantage of her mischievous grin.

She dropped an arm and cupped him. "I'm glad you believe me."

"I'll always believe you." If he believed her any more, he would set her on her feet, spread her legs and make good on the promise straining his pants. Jaw resolute, he marched toward the bedroom.

She tightened her grip.

At the exquisite pleasure, his entire body jerked. He stopped to claim a kiss, but he caught her smothering a yawn against his shoulder. Reaching the bedroom, he lowered her to her feet, centered his hand over her hand and pressed against her palm. "I want you, tight, wet and wrapped around my cock."

Pressing a kiss beneath his ear, she tilted her head. "Done."

He groaned. Why had she yawned? "You're exhausted."

"Dante"—she stroked his length—"we've been together. I know you want me. What's holding you back?"

Leaving his family had hurt him for many years. No matter how he examined their sins and his role, uncertainty plagued him and stole his rest. Voicing his memories might send her straight back to the prison she escaped, and he feared losing her forever.

"Dante?"

Her persistence almost teased the truth from him, but she felt good cradled against his chest and her fresh emotional wounds needed time to heal. If he misjudged the timing and burdened her with his regrets, the similarities might tip her over a precipitous edge. She might want him, but she didn't want to *be* him. "You've had a rough night."

"Antonio will pay," she said.

The cur's actions would catch up to him. Dante tried for a lighter tone. "Does that mean I get to keep the fifteen million?"

She skewed her jaw. "I don't know. Do you want to keep me?"

He tightened his hold. "Yes."

"Good. I'm planning to keep you, too. Italians don't do divorce."

"I know." Her scent wrapped around him like her long, graceful arms. He could still taste her desire on his lips. Admitting his need would end the conversation before he revealed too much. She would follow his lead, but at what cost? He wanted more than a lifetime of casual fucks, but he was a bit hazy on the specifics. Instead, he cupped her chin. "You're tired."

She squeezed his balls. "I'm not."

He closed his eyes and bore the pressure. South beach's mimes could take lessons from his self-control.

Exhaling, she released her hold. "You keep me on edge. Being with you is like a battle between impulsivity and caution, recklessness and control. How can you stop when I know you want more?"

Inhaling, he made eye contact. "You have no idea."

"Show me." She raised her hand and skipped the pad of her finger from button to button on his shirt. Pausing at his belt buckle, she looked up. "I want you."

"Tomorrow." He choked out the response.

Dropping her hand, she flounced toward the bed and flopped on the linen duvet cover. Arms spread, she stared at the ceiling. "Fine."

Lying down beside her, he traced her body's swells and dips.

"Tease," she said.

He smiled. "Go to sleep."

"And what will you do?"

"Take a fucking hot shower."

She rolled toward him.

He spread his fingers and stopped her momentum. "Just sleep, Gisella. I'll be here in the morning when you wake up."

She turned her head. "Will you?"

He pressed a kiss against the corner of her lips and felt her sigh. "I will."

"You're getting a bum deal. Do you think I don't know my wants and needs?"

Laughing, he tugged her against his chest. "I took copious notes."

Fitting her head in the hollow below his shoulder, she unbuttoned his shirt and slid her hand along his chest.

If she slid her hand lower, he would have a hard time ignoring the buzzing friction of skin against skin. Pushed to his limit, he might cave and claim the release she offered. He had time to coddle her and keep her safe. If she pushed him, he would gladly concede.

Rubbing her nose against his shirt, she scratched an itch and settled her hand over his heart. "Why are you marrying me?"

"Sex."

"Liar." She raised her head and propped herself on one elbow.

Reaching past her, he pressed a kiss to her lips, toppled her onto her back, and turned off the lamp. Shrouded in near darkness, he repositioned her on his shoulder.

"I've always known how to look into a person's eyes and tell the difference between someone willing to fight and someone who enjoyed pain. I don't want to fall into the trap of treating my childhood as some kind of testing ground. It sucked. I know how much fearing your father can tether you."

"I never feared *Papà*."

He stoked her hip and smiled. At least he wouldn't have to kill the asshole for past transgressions. "Good. Fear also breeds determination. When people exhaust their options, they lash out. I don't want you to experience the regret I carried. You're going to find out that I struggle to trust and relax. The hard exterior I've developed keeps me sane, but you're still soft."

Picking up a strand of her hair, he rubbed it between his fingers and wondered how it shone with so little light. "Your family's a piece of work, but you still dance. I don't think you have a malicious bone in your body. You tease Martin and turn to Tia." He struggled to piece together his thoughts. Competition, sex and a haughty smile had hooked his interest, but every time he looked closer, he discovered a new facet he admired. "You're like a precious gem, Gisella. I won't lock you away, but I can't stand the thought of someone dulling your shine." He waited for her response. Her chest rose and fell against his side, and her hand lay heavy over his heart.

She snored and shifted in her sleep.

"And now you're finally following orders." Tucking her closer, he told himself he'd wait twenty minutes, slip out of bed and finish his work. His cock ached, but he could bear it, and a hot shower would rein in his lust. If everything went according to plan, a night of restraint would fade from his memory, she would reclaim her lithe strength and he'd never have to bear the pain of watching her leave.

Chapter Fourteen

"I heard you last night." Gisella rolled to her side and traced Dante's spine. Each corded muscle eroded her desire to leave the bed. Men shouldn't be able to tempt a woman without trying.

When she awoke, she expected to find an empty sheet and a lingering scent, but the man beside her was definitely warm enough and alluring enough to steal her momentum. Reaching around his waist, she slid her hand over his abdomen and ascertained his interest. The closer she got to his heat, the wider she grinned.

"Heard what?" he asked.

She stilled her hand. "I'm not a precious gem. I don't want you to think of me as something to store away and protect. The dance company will have to pause performances, but I'm under contract. I'll earn my keep."

He rolled to his back.

Bracing her forearm across his stomach, she toyed with his hair. "I'm a modern woman."

"You're also a beautiful, spoiled, pampered woman." He yawned.

She slapped his chest. The man hardly moved. Pulling her fingers across his pecs, she made for his happy trail. "I can help you trust and relax."

Wrapping an arm around her waist, he flipped her and caged her against the mattress. "I'm sure you can, but I'm not a project. The suffering made me stronger. That's one of the blessings and the curses pain leaves behind."

"But it scars you. You don't forget."

"Suffering doesn't let go of a person. I can bury it, but I recognize people in pain. You haven't suffered. You're a bright light, and I don't need a hobby." He dropped his head and kissed her collarbone. "Taking care of you will keep me plenty busy."

She shoved at him, ducked under his arm, and rose to her knees. "So you get to be the big, bad protector and I'm back to" — she shook her head and climbed from the bed — "a cloistered existence."

"No." He rubbed his jaw. "That's not what I meant. Let me take care of you."

The man wanted to set limits, but he also wanted to start his morning with a solid fuck. Well, fuck him. She left her father's house to stand on her own two feet, and she wasn't about to trade one overbearing Italian scion for a stubborn West Coast husband.

"Where you going?" he asked.

"To make eggs." She walked toward the living room and hoped her clothes still littered the floor. Stepping into the bright, light-filled living room, she made eye contact with a woman tidying the coffee table books. "Shit!"

"Your clothes are on the stool." The woman aligned the book spines.

Stark naked in front of a stranger, Gisella raced toward the stool, pulled the sweatshirt over her head, and shimmied into her sweatpants. "I'm sorry. I didn't know anyone was in the apartment."

"I clean the penthouse every day from nine to twelve." The woman straightened and crossed her arms.

She wore her salt-and-pepper gray hair pinned back in a bun. Beneath her pale pink service uniform, sheer black tights and sensible shoes shielded her skin. How the hell did anyone in Florida wear tights? "I'm Gisella."

"Linda."

The woman looked like she could organize a card catalog in record time. Gisella moved toward the kitchen and realized how much she would miss Tia's warmth. Linda didn't look like the type of women who enjoyed steaming milk for cappuccinos or baking fresh *cornetti*.

Dante walked into the kitchen bare chested, approached Linda, and kissed her cheek. "Did you miss me?"

"Mr. Dante, I always miss you." Linda blushed.

Gisella opened her mouth and stared.

"If I'd known you were coming back to the penthouse, I would have ordered groceries. I'm afraid all you have are eggs, butter and a few leftover oranges. I threw out the rest of the produce before it could spoil."

"No big deal," Dante said. "We'll order breakfast."

Gisella turned and faced down the gleaming refrigerator. Opening a door, she found the ingredients

Linda named, as well as a carton of half and half. "I can make eggs."

Nobody spoke.

Turning, she found Dante and Linda staring. "Really, I can scramble eggs."

Linda pursed her lips.

Dante grinned. "Great!" He turned to Linda. "You want eggs?"

"Good luck." Clearing her throat, Linda picked up her cleaning supplies and walked toward the door.

"I make very good eggs," Gisella said. If Dante treated the woman like a friend and a guest, she would do the same. "You're welcome to stay and tell me everything you know about Dante. Can I get you anything? Coffee?"

"Thank you, but no." Linda opened the front door. "I'll be back tomorrow at nine."

Gisella smiled. "Wonderful."

Linda let herself out of the door.

"So, she seems nice." Tia had technically taught her to make scrambled eggs, but a couple of years had passed since she'd tried to improve Gisella's nascent cooking skills. Crack eggs. Whisk. Pour in hot pan. Gisella didn't need a college degree to make breakfast. She pulled the eggs from the refrigerator. "You must visit a lot."

"Alessio has hosted a few corporate retreats down here, but Linda only took a liking to me when I arrived for the CIH deal."

She opened cabinets until she found a bowl, pulled a skillet from the drawer, placed it on the front burner and turned up the gas. Cracking the first egg, she realized she needed a discard bowl. Instead of washing her hands, she chucked it into the sink.

"Are you sure you want to cook?"

Dante claimed the stool that once held her clothes. Shirtless, he looked like a calendar model. How had she ever pinned him for a corporate classic? Knowing he would run CIH soothed her nerves, but she expected a bumpy road. "I can cook."

How many eggs did this man eat? Instead of asking, she cracked three for herself and decided to crack a complete dozen. Eggs could keep, couldn't they? They weren't like rice. Tia refused to reheat rice. She swore off botulism like the bubonic plague. Dropping the final eggshell into the sink, Gisella washed her hands and wiped them on her pants. "Do you think you can make coffee?"

"Sure." Standing, Dante opened a cabinet and revealed a high-end machine.

She suddenly wanted to hug the faceless Alessio.

"How strong?" Dante asked.

Whisking the eggs, she chewed her lip. "Strong." While the coffee machine whirred to life, she eyed the skillet and tried to remember Tia's instructions. Salt and a splash of milk? Pulling the half and half from the refrigerator, she judged the soupy eggs and added close to half a cup. Sprinkling a few salt crystals into the mix, she figured she could always add more after the eggs finished cooking.

Dante set a cup of coffee on the counter.

The rich, velvety aroma stole her focus. Clasping the cup in her hands, she closed her eyes, took a long sip and knew everything would be fine.

"I think your pan's hot," Dante said.

"Great!" Setting aside the coffee, she poured the egg mixture into the pan.

Steam billowed into a tiny mushroom cloud. The eggs sizzled and popped. In the center of the pan, a dome grew taller than the pan's width. "Shit, I need to stir them." Opening drawers, she searched for a familiar wooden spoon. Finding nothing she recognized, she grabbed a rubber spatula, popped the growing egg bubble, and mixed up the steaming mixture. "*You just have to keep scraping down the bottom.*"

Tia's careful instructions echoed in her memory, but the eggs refused to move. Rubbing the spatula along the middle of the plan, Gisella tried to scrape off a seared layer, realized the eggs wouldn't move and turned to the pan's sides. *Why are they so watery?* "Shit."

"Stick with it," Dante said.

"I'm trying!" No matter what she did, the bottom seared into a caked mess, the top oozed and nothing she did created the golden, buttery eggs she loved. "Stupid eggs!"

Dante rounded the corner, turned down the gas and pulled the spatula from her hands. "Are you crying? Over eggs?"

She turned her back on the soupy, burnt monstrosity and pressed her cheek against his chest. "We're going to die of starvation...or go broke ordering takeout. I only make fifty thousand a year." She hiccupped. "Who can't cook eggs?"

He laughed, and his chest rumbled beneath her cheek. "We won't go broke."

Pulling back, she wiped away her tears. "I know. You'll make CIH successful. We won't be poor forever."

"You think we're poor?"

She nodded. "I mean, how much do corporate jobs pay? *Papà* always says *Ai mali estremi, estremi rimedi.* I have to learn how to cook."

He cupped her face and stole a kiss.

His warmth calmed her agitation, and she exhaled.

"We're not poor."

"I know." She wet her lips. "You work hard. I work hard. How difficult can it be?"

Shaking his head, he released her face, pulled out his cell phone, and made a call. "Linda, can you run to the corner bakery and pick up those almond croissants I love?"

Gisella covered her face. "Come on, not Linda! Don't you have an app? I have an app. I can have breakfast here faster than Linda can walk."

"With what? Your daddy's credit card?" he asked.

She frowned. She had a bank account and a credit card, but her father had opened the account when she turned sixteen. She needed to change the passcode and cancel the credit cards she normally used. "I can buy breakfast."

Ending the call, he set aside his phone. "I'll give you everything you want and need. Trust me, Gisella. Let me take care of you for a few days. After things calm down, you can buy a slow cooker and make every stewed meat recipe your heart desires."

He must be joking. Didn't people slow cook roasts in an oven? "But I don't need you to take care of me. People have taken care of me my entire life."

"And you're a talented dancer." He eyed the abandoned eggs. "Not so much a skilled cook."

She narrowed her gaze. "Dante, if you think I swapped one gilded cage for another..."

He raised his hands over his head in a stretch.

She lost her train of thought. The male chest shouldn't fascinate her. During rehearsal, Jandro and the rest of the dancers routinely stripped to their tights. The gardeners sweated through their shirts. Dante's chest had to be special. She counted the abdominal muscles. *Eight.* Well, that made anatomical sense, but even Jandro didn't have eight defined pecs. "I need to see him."

"Who? Your father?"

She sat on a stool, bent her arm across the counter, and dropped her head. "Jandro. Antonio beat the shit out of him. He must be terrified and in so much pain. I have to go see him."

Dante stroked her back.

She didn't deserve comfort. Shrugging off his touch, she tried to ignore the sour smell of burnt eggs, her fumbling desires and the ease with which she had accepted her old life. After the bank, she needed to call Ursula and dig through their shared memories. What fatal flaw in their DNA permitted so much selfishness?

"I'm sure the hospital has Jandro medicated," Dante said. "Go shower and we'll ride over there. Call his wife and see if now's a good time for us to visit."

She raised her head. "You're coming with me?"

He crossed his arms and glanced at the windows. "I'm not leaving your side."

Following his gaze, she moved toward the windows and looked down. One of her father's men stood on the corner. He looked as inconspicuous as a nun on a beach. If he wanted to go incognito, he should have ditched his newspaper and scrolled through his social media feeds like any other human on the Florida peninsula. She drew a steadying breath. "He's harmless."

Linda walked out of the bakery, pivoted, and swung her purse into the man's newspaper.

He jumped to his feet and glowered.

Matching his stare, Linda righted her purse, lifted her chin, and walked back toward the building.

Gisella smiled. "I think our breakfast's almost here." Turning from the window, she walked past Dante's imposing form and trailed her fingers along his abdomen. "I'm going to shower. Care to join me?"

Loosening his stance, he nodded.

She reached over the counter and triggered the garbage disposal. The satisfying whir and crunch erased her misgivings about the morning. This wasn't the 1950s...

The disposal shuddered to a stop.

Frowning, she flipped the switch a few times and turned to Dante.

He caged his hand over his mouth. "Um. Eggshells aren't recommended for garbage disposals. The egg membranes can tie up the blunt impellers and cause damage" — he dropped his hand — "or something."

She rubbed her temples and imagined her bank balance swirling down the drain. "Right, um, have Linda call a plumber."

"Don't worry about it, Gisella." He reached toward her, grabbed her hand, and tugged her across the kitchen floor. "We'll take care of it."

Hands braced on his chest, she looked up. "I don't want to be a burden, or a disaster, or a...burdenaster?"

"That's not a word."

"If you leave me unsupervised in the kitchen, it might be."

He laughed. "I appreciate the effort." He lowered his head.

A second before his lips erased her embarrassment, she pulled back. "Can you cook?"

"Eggs? Yeah. I've lived alone for a while."

Pushing off his chest, she wrapped her self-confidence around her like a fur coat. Letting her hips sway, she walked toward the door and looked over her shoulder. "Next time, you make breakfast."

"Gisella…"

She kept walking.

"Only if you burn those sweats."

She bit back a laugh, pulled her sweatshirt over her head, and trailed it along the hallway. "Are you coming?"

"As soon as I call a plumber."

Flipping him the bird, she headed straight for the shower. She would drown her embarrassment in scalding hot water, find a button-up to replace her sweatshirt, and walk out of the building with her head held high. Jandro wouldn't give two shits about what she wore to the hospital. If Dante had ideas about the wardrobe, he could bang on her father's door or accompany her to the clothing boutiques.

But she couldn't afford those boutiques. Ursula's jibe surfaced in her memory. When was the last time she'd entered a public mall? As soon as she saw Jandro, she'd reset the counter and embrace the life she intended to live.

* * * *

The taxi driver navigated away from the beachside building and the surf shop where she'd acquired a pair of cheap plastic flip-flops. The band irritated her toes, but the squishy soles were surprisingly comfortable.

Settled beside Dante in the taxi, she looked past her window, watched the buildings pass and contemplated her new life.

"So, what kind of wedding do you want?" Dante asked.

She started and turned her head. "Excuse me?"

"We're getting married."

Swallowing, she nodded. "I'm aware."

"Fifteen bridesmaids?"

"Hardly." She cleared her throat. She could never imagine the wedding, but the night before the big event, her groom would organize *la serenata*. Kept completely kept in the dark, she would wake up to love songs, an eager groom and cheers from her friends and family. "Something simple."

"You want something simple?"

"Maybe the mayor can officiate." She winked.

He picked up her hand. "I know the circumstances aren't ideal, but tell me what would make the day more meaningful."

She wanted Ursula by her side, sweet flowers, a booming organ and overflowing pews. Given the idiot on the street corner, her *Papà's* foul mood and Antonio's vitriol, she doubted planning a traditional church wedding would be a good idea. "Really, Dante, something small."

"How small?" he asked.

"You, me and a judge." She pulled free her hand.

"Don't shrink away." Drumming his fingers on his knee, he shook his head. "Just because you're walking away from your family, you don't have to walk away from the things that make you happy."

"I agreed to marry you, and I'm committed. The location doesn't matter. The guests don't matter. Don't worry. I won't skip the wedding night lingerie."

"Gisella, if I wanted you in lace, I'd go to the ballet."

Smiling, she stilled his hand. "What kind of wedding do you want?"

"An ironclad one."

"Well, at least we don't need a prenup."

He rubbed his jaw. Linking their fingers, she pulled the heavy weight of his fist into her lap. "Let's find a judge, charter a boat and go for a sunset cruise."

"That's what you want?"

"It's simple and sweet. It takes the pressure off the evening." She didn't mention how much she feared the water. After her mother read her *Pinocchio*, she imagined the terrible dogfish swimming beneath the waves.

A psychiatrist chocked up her fears to humanity's deep-rooted primal fear of monsters in the deep. Gisella wondered if her subconscious recognized the monsters closer to home.

With Dante at her side, she doubted she would encounter a gigantic dogfish with three rows of enormous teeth. Instead, she would have a pleasant association to cap off a practical deal. Remembering how Dante coaxed pleasure from her body, she squeezed his hand and admitted the deal offered more than practicality.

"If that's what would make you happy?"

She smiled. "It is."

The driver slowed for Charity Hospital's imposing edifice.

The five-hundred-bed hospital was Miami-Dade County's only Catholic hospital, and its waterside location gave patients' rooms picturesque views. Despite the city's growth, the building retained its 1950s boxy charm, pink color scheme, and spiritual alcoves. Modern medicine updated staff protocols, but the hospital remained dedicated to caring for the physical and spiritual needs of the patients. Gisella smiled. "For my high school community service hours, I used to visit sick patients."

"What did you do? Read to them?"

She laughed. "Mostly watch television and listen to them complain about the nursing staff."

"Are they bad?"

"No, but people in pain have little patience."

"Tell me about it." She looked away from the building and considered his profile. How many men could land in Miami and pivot their lives in a matter of days? If the money lured him into marrying her and she took it, what compelled him to stay? She understood the parts of his life he shared, but daylight cast so many shadows. "You know, we don't have to do all this. I can hawk my jewelry and pay down Jandro's medical bills. I can…"

"Shh." Dante reached across her chest and unlocked the door. "We made a deal. Don't get nervous and back out. You still owe me watercolor classes. Hand-built pottery. Pickleball…"

She opened the door and exited the vehicle before he delved into crochet hooks, pint glass collections and antique gun ownership.

Rounding the sedan, he took her hand and squeezed it.

She led him through the hospital's automatic glass doors and aimed for the information desk. The hospital smelled antiseptic, but the linoleum floors gleamed, and the families milling in the coffee shop sipped overpriced drinks.

Following the nurse's instructions, she stood outside Jandro's door and took a deep breath. Her cousin had shattered his dance career. Her father had condoned the action. If she had more than fifteen million dollars to give him, she'd empty it onto his bed, dry her tears and apologize until a burly nurse evicted her from the floor.

"Jandro?" She opened the door, stepped inside the curtained antechamber, and listened. "Are you up for visitors? It's Gisella."

Metal creaked, and a monitor beeped.

"If now's not a good time, I can come back later." She held her breath.

A minute passed.

"Come in, Gisella," Jandro said.

His voice sounded strained. Pulling back the curtain, she found his legs suspended in the air. Thick casts obliterated their sinuous strength. How many times had he leaped and landed perfectly on stage? She wondered if he would ever dance again. Raising her gaze from his injuries, she found his wife, Annie, staring at her like she'd ordered the hit. She pulled free from Dante and stepped forward. "I'm so sorry."

Annie opened her mouth.

Patting the white hospital blanket, Jandro shook his head. "Sit. Visitors lighten recovery. Do you know how many times they've taken my temperature? Thank you for coming."

"Are you sure?" Gisella asked.

"Feeling guilty?" The lines on Annie's forehead deepened.

Gisella looked away and focused on Jandro. "Yes."

"I know you had nothing to do with this mess. I know of your father. Why do you think nobody else would partner with you?"

She gasped.

He smiled. "I'm kidding. I told the police everything, Gisella. They'll come for him. He won't get away with this harassment. What else can he do? Shoot me?"

Silence seemed like the safest answer. Looking over her shoulder, she nodded toward Dante. "I hope you don't mind that I brought him along."

"Who is he?" Annie asked.

"Daniel Johnson," Dante said.

Annie covered her mouth. "I thought your email was a hoax."

Gisella frowned. "What email?"

"I told Annie I'd wire her fifteen million dollars after you married me," he said.

Jandro slapped his chest.

Gisella stood. "You don't have the money yet. Maybe *Papà* won't follow through. I might not..." She frowned. The thought of backing out of her deal left a sour taste in her mouth.

Dante cleared his throat. "Gisella, I'm not exactly poor."

She narrowed her gaze. "What does that mean?"

"I've worked for Alessio for nearly a decade. I'm good at what I do. CIH is a deviation, but I'm not exactly an inept businessman."

The room's walls couldn't contain her frustration, and she stamped her foot. "You led me on! You tricked me!"

"You assumed," he said.

"So you don't have to marry me?"

He stepped forward and caught her hand. "Don't even think about backing out of our deal. If you want Jandro to have the money, you're stuck with me. I'll collect what your father promised me. Where it goes doesn't concern him."

She turned and sought reassurance from Jandro. Instead of sympathetic outrage, she found Annie crying on his chest and him rubbing her back and murmuring Spanish endearments. "We should leave."

Looking up, Jandro smiled. "Thank you."

"It's not enough," she said. "Look at your beautiful legs!"

He grimaced. "I'd rather not."

Covering her mouth, she nodded.

"The surgeon says she can perform a full Achilles reconstruction. She'll go into my lower leg, pull down the snapped tendon and reattach it. The bones?" He shrugged. "They'll heal, and I'll learn how to walk again."

"To walk!" She widened her eyes and understood Dante's classification system. Antonio enjoyed causing pain, but until seeing Jandro's injuries, she would have argued a third classification existed. Some people turned their emotions into art and walked softly through life. Now, frustration and helplessness mocked her control, and she understood the compulsion to fight. Taking deep breaths, she focused on what Jandro needed. "You'll walk."

"Then dance. I'll finish rehab and return to the stage. While I'm home for rehab and therapy, my children will have months to annoy me." He jerked his chin toward the small metal crucifix on the opposite wall. "Remember, Gisella. You're not responsible for life's messes. Be at peace."

"And if you can't dance professionally?" She whispered the question.

"I'm alive, aren't I?" He stoked Annie's shuddering back. "My children are healthy. I'll find a new artistic outlet. I've always wanted to paint."

Annie wailed.

"You'll come back stronger," Gisella said. "We'll be waiting for you."

"I hope so." Jandro smiled. "Thank you for checking on me. Since posting about the accident, my follower count is through the roof. Most people are good, decent humans. I'll respond to every comment, and I'll see you again soon?"

She nodded.

Dante opened the curtain.

The metal scrape inflamed her raw nerves, but she recognized her exit cue. Pressing a kiss against Jandro's forehead, she backed out of the room, eased shut the door and turned on Dante. "What the fuck?"

He held up his palms. "I can explain."

Her frustration needed an outlet, but his handsome strength and sun-streaked, wavy blond hair made a crappy target. He'd given her dance partner fifteen million dollars, promised to marry her and helped her leave her father's house. If his transparency fell short of her standards, she'd deal with his flaw. She'd certainly learned to live with bigger defects. Refusing to make a scene, she strode toward the stairwell, raced down the flights and pushed open the exit door. Blinding sunlight made her blink, but she headed toward the water and the cool, refreshing breeze.

"Gisella, wait!"

If they needed couples therapy before their marriage ceremony, how could a rite keep them together?

Chapter Fifteen

With hands wrapped around her middle, Gisella stood on the bulkhead and let her toes hang over the edge. Biscayne Bay's gentle, lapping waves barely broke the water's surface. If she dropped her flip flop into the water, it might float all the way to the tropics. She wouldn't be so lucky, but she understood her father's desire to flee the mess he'd created for an easier life.

She knew Dante would join her in a second. She had sprinted across the grass, but he was too dignified to run. In the time she'd claimed, she took deep, salt-tinged breaths and tried to add perspective to her plight.

As Miami's population grew after World War II, the Florida diocese acquired a stretch of swampy land south of the Villa Vizcaya. With the site for a new hospital on the map, the church collected donations door-to-door, in movie theaters and in area schools. The hospital served the growing regions, opened its doors to exiled Cuban physicians and offered medical care to the Bay of Pigs Brigade. How could her losing a principal dancer matter more than global conflict? The smaller a person's world shrank, the more significance its players assumed.

"You look like you're about to jump," Dante said. "Should I call someone to save you?"

She turned her face from the wind. "Would you let me fall?"

"Maybe. How deep can the water be?"

The water depth wasn't the problem. She faced the bay. Before her mother died, she'd spent laughing days among the waves, but the waves had betrayed her. "The maximum depth's about twelve feet. By the sea wall?" She shrugged. "Three?"

"So you won't drown."

She exhaled. "I hate the water."

"Didn't you just ask me to rent a boat to celebrate our nuptials?"

"Boats float." She smiled. "Mostly."

"Can you swim?"

She nodded. "But you don't know what's out there. Underwater sea-grass beds. Shrimp, lobsters, fish, sea turtles"—she shuddered—"manatees."

"You don't like manatees?" Picking up a pebble, he skipped it across the water.

She watched the pebble sink into unknown depths. "They're huge, lumbering monsters. Have you seen one? It could crush me. The farther you go from the city, the wilder the coastline becomes. Toward the edge of the bay, mangroves creep into the water. Their roots look like gnarled hands."

He huffed. "Okay, so we won't go to Key West for a honeymoon."

"At least the water's clear!"

Tucking her under his arm, he rubbed her shoulder. "Nothing's going to harm you out there. You can swim. You'll never be alone. Help is only a shout away."

"You say that, but you can't promise it's true."

Turning her, he lifted her chin.

She looked into his light brown eyes. Standing on the green lawn, the colors in his eyes shifted toward hazel, and his thick, dark lashes intensified the concern in his gaze. If primal fear kept her from the bay, recognition rooted her in his arms.

"I'll take care of you."

"You lied to me," she said. "You're rich."

"I'm nowhere near as rich as your father."

"You just gave away fifteen million dollars."

He stroked her cheek. "I'll get it back. In the meantime, content yourself with a few million."

She sighed. "You are rich. You don't need me."

Shaking his head, he dropped a kiss to her lips, pulled back, and smiled. "You're wrong. I'm nowhere near real rich. I'm not a billionaire. I don't have the world at my beck and call...yet."

"What's the difference between a million and a billion."

"About a billion," he said.

She pulled away from his teasing smile. "On a dancer's salary, they're the same thing."

"Well, good thing I'm not a dancer." He lowered himself to the bulkhead and swung his feet over the edge. "Come sit with me."

Dropping to his side, she sat with her legs tucked beneath her.

He pulled her into his lap.

"Are you going to drop me in the bay?"

"Tough-love style?" he asked.

She nodded. His warm lap and wide thighs supported her weight, and she relaxed into his chest. She had no idea what love language Dante spoke, but if it involved submersion, she wanted nothing to do with it.

"No." He nuzzled her neck. "But I have been thinking about our wedding."

"So you can recover your funds?"

"Among other things."

"Italian brides spend the night before their wedding separated from their intended grooms." She dipped back her head and exposed more skin for his warm, trailing kisses.

"Maybe we should delay the wedding a few days."

She smiled. "I'm sure there's a waiting period for a marriage license."

"Three days," he said. "I petitioned a judge to waive it."

Pulling free from his kisses, she stared. "When?"

"When I killed your cousin Luca, when I realized how deeply the CIH deal would pull me into your world. The minute I had Gregorio in position, I wanted the power to act."

She chewed the inside of her lip. "So, it has nothing to do with me."

Running his hand up her spine, he spread wide his fingers. "Marrying you or your sister started as a business decision, but I never imagined how much I would enjoy your company. Don't let that legacy haunt our relationship. You have to move beyond it and trust me. Let Fr. Pietro marry us, and let me spoil you."

"He's a priest."

"Would you prefer Linda?"

Covering her mouth, she shook her head. "When?"

"Tonight at sunset."

She looked at her flip-flops. "No, I need more time."

"Your sister's at the penthouse with some clothes. Find something suitable for a wedding, open a bottle of champagne and take a deep breath."

"That's it?"

"Well, no, that's just the beginning." Lifting her to her feet, he stood and brushed off his slacks. "The hard part comes next."

She was afraid to ask. "What's the hard part?"

"Teaching you to cook."

Slapping his ass, she turned her back on the opaque bay and let her arms swing in the breeze. Marrying Dante might not be the worst decision of her life. He had a bit of money, satisfying rhythm and enough muscled contours to distract her for years.

Her phone vibrated in her pocket.

Pulling it free, she saw her father's name and winced. "Hello?"

"Come home, Gigi. Stop this nonsense."

"Is Antonio there? Have you surrendered him to the police?" she asked.

"God no."

She rolled her eyes. "Of course not."

"Quit playing this game. I have better things to do than assign one of my men to babysit you."

She scanned the hospital's shoulders for a familiar silhouette. "Well, feel free to call off your goon." Switching to Italian, she sought to spare Dante her opinion of *la famiglia*. "Men and women have equal rights under the law, but in your house, I'm a pawn. I refuse to sit by and wait for your next joke of a suitor.

You think I would marry Marco? I'm your daughter! If you don't treat me with respect, who will?"

"You're Gisella Santa Maria Vitella!"

"Exactly!" She ended the call.

"So…" Dante matched her step.

"Who's in the mood for a wedding?" she asked.

He raised her hand to his lips.

"You just want your money and your leverage."

"Maybe I want you." He brushed his lips across her skin.

The warmth stole her breath, but her father's disregard lingered like a bad aftertaste. Pulling free her hand, she linked her fingers and drew a deep breath. Her father's overbearing approached stifled her, but she remembered her childhood freedoms. Sometimes people found happily ever after. "Maybe."

* * * *

"Gisella," Dante said, "I believe we're about to have company."

Blinking away her introspection, she stared. "Who?" She widened her eyes. "Wait! Is Linda coming back?"

He cleared his throat. "This isn't my penthouse."

She cupped his cheek. "I know. I could be happy anywhere with you."

"I doubt you appreciate what that means, but thank you." He nosed away her gesture and ran a hand through his hair. "Alessio and a few of his associates are coming to Miami."

Laughing, she walked toward the refrigerator and hoped for a few slices of cheese or an apple. Opening the door, she leaned inside the chilled appliance and shifted stacked organizers and rummaged through spotless drawers. Cheese must exist somewhere in the stupid appliance. "Oh, is that all?"

"The jet landed at Miami Executive Airport half an hour ago."

Bumping her head against the fridge ceiling, she backed out of the chilled space and stared. She loved Miami, but it was the sixth most densely populated city in the country. Nobody with means navigated their way through the main airports. Instead, they chose one of the smaller jet airports that catered to the privileged.

The MEA had a boring but descriptive title. Business aviation chose the much smaller and quieter airport over Miami International Airport because they could get wheels on the ground and head straight to their inane, corporate meetings. "Sometimes I forget why you're here."

He braced his hands on the counter. "With you?"

"In Miami," she said. "You don't belong here. My family drama is a footnote in your business contract."

Flexing his fingers against the polished stone, he made eye contact. "Gisella, I'm building a life here with you. We made a deal. Alessio and his team have every right to visit, but I don't want you to feel ambushed."

Her friend lay in a hospital bed with multiple broken bones, and his friends fought for leg space in chauffeured SUVs. If someone wanted a character sketch, she had nothing but shadows, backstage secrets and distant memories to offer. "How long?"

The doorbell rang.

"Oh, come on."

Dante worked his jaw. Shaking his head, he turned and approached the front door.

"Sweet of him to announce himself in his own home." She tossed out the platitude and looked for a reflective surface to fix her hair. After traipsing across town and standing on the edge of the bay, she looked ready to scrub floors, not dance across them.

"Gisella, this visitor is for you," Dante said.

Peering around his frame, she found her father standing in the foyer with his arms crossed over his chest. An apparent sleepless night left him haggard, and dark bags puffed the skin near his eyes. The silver streaks threading his black hair looked denser, and he wore the same wrinkled dress shirt he'd worn the prior evening. "Rough night?"

"I couldn't find you," Gregorio said. "We looked all over the house. Tia finally admitted she'd seen you slip into the garden. When I found the back gate unlocked, I knew you'd run, but I never thought you'd run to him."

Dante grunted.

Gregorio stepped into the penthouse. "Come home, Gisella. He's a dalliance. You belong with your family."

She laughed. "You offered him fifteen million dollars to take a daughter off your hands. Who sells their daughter's hand in marriage?"

"He was supposed to pick Ursula."

Throwing up her hands, she walked to the wide, glass windows and put her palm against the glass. She should have felt warmth, but engineered panes reflected the sun's heat. The mansion's energy efficiency should impress her, but so much of her life remained rooted in the Dark Ages. "Well, he picked me — or I picked him. We're getting married, *Papà*. Write the man a check. As soon as he cashes it, he'll wire the money to Jandro."

"That spic!"

Turning her back to the sun, she walked up to her father and slapped him.

He caught her hand and turned her wrist.

Dante surged forward.

She shook her head. "He won't hurt me." She dropped her voice. "I remind him too much of my mother."

Gregorio dropped her hand and pulled a handkerchief from his jacket pocket. Patting his face, he shook his head. "She was insolent, headstrong and stubborn." Pocketing the handkerchief, he shook his head. "She was also beautiful."

"And she drowned," Gisella said.

Narrowing his gaze, Gregorio exhaled. "I've kept you safe all these years. You pick this man?"

Turning, she looked at Dante. Despite the penthouse's size, he filled the room, and she recognized the depth hidden beyond his casual, arrogant irrelevance. She would find time to strip off his socks and leather loafers, lead him onto sun-warmed sand and teach him to let go of his worries. "I do."

"Fine," Gregorio said. "Plan the wedding. Order a dress. Book the venue."

"Today." She whispered her commitment.

Dante raised his eyebrows.

Gregorio coughed. "Be reasonable, Gigi."

Turning, she met her father's gaze. Dante's light brown eyes bordered on hazel, but her father's mercurial, quicksilver gaze revealed his profession. He could walk out of the penthouse, lift his phone and order a hit on Dante. In her father's realm, Dante's corporate resources and holstered gun offered him little protection. She would claim him, then she would figure out what to do next. "I am being reasonable. Four o'clock, *Papà*. Change your shirt, and I'll see you at the courthouse."

"No daughter of mine is getting married at the courthouse. You will be married in a church!"

She winked. "Too late for a white dress."

"Gigi!"

His cheeks looked red enough to pop veins.

Dante settled his hand on her lower back.

His comforting presence reminded her to breathe, but her father had to acquiesce to her wishes. She needed nothing from him — a smile tipped up her lips — except fifteen million dollars. "Maybe the judge will let us livestream it."

"Gisella Santa Maria Vitella!"

"*Papà*." She smacked her lips. "Or should I start calling you Gregorio?"

He stepped forward.

Dante dropped his hand from her back and matched her father's advance.

Shaking her head and turning her back on the pair, she walked into the living room. Miami was beautiful and intriguing, but its flawless sandy beaches, bustling art deco streets and vibrant Latin district rarely registered in her dreams.

For hours, she'd pounded the beach for long, sweat-soaked runs, laced her ballet shoes as tight as she could stand and looked for connections in the city, but she dreamed of Italy, not overbearing Italian men. How much of her father's shade had seeped into her life?

She dropped into an armchair, closed her eyes and leaned back her head. "Take it or leave it, *Papà*. Dante and I are getting married tonight. It's a new world, and you don't belong here. Take Lisette back to Italy. See how long she lasts with *la famiglia*."

Gregorio peered around Dante's shoulder. "This isn't about Lisette!"

Cracking an eye, she stared. "No, it's not, but she's a foolish choice for a companion. Do you want a family or an employee? Hire a hooker. At least I won't have to be nice to her."

A dark shadow passed beyond the front door.

Looking past Dante and her father, she saw a man with shoulder length dark hair, weathered skin and a cold stare. She recognized power, and the crowd of men standing at bay behind the man radiated it. A single woman in a red dress, her curves as fierce as her interest in the apartment, stood at Alessio's side.

Gisella stood. "You must be Alessio."

"Correct." He offered the woman his arm, stepped into the penthouse and looked at Dante. "And she is?"

"My future wife," Dante said.

The title sent a rush of pleasure racing along Gisella's skin.

Alessio rubbed his chin. "Apparently we're just in time." He led the woman beside him to a chair, whispered in her ear and kissed her cheek.

Gisella would give her last dollar to know what he'd said. Instead, she faked a yawn to cover her uncertainty. Alessio didn't need permission to enter his house, but he waited outside until Dante granted it. "The ceremony's at four." She gestured to the living room. "Make yourself at home."

Alessio straightened and cracked a smile.

"Six o'clock on the yacht." Gregorio cleared his throat. "Everyone is invited."

Dante looked over her shoulder and raised an eyebrow.

She hated the five-million-dollar behemoth sitting at the marina. It's black hull and white topside made her skin crawl. Built by a British yard in 2008, the model had eight generous cabins with connected en-suite facilities, but her father used the VIP wing like a floating conference room. The vessel would have been her last choice of venue for a wedding ceremony, but she would marry Dante before the sun set. As much as her father deserved her ire for protecting Antonio, she wanted him to witness and accept the moment in her life when she chose her future. "Fine. Six o'clock."

Alessio walked toward the bar, pulled out a bottle of champagne and popped the cork. "You must be the proud papa."

Nobody in the room could miss the feral glint in his gaze or the way Gregorio suddenly found himself outnumbered and alone. Shaking his head and mumbling Italian obscenities, he parted the clustered associates and called the elevator.

Alessio's men examined him like a pinned bug.

A man with a reddish-brown beard and curious blue eyes rocked back on his heels and waited with his hands in his pockets. A second man, his face bearing several raised scars, wore his hair and his beard the same length. She couldn't quite tell, but the man might be wearing a utility kilt.

The shortest of the associates tapped his phone. A pair of intense-looking blond twins made eye contact with each other and shrugged. She hoped they weren't about to take things into their own hands and engage her father.

The elevator door opened, and Gregorio stepped inside.

As the stainless-steel doors closed, she released her breath.

The associates turned en masse toward the penthouse, bumped shoulders trying to enter first, and good-naturedly pushed each other out of the way.

The shortest one slipped through the scrum.

Bending down, she pulled out another champagne bottle and handed it to Alessio. "Where do you keep your extra glasses? I think we're going to need them."

Chapter Sixteen

Accepting a glass of champagne, Dante raised it to his lips and let the sweet, dry liquid subdue his sarcasm.

His associates leveled curious looks and waited for a signal.

He withheld it.

Left undirected, the over-educated bevy of jocks lounged on the furniture or rifled through the cabinets.

He focused on Gisella's vibe. Her back straight, she stood at his side like a department store mannequin. He rested his hand along her lower back. "You don't like the water."

She sipped her champagne. "Nobody gets wet on a yacht."

The vessel had appeared in his research, but he knew little about it. Gregorio maintained *The Grace* at a deep-water super-yacht marina. The marina enabled yachters to transition directly from their vessels to Miami's sandy shores. Well, the sissy boaters had to make use of an island causeway, but if they wanted direct access, they'd have to swim. He removed his hand and set down his glass.

She followed.

Placing a hand over hers, he stroked his thumb along her smooth skin and pulled her to face him. "Are you sure?"

She looked up. "Yes."

Jerking his head over his shoulder, he indicated the master suite. "Go freshen up. Call Linda. See if she can find something you want to wear."

"Do you care what I'm wearing?" she asked.

He smiled. "Absolutely not."

"Interesting. Aren't you going to make introductions?"

Raising his head, he scanned the room. "She's mine."

Everyone from Charon to Driver nodded.

"Asshole," Gisella said.

He shrugged.

Pulling free her hand, she waved, walked into the main bedroom and slammed the door.

His gut told him to go after her, but he couldn't claim that right. After everything she'd gone through and the upheaval in her life, she deserved time to examine the pieces and weigh the decision she was about to make. If she changed her mind, she would break his heart, but he owed her the escape route.

Nina pressed a kiss to Alessio's lips, pulled back and held his gaze. "Behave."

He smiled. "Only for you."

She laughed, made her excuses and headed toward a second bedroom to shower after the long flight.

Alessio sank into a chair and kicked up his feet on the center table. Rubbing a champagne glass's exterior, he cocked his head. ""I sent you down here to buy a company. The daughter's a nice catch, but she wasn't part of the deal."

"Side deal," Dante said. "I'm staying to run CIH."

Alessio squeezed the champagne glass until it shattered. Shaking off the wetness, he pulled a handkerchief from his pocket at dabbed at the blood. "I told you to leave me out of the nitty-gritty details. I didn't tell you to go rogue."

Charon coughed.

Slipping Alessio's bearded number two man a wry look, Dante shrugged. "What's wrong, Pops? You getting old and nervous?"

Alessio pocketed the handkerchief, leaned back and closed his eyes. "This is why I never had children."

* * * *

An hour before sunset, Dante and Gisella led a caravan of black SUVs toward the deep-water marina on Watson Island. Alessio had commandeered his favorite sports car, but Miami's traffic snarled the vehicle's horsepower. Dante tried not to smile. "You're sure?"

Closing a vanity mirror, Gisella rubbed her lips together and blotted her lipstick. She wore the same borrowed button-up. "You have to take me for rich or for poor, for perfume or for BO." She snapped closed the mirror, and her lips look flawless. "If you ask me again, I'll assume you're getting cold feet."

"Noted," he said. She couldn't be further from the truth.

At the marina, he parked and waited for her to lead.

Waltzing into the luxurious marina lounge, she paused at the receptionist desk. "Is anyone on *The Grace*?"

The uniformed man lifted a radio and exchanged static with the marina crew. He looked up. "Just your family and the crew."

Gisella wrinkled her nose. "I hoped we'd be first."

The man looked past her and paled.

Dante suppressed a smirk. He got it.

Jerking her thumb over her shoulder, she indicated Alessio's associates and Nina, Alessio's girlfriend. "This lot's with me."

At some point, the two women had made friends, because they kept exchanging conspiratorial smiles. He had yet to say two words to the woman Alessio had claimed, but the thought of Nina getting a step ahead of him made him smile. He would catch up.

"All of them?" the receptionist asked.

She leaned forward, rubbed her lips, and worked her lipstick.

Her breasts tested the white linen shirt, and if the receptionist so much as glanced at them, Dante would slam him against the wall.

"All of them," she said.

The receptionist tapped a tablet. "Their names?"

"Bob." She turned and counted the men. "One through seven. This is Dante Johnson. The long-haired pirate is Alessio Chen."

Dante crossed his arms across his chest.

The receptionist nodded like a bobble head. "Have a nice cruise."

Taking her elbow, Dante leaned close. "Do you want to know their names?"

Smiling sweetly, she scratched her mouth's edge. "Eventually. Nina filled me in, but I forgot the specifics." Walking toward the main doors, she waved at familiar staff and led the parade of men toward her father's yacht.

Dante exhaled. With his friends at his back, he couldn't doubt his security, but the trip would hardly be a pleasure cruise. Instead of arguing, he followed.

The vessel loomed over the gangway and flew a yellow, green and blue flag. At full speed on the water, the sleek lines would disappear into the horizon, but up close, *The Grace* commanded respect.

"Guns and cell phones," the porter said.

He blinked. "Excuse me?"

The man held up a black canvas bag. "Guns and phones stay on the dock. Owner's orders."

Dante turned to Alessio, who never carried a gun, but who wouldn't relish relinquishing his satellite connection. "You don't have to come. Lend me Charon and Driver, and send the rest back to the penthouse."

Dropping his phone in the bag, Alessio shook his head. "They'd kill me. Who wants to miss this spectacle?" He offered Nina his arm, walked onto the gangway and boarded the yacht.

One by one, Alessio's men dropped their guns and phones into the bag, slapped his back and followed Alessio's lead. The chatter of metal and high-price silicone would entice criminals to target the bag, but Dante added his gear. "Lucky number eight." If Nina wanted to be number eight, he would drop down to nine. So many things in his life had changed in the last few days that he counted himself lucky he remembered his name. The exaggeration amused him, and he gestured for Gisella to precede him.

She smiled and gripped the lines.

"You too, Miss Vitella. Your father's orders," the porter said.

One hand on the rope, she turned with a dancer's control and extended her phone. "Take it."

The porter swallowed, reached for the phone and grabbed it like he'd dodged a snakebite.

Dante suppressed a grin. Gisella had strength and endurance, but she'd learned a few things growing up in her father's house. If she wanted the porter gone, she'd mention it to her father, and the lackey would be out of a job. Watching her terrify the porter amused him, but he wanted the woman behind the act who never pulled the trigger.

She fretted over her independence, but he understood relinquishing power left a void. Leaning close, he dropped his voice. "He's following orders."

She stiffened.

"We don't have to board the boat."

Turning, she raised her chin. "I agreed to this marriage and this time and place. Are you getting cold feet, Daniel Johnson?"

He swatted her ass. "Stop stalling."

She strode up the gangway like a queen, dropped her shoes in a waiting basket, and entered the main cabin.

Gregorio obviously subscribed to the barefoot rule. High heels and black soles left dents and scuffs in teak decking. Following her lead, he tried to remember the last time he'd boarded a yacht.

Alessio's social circles pulled him in for various fundraisers and business meetings, but onboard, Dante felt like a guest and spent most of the time observing the crew. Being nice to the crewmembers had two perks. He had a vague sense of how to run the boat, and he received more attention than the drunken buffoons boasting about their hobbies. Then again, Gisella thought he still needed a hobby.

On this vessel, four freestanding sofas surrounded a rimmed center table in the main salon. In the corner, a granite top bar reflected bottles behind rails. On the opposite side of the salon, a touchscreen controlled a full entertainment center and a fifty-inch flat screen. Gisella moved through the space like a graceful queen, and he grinned at the thought of her by his side.

The ADC Crew settled themselves on the sofas like a pack of dogs.

He claimed those animals, too.

Gisella nodded toward a stewardess. "How's your daughter?"

"Studying to be a veterinarian at Ross University on the island of St. Kitts." The woman pulled a phone from her back pocket.

"Oh, I love St. Kitts, and she looks like she's having a great time."

"Of course," Dante said.

Both women stared.

He shrugged.

The stewardess approached the crew and took their drink orders.

Gisella walked toward him. "What's wrong with St. Kitts?"

"I've never been there," he said.

She smiled. "We deserve a honeymoon."

"For a woman who doesn't like the water, you're fond of beaches." He wrapped an arm around her waist and drew her close.

"Take me skiing." She looked up. "Make me hot cocoa."

He laughed, pressed a kiss against her lips and spun her into the catcalls and whistles filling the cabin. "As you wish." Walking away from the pack, he approached the forward dining area and considered how to celebrate the wedding on their terms. As far as she knew, hot cocoa was in the budget, but he couldn't claim dimes and pennies without labeling himself a liar.

Alessio pulled out a chair in the dining area.

Seating for twenty took up a lot of room, but stainless-steel doors led to a large aft cockpit with ample space for al fresco entertaining and dining. Dante would give his left nut to be outside, but he carved out a moment with his mentor.

"You're taking on a lot," Alessio said.

"She's worth it." He thought about his first impressions. Her ridiculous speech about trash belied a sensitivity she'd suppressed for so long that it became her nature. Up against his stubborn brute force and her family's idiocy, she'd cracked, but he would do everything in his power to help her pick up the pieces and shape her life into the adventure she wanted. "I wanted her the moment I saw her."

"Wanting something and chaining your life to it for decades are two entirely different things," Alessio said.

"Marriage doesn't have to be a life sentence." He'd considered divorcing her and leaving her ass in Miami, but now that he knew her better, he knew she'd track him down and say her piece wherever she found him. He smiled and welcomed her spirited presence in any corner of the world. "Maybe it's time you caved."

Hands in his pockets, Alessio rocked back on his heels with a fighter's grace and snorted. "Unlikely. I prefer thinking of my relationship with Nina as a mutually beneficial agreement."

"Is that so?"

Alessio grinned. "Today's the first day I've felt like punching someone."

Opening the stainless-steel doors with both hands, Gregorio stepped into the cabin and surveyed his newest guests. "I see you brought everyone."

"Well, there's he is." Alessio pulled a hand from his pocket and made a fist, but he dropped the hand and shifted with a fighter's lethal grace.

Dante stepped up to his future father-in-law. "Of course the men came. They're like family."

"Family can disappoint you," Gregorio said.

"Hmm." He traded glances with Alessio. *How many times had Gregorio disappointed the people in his life? How many times had Gregorio draped familial guilt across Gisella's shoulders like a heavy mantle?*

"Now can I beat him?" Alessio asked.

"Hey, Babe," Nina called out, "can you help me with something?"

The woman, who he'd learned commanded six figures as a mediation lawyer, had beaten him to the punch. As Alessio strode to her side, Dante faced Gregorio and cracked his knuckles. For the first time in a while, he appreciated how a show of force could lead to a win.

Ursula and Antonio followed their father into the dining room with heavy footsteps and chattering Italian.

Dante acknowledged the pair with a nod. So far, he liked the odds.

Fr. Pietro stepped inside and rubbed his eyes.

In a fight, the man hardly counted.

Chattering in Italian, four hotheads wearing black suits entered the cabin.

He'd wager his net worth someone in the squad retained a weapon or kept the key to the onboard gun safe. Looking toward Alessio, he raised his eyebrows.

Alessio cracked his knuckles. "Beautiful day for a cruise."

Lisette stumbled from the hallway. "I'm thinking navy and white. Brass accents!" She hiccupped. "Or patriotic!"

"Inspired." Gisella covered a yawn.

One of the associates chuckled. He'd give Driver the credit.

After a safety briefing from the captain on life jackets and life rafts, the captain went below in less than twenty minutes.

Breezing through the crowd carrying a glass of champagne, Gisella took her sister's arm and pulled her toward the prow. "*Spostati!*"

The men split like racked bowling pins.

Dante grinned.

"Hell of a woman," Alessio said.

"I know it." Dante saluted him and followed her.

The wheelhouse had two helm chairs facing a comprehensive electronic navigation system and a sofa for interested observers. She passed right by it and climbed up to the flybridge. A teak dining table, an upholstered seating area and a bar provided plenty of room for sunbathing, al fresco entertaining and dining.

Ursula stood at the railing taking selfies. For a woman who wore black from head to toe, she looked remarkably confident mimicking *Titanic*.

Gisella dropped into a chair and ran her hand through her hair. "How're you holding up?"

"That's my line," he said.

Smiling, she sipped her champagne. "We'll motor out to the open water, let Fr. Pietro do his thing, pop the champagne and toast our future."

"That easy?" Some people privately spent massive amounts of money. *The Grace* probably boasted a professional-grade galley, a helicopter landing pad and below deck quarters for twenty staff members. If Gregorio wanted sushi in Monaco, the captain could make it happen.

"Why should this be hard?" she asked.

"Your daddy's a mafia boss who changed his mind about liking me. You brother's a pretentious asshole."

She waved her hand in the cooling late-afternoon air.

"Your sister's about to audition for *The Addams Family* reboot."

"I heard that!" Ursula puckered her lips and took another selfie.

"They're not perfect, but they're everything I had until I met you. Now, *we're just a boy and a girl in a little canoe...*" Gisella hummed the rest of the tune and smiled. "I loved summer camp. I pretended I lived in a little suburban house, wore gingham bikinis and stockpiled teen magazines like all the other girls."

"What else do you love?" he asked.

She tilted her head. "You're my escape."

A smile tugged at her glossy lips, and the wind blew her sleek hair across her face. He feared her answer as much as he craved it. "And when you're free?"

She shrugged and brushed the hair out of her face. "I'll dance. I'll keep working toward my goals—

Principal Dancer, a few rowdy kids and room to stretch my legs." Turning, she extended her limbs along the low white couch. I'll be a good wife."

Sitting next to her, he tucked her under his arm, pressed a kiss against her hair and turned his face to the wind. At one point in his life, he thought he'd be the kind of man drumming up crew work at Antibes on the Côte d'Azur, but he'd managed to shape his life into a success. "I believe you."

As Miami's lights fought the sun setting in the west, *The Grace* slowed in open water. Part of him worried the captain would take them into international waters, sound the horn and give Gregorio's men free rein to wreak havoc on Alessio's associates. To avoid registering in any country and avoid paying any taxes, many yachts floated around the world and spent limited time in port, but international waters held lawless dangers, too.

Gregorio walked out of the cabin. "We're celebrating a wedding!"

Gisella yawned.

"Bored already?" he asked.

She pressed a kiss against his cheek. "When I'm on stage, I expect theatrics."

The crew unlocked the couches and slid them out of the way. The stewardess unfurled a long, white satin cloth, scattered rose petals over it, and lit two candles in tall stands.

Ursula rocked a candleholder. "Papa, where did you get all this shit?"

Lisette raised her hand. "I had it in storage!"

Gisella and Ursula looked at each other and laughed.

Gregorio pointed toward a crew member. "You, get a camera and climb as high as you can to take pictures."

"Papa, that's the second engineer. He does engine maintenance," Gisella said.

"He should be able to work a camera!"

The engineer nodded and scrambled toward the highest point.

Taking his place in front of Fr. Pietro, Dante waited for Gisella and her family to iron out the ceremony logistics. He'd be happy enough with a kiss and a legal signature. Ten minutes later, Alessio and his crew stood on one side of the aisle while Gregorio and his henchmen manned the other side.

Gisella took a bouquet from the stewardess.

He released his breath and wondered how a punk kid from the West Coast ended up such a lucky man. If search terms and self-preservation saved his ass from a life of crime, he would spend the next decades making sure he deserved his beautiful, lithe, feisty reward.

A wedding march piped through the vessel's entertainment system.

If Fr. Pietro ordered him to love, honor and obey, he would have to clarify whose orders took precedence. Every step Gisella took brought her closer to him. In another moment, she would be close enough to grab, and any asshole who interfered with his plans would answer to the knife he kept strapped against his calf.

The engineer raised the camera.

A gust of wind buffeted the vessel.

Arms flailing, the engineer fell from the top of the yacht.

Time slowed, and Dante watched the man fall. Each time the crewmember bounced and made contact with a piece of equipment raised the probability of severe brain injuries.

When the engineer hit the siderail and landed in the water, Lisette screamed.

Several crewmembers jumped in.

Dante tightened his grip on Gisella's hand. "Let the captain handle the rescue."

She tugged against his hold.

Most likely, the man had fractured his skull, and Dante didn't want her to see the aftermath. "Please."

Closing her eyes, she counted aloud in Italian.

The bosun lowered a rib containing two crewmembers. The small boat used to ferry passengers to and from the yacht launched quickly, but the engineer slipped beneath the surface. The nearest crewmember dove toward the disappearing figure, and every passenger on *The Grace* held his or her breath.

Gisella opened her eyes.

The crewmember surfaced, sputtered and waved toward the rib. "I've got him!"

Releasing her breath, she pressed her face against his shoulder.

He rubbed her back. "We'll get him ashore."

"Dump him," Antonio said.

Dante dropped his hand and turned. "The fuck?"

"Throw some flowers over the side and give his belongings to the port police." Antonio picked at his nails. "He's replaceable."

If the asshole couldn't stomach his proposal, he shouldn't have made it, but his words hovered over the deck like a foul miasma. Guests shifted, and the crewmembers averted their gazes.

The compulsion to act coiled in his muscles, but Gisella remained his only concern. Monitoring the onboard tension and making eye contact with Alessio, he peered over the railing to ascertain whether Antonio's shit suggestion applied.

A crewmember performed CPR on the engineer, but the man lay unresponsive in the rib.

Shaking his head, Dante straightened. *The Grace* needed to return to shore as soon as possible. Turning his back to the railing, he ignored Antonio's greasy suggestion and looked toward the captain for leadership.

Hands locked behind his back, the captain waited.

Gregorio walked toward the railing. "Discretion has its merits."

Gisella raced to her father's side. "*Papà*! He might live!"

He shook his head and turned to her. "You saw him fall, Gigi. What kind of life will he have? Months in a hospital coma and constant care? What kind of life is that?"

She gripped his arm. "Let his family decide."

Resisting her entreaty, he sighed. "His family has no resources."

"Would you let them dump me overboard?"

Gregorio recoiled. "I would never let you fall into this position. My daughter would never crew a yacht." He lowered his voice. "You are two different types of people."

The crewmembers shifted.

Charon and Driver exchanged looks.

Dante held up his hand. The hairs on the back of his neck stood at attention, and violence simmered on the deck, but nobody threatened Gisella. He couldn't save the engineer, but he could keep the testosterone-fueled crowd from erupting into a pissed off melee. He shifted closer to Gisella and hoped his associates would stand down unless absolutely necessary.

Driver pumped his fist into his palm.

"C'mon! You don't need this shit." Antonio slashed his hand across his throat. "Dump him!"

Gisella pivoted. "That's murder!"

"It's your fucking fault we're on this boat." He jabbed his finger toward her. "Why can't you do what you're told?"

Advancing toward him, she stopped, squeezed her hands into fists and screamed. "Why can't you be a decent human being?"

Antonio raised his hand and swung.

Surging forward, Dante caught his arm and held it inches from Gisella's face. Since the moment he'd met her on the beach, he'd inched closer toward her passion and loyalty. Watching her idiot cousin threaten her life over dinner had set off his protective instincts, but he'd worked hard to tamp down the impulses and let discretion rule his impulses. Antonio's brunt aggression released the hold on his emotions. If Antonio's hand moved an inch closer to Gisella's face, Dante would beat the shit out of him, and the man would beg for a gun. "You don't touch what's mine."

"She's not yours. She's…"

Raising her knee, Gisella slammed it into Antonio's groin. "I don't belong to any man!"

Antonio doubled over and moaned.

"If I want your advice, brother, I'll ask for it." Tucking her hair behind her ear, she scanned the deck and made eye contact with every passenger. "If the engineer isn't on deck in the next few minutes, I'm going in the water, and you won't dump my belongings overboard with a handful of flowers!"

The four hotheads wearing black suits exchanged glances and turned toward Gregorio.

He shook his head. "Daughters. Your mother was *una donna dal cuore tenero*. Bring him up!"

The captain gave the order.

Dante exhaled. For a decade, he'd worked to bury his hot-headed roots and align his future with Alessio's dispassionate, refined control. Gisella upended his quest, and choosing a life with her summoned ghosts he'd long buried.

The more time he spent in her world, the more he wanted to protect and cherish her, but navigating two hierarchies upended his control. He understood Alessio. The asshole would drag him into the boxing ring and settle an indiscretion in twenty minutes, but Dante played by the rules.

Gregorio's patriarchy had brought him to Gisella, and Jandro's injuries ensnared her, but he had to convince her to stay with him. Marriage seemed like the easiest solution, but putting a ring on her finger was turning into a fucking Olympic sport. Afraid she would make good on her threat, he pulled her to his side. "Stay close where I can protect you."

"With what? Your fists?" Her teeth chattered.

He cupped her elbow and looked for a way to extract her from the situation before her worldview collapsed at her feet. "Don't test me."

Ursula cleared her throat and checked the barrel of a sleek, black pistol. "Are we done here?"

Gisella turned on her sister. "Since when do you carry a gun?"

"Since when do I not?" Ursula smiled and turned her head. "*Papà?*"

"Put away your toy, *Ursuluccia*. The engineer's coming aboard. We'll go back to shore and play nice with the authorities. Accidents happen."

"Accidents," Gisella said.

"Fucking waste of fuel." Antonio spat on the deck.

Dante wondered whether the asshole had ever lifted a mop in his life.

Gregorio exhaled. "Clean it up, Antonio. Respect your assets."

Heads raised, the assembled guests waited with bated breath.

Dante had one hundred bucks on an Italian-fueled temper tantrum.

"Bring me a fucking rag!" Antonio yelled.

A crewmember handed him a worn, dingy ship's rag.

Snatching the rag, Antonio glared at Gisella and Ursula. "Stay in your lane, sisters."

Ursula lifted a finger and mimed shooting him. "Noted."

The captain fired up the twin eighteen hundred horsepower engines.

Dante led Gisella back to the salon. *The Grace* had a cruising speed of twenty-one knots, but stabilizers ensured the vessel could top out near thirty. He beckoned the stewardess. "How much food's onboard?"

"Enough for a wedding feast," she said.

"Set out the food and bring me a small plate. Keep the wine and champagne flowing but curtail the hard liquor."

The stewardess nodded.

He turned to his intended bride. Gisella sat on a sofa and stared out to sea with a blankness that worried him. She was a haughty mafia princess in her father's world, a lithe dancer on the stage and a passionate lover in his arms. Her identity remained in her hands, but he wondered who would emerge. "Are you okay?"

"He followed orders," she said.

Lowering his frame beside her, he nodded.

"He shouldn't have gone up there without a harness. A foothold. Something."

Stroking her silky hair, he let her talk.

"*Papà* was right. I'd never be in his position." She turned her head and frowned. "What made me think I could survive in this world? I've been cosseted my entire life. Doors opened. People averted their gazes. I'm just a woman who likes to dance."

He cupped her cheek. "And shop."

Wetting her lips, she shook her head. "Dante, that man died trying to take my photograph."

"He fell at work." Raising his other hand, he steadied her. "His fate and your reaction to his fate are two different things. You spoke up. We're headed back to the marina. He'll receive medical care, and Fr. Pietro will pray for a miracle."

"It won't be enough," she said.

Lowering his head, he kissed her forehead. "No, I don't think he'll survive."

"And that's not my fault?"

He sighed. Her sweet, tempting warmth lured him toward platitudes, but his soft words would never erase her memories. "No, it's not your fault. The engineer needed the courage and empowerment to stand up for himself, but any order could have put him in that position. Maybe luck kept him safe for a few shifts, but unless he exercised good judgment, he was eventually going to fall."

"Luck shouldn't determine fate." She buried her face against his shoulder. "How many people lost their lives to enrich my family? Ursula has the right idea. I should be on my knees, praying for forgiveness."

"You spoke up." He stroked her back. "You kneed your brother in the groin. It's a start."

She nodded against his shoulder, raised her gaze, and wiped her eyes. "I should have punched him."

"Do you know how to throw a punch?" he asked.

She shook her head.

Shaping her fingers into a tight fist, he cupped them and raised them to his lips. "I'll teach you. Anytime you want to stand up to your family, I'll be right beside you. You're a good person, Gisella." Pressing a kiss against her fingers, he pulled back and smiled. "Do one thing for me?"

She nodded.

He took the plate from the stewardess. "Eat every bite on this plate. Let me watch over you until we're back at the marina. Let Alessio and his crew manage your family."

Biting into a strawberry, she looked up.

Every associate had claimed a Vitella family member. Using man-to-man defense, they'd isolated the cousins, prima donnas and surly men from causing mischief. Alessio kept Gregorio engaged near the aft cockpit, Charon stared down Antonio, and Stefano flattered Lisette into drinking so much champagne that she snored on the couch. Ursula and Fr. Pietro played cards with the twins, Anders and Fell.

Somewhere above deck, the engineer waited for his fate.

Dante credited the human body with amazing feats, but rash acts of madness ended lives. Having feared for his safety, he regretted killing his father but knew his priorities. He pulled Gisella closer to his side. Acts of madness, moments of lust and pliant levity could begin lives, too.

Chapter Seventeen

After sunset, the ambulance carrying the engineer roared toward the nearest hospital, and Gisella stayed to address the fallout.

Hands braced on her hips, she stood in the luxurious marina lounge and spoke to the officer recording the accident's details. The Florida Fish and Wildlife Conservation Commission handled crash investigations in state waterways, but the officer looked like he would be comfortable on a football field or a patrol boat. Shifting her weight, she longed for a hot bath and sleep's oblivion.

"The engineer's name is Aiden Andrews. His family lives in Montreal." She handed over the slip of paper containing his family's contact information. She'd requested the information from the stewardess and promised to take care of Aiden. "I already called them and told them about the accident."

The officer looked up. "Good on you. And you're sure it was an accident?"

"Aiden worked his way up from a deckhand on smaller boats. He had his sea legs." She considered her next words. Gregorio registered his yacht in Saint Vincent and the Grenadines, but the island nation had little sway over him or his vessel. No matter what she said, the Florida commission officer would record the accident, but she doubted an investigation would follow. "Nobody was near him."

"But he fell."

She swallowed. "I won't ever forget the sight."

The officer nodded and ended his recording. "Boating in Florida can be deadly. Over the past year, we've seen a surge in crashes and fatalities. Everyone calls this state the Sunshine State, but it leads the nation in vessel crashes."

"It also leads the nation in coastline."

He scratched his head. "I believe that honor belongs to Alaska."

"Right," she said. Sometimes her isolation embarrassed her. She could speak about fifteenth century Italian Renaissance courts, but she stumbled over her country's geography. "The Vitella family will cover his medical bills."

Antonio breezed past. "You're running out of pin money, sister."

She ignored his rebuke in Italian and kept her gaze focused on the officer. Gregorio couldn't leave the marina fast enough, but Antonio stayed to pass out hundred-dollar bills. She doubted his tips would keep the story from the media. The same Miami citizens who gawked at his red sports car anticipated his downfall splashed across the gossip sites. If he were a gladiator, they would have lusted for his blood.

"What did he say?" the officer asked.

"He hopes Aiden makes a full recovery." She plastered on her dutiful smile. "We all do."

Dante walked up and cupped her elbow.

His steady presence gave her courage to preside over the accident. Even though her father and Antonio distanced themselves from the report, she would make sure Aiden had the care he required.

"Do you have everything you need?" Dante asked.

She looked at him. "Thanks."

While she dealt with her family, the officer and Aiden's prognosis, he organized removing remnants of the wedding ceremony and ferried the catered food to waiting vehicles. His competence soothed her, but it couldn't erase reality.

She wondered how long Aiden's fall would haunt her nightmares. She saw his body ricochet off the railings, but competency and compassion couldn't alleviate his fate. She let her shoulders slump.

If Aiden survived the night, his family could say goodbye. She barely knew him, but stepping into the world brought the difference between life and death into sharp focus.

If Antonio's antics had escalated outside the theater, Jandro could have lost more than his season. How many times would she skate by without incurring personal consequences? Leaning against Dante, she feared who could be next. "We're taking care of it."

"Your father and cousins went home," he said. "Antonio was the last one."

She nodded.

"You should do the same," the officer said.

She pondered the meaning of the idea. Dante occupied a friend's penthouse, but when she aligned her fate with the man, she chose to shape his future. For the time being, the penthouse would be their home. If Alessio booted them, she'd google hotels and check into whatever bleached haven she and Dante could afford.

Pulling her away from the officer, Dante dropped his head. "This isn't how I expected the night to end."

"Me neither." Shaking her head, she pulled free her arm and linked hands. "I'm sorry I upended your life."

He tightened his grip on her fingers. "You began it."

* * * *

Following Dante into the penthouse, Gisella stopped and stared.

The exterior doors stood wide open, and a soft evening breeze rolled through the penthouse's open living room. Jazz piped through hidden speakers, and trays of food sat uneaten on the kitchen island. Alessio's crew occupied the living room and played cards like rowdy fraternity brothers. Nina sipped a glass of wine and chatted with a steward. Ursula, Lisette and Martin occupied the outdoor patio furniture and clutched cocktails. If they were last bastions of the life she knew, she might be screwed.

She cleared her throat.

Every person in sight made eye contact, but none moved.

"What are they doing here?" she asked.

"Checking on you," Dante said.

She swallowed.

"But Aiden…"

He rubbed her knuckles. "Nobody blames you."

Exhaling, she turned her face to the sky. A lone seabird hovered past the patio before turning and flying away. If the wildlife had given up hope, maybe she should too, but Dante's allure drew her closer. She moved to his side but avoided collapsing into his arms.

Ursula listened to Martin, and her laughter mixed with the soft sea air.

If her wide black pants didn't look so familiar, Gisella would have double-checked she had entered the right penthouse. She pulled free from Dante and strode onto the patio. "What are you doing here?"

"Drinking." Ursula raised her glass. "Planning your wedding."

"Cursing it, more likely."

Martin frowned, and the penthouse conversation lagged.

In the silence, Gisella shifted.

Ursula set down her glass, stood and gripped Gisella's arms. Her wide, black-rimmed eyes held steady. "Pietro said he would officiate your wedding, and nothing has changed. Dante is your freedom. Take it."

Gisella swallowed. Visiting Jandro had helped her reclaim her balance, but she needed a liter of prosecco to face this crew. Then again, Lisette probably couldn't see straight. Teetering on the edge of violence had worn down her reserves, but appearing weak was never an option. She smoothed the borrowed button-up and kissed Ursula's cheek. "Thank you, but why did you bring Lisette?"

"Cover story." Ursula patted her arm. "Also, she donated a rack of white cocktail dresses. One of them will fit. Tomorrow, we'll see you married and out of the reach of *Papà*."

"Fit me?" Gisella turned from her sister's embrace and considered the clothes. They looked so mundane and innocent on the rack. She didn't want fear and terror to launch her marriage to Dante, and a touch of mundane might help. She reached for the rack of sequins, lace and soft white silk. "Thank you."

Ursula released her.

A toilet flushed, and Pietro stepped out of a bathroom. "Gisella!"

"He speaks," Dante said.

One of the associates laughed.

Blinking, she broke free of the clothing's sequined spell and considered Dante's friends. "You arranged for them to be here? What's going on?"

"You need company. You're not" — he loosened his collar — "a solitary creature."

"I'm not a creature at all! You should have asked me."

"Asked you what? If you wanted your family by your side on your big day? These men are my family. Tia and the aunties will meet us in the morning."

His admission stole her thunder, and she considered her response. "Thank you, but Lisette is not family."

"I made calls while you were busy with the office. Juniper and Julietta insisted we include her. Maybe they just wanted her out of the house."

Making fists around her hair, she pulled until it hurt. "How do you have everyone's phone numbers?"

He jacked her against his hips. "I will take care of you."

Suddenly constrained, she dropped her hands and drew a deep breath against his iron grip. His whispered pledge kept her from cracking. "I'm fine."

"And I'm capable of conducting research." He raised a hand and trailed a thumb along her side. "In fact, I am very good at research. The minute Juniper left her phone unlocked, I downloaded every single contact they had. I can probably call your first-grade teachers."

"Cheater."

Beyond the crowd's view, he teased her breast. "Winner."

Someone whistled.

Discretion had its limits. She wanted to lean into his touch, but she straightened and faced Lisette. "You didn't have to bring the dresses. Thank you."

Lisette waved off the comment. "Oh, those are the reject dresses."

If Gisella smiled any harder, her cheeks would crack.

"Go to bed," Driver said. "We'll keep her in line."

She'd learned their names on *The Grace*, but the interplay between the men fascinated her more than their names. Alessio held court, but Charon and the other associates moved around him like orbiting planets. Dante, aloof and untethered, touched base with each man and pulled back like a comet retreating to the edge of the solar system.

His independence fascinated her, but she feared his friends would remind him how much marriage would change his life. Maybe he didn't want it to change.

Dante tugged her toward the bedroom. "Unless you want to stay up?"

"But where will they all sleep?"

"Don't worry," he said. "They can take care of themselves. Ursula, Lisette and Martin will go back to your father's house. My friends can bed down in spare rooms or bunk on the couches."

"But Alessio..."

Shaking his head, Alessio laid down his papers. "I'm fine."

The subtle acknowledgment that everyone in the room knew her business increased her shyness. "Okay."

Dante closed the bedroom door behind her and turned on the faucet for the large, freestanding bathtub. "You need downtime."

"You're drawing me a bath?" She stood in the middle of the bedroom and stared at his large form hunched over the tub. The care and attention almost terrified her. She could work the room of friends and acquaintances, but Dante's efforts left her on unsteady ground.

He straightened. "You don't like baths?"

"Love them." She swallowed. The level of intimacy existing beyond stifled moans and slick pleasure held repercussions. She thought she would have time to ease into it, but steam clouded the mirrors. "Will you join me?" She rubbed her hand over her face. "Wait! You probably want to see your friends."

"I'll join you," he said.

His pledge uncoiled the tension gathering between her shoulders. Unbuttoning the shirt, she stripped off her clothes and stepped into the steaming water before she lost her nerve.

He squeezed shampoo into the tub. The mandarin and vetiver steam smelled like a paler version of him, but she missed the strength and spice she associated with his skin. "Aren't you joining me?"

"In a few minutes."

"Oh." She tried to keep the disappointment from her voice. "Of course."

He kissed her forehead and let himself out of the room.

Alone, she relayed the night and scrubbed her skin until she removed the taint of salty sea air. Replaying Aiden's fall, she convinced herself that sticking up for the engineer and overseeing the official report had been the right things to do, but she wondered if she had done enough.

Short of calling up the local news station and exposing everything she knew about her family, she held them accountable and expended the resources she had to remedy their mistakes, but Antonio's taunt hit home, and her muscles ached with coiled tension and the need to move.

She missed the freedom and artistry of her old life. The further she stepped from her glittering confines, the more she understood the cost of her choices. Carefree, glittering magic enabled her to dance, but responsibility might ground her jumps.

Lost in thought, she almost didn't hear Dante approach the tub.

He sat on the bath rim and dipped his fingers into the water. "You like it hot."

She blinked. "Always."

His gaze darkened. "I should let you get some rest."

"Why? You don't think I can handle more excitement."

He looked at his fingers and rubbed the suds between the pads.

The steam gathered and grew heavy with spice with expectation. His intensity tightened her chest and restricted her breath. Aiden's fall had pained her, but she'd managed the aftermath. She could learn to manage anything. "I can stand the heat. Can you?"

He looked up. "I can."

His voice was deep and sultry, and she wondered if his heated pledge blew the last remaining fuse her brain possessed. Part of her burned so hot for him that she met him in hallways and hidden recesses, but the other part longed to shine a light on her feelings for him and examine their depth. Throughout the showdown on the yacht, she'd felt him at her side, coiled and ready to come to her aid. She trailed her finger along the tub's edge. "Get in."

His gaze focused, and he stripped off his clothes.

His corded muscles and proud erection flamed her desire. She knew his body and the aching pleasure of his touch, but the proof of his interest spiked her confidence. Pulling in her legs, she made space for his bulk and wondered how much water would slosh onto the floor.

Settling into the tub, he closed his eyes against the heat. "Impressive."

About a gallon slipped over the sides and ran along the floor.

She shrugged and watched the ripples travel. "Wait long enough, and the water will cool."

"I have a hard time waiting for anything with you." He reached out and drew a finger across her cheek. "Gisella, I owe you an apology. I wanted to beat the shit out of your brother."

Closing her eyes, she sighed. "He deserves it. If life has a hierarchy, he thinks he's at the top."

"If he keeps shitting on the little people, he'll fall. If it's not me, it'll be someone else."

Drawing a deep breath, she opened her eyes. "I'm counting on it. Should I do more? Say something?"

"Do you have any proof?" he asked.

She shook her head.

"I figured as much." Trailing his fingers along her neck, he traced her collarbone and cupped her breast. "Second thing... You deserve romance, but I keep giving you lust. I don't have any excuses for my selfishness. I want you beside me."

Her nipple tightened, and a chill raced through her body. "I want you, too."

His hand stilled. "That's the first time you've said it."

She managed to look at him and found him studying her.

"Are you sure?"

"Yes."

He wrapped his hands around her waist and lifted her into his lap.

More water slipped over the rim, but she settled against his chest.

"When I touch you, your breath hitches. When you're thinking about me, your skin flushes. Your body wants me." He kissed her shoulder and trailed his fingers between her breasts. "But you're more than a passionate woman."

She fit against him like a second skin, and his arousal pressed into her thigh, but she understood his statement's magnitude. She also understood the fear that was keeping him from meeting her gaze. For so long, he'd obviously felt like an underdog fighting his way to the top, but he'd arrived, and she would help him enjoy his life. "Dante, I choose you." She wiggled her ass and felt his muscles tighten. "Stop stalling."

Pressing a kiss to her heated neck, he brushed his hand along her stomach and cupped her sex. Dipping his fingers through her neat curls, he grazed his thumb against her clit and sent a bolt of pleasure spiraling through her core. "Stalling?"

She gasped and arched against him.

He tightened his free hand around her waist and pinned her. Toying with her, he stroked and circled until she strained against his hold, looking for release.

"Let me take care of you." He grazed her shoulder with his teeth.

She drew a deep breath and exhaled on a sigh. "Yes."

He sank his fingers into her flesh and hooked upward.

Dropping back her head, she groaned. His mouth was warm against her skin, the water lapping at her nipples, and he moved his skilled fingers in and out of her until she embraced the building pressure, arched her back and rocked against him.

The building pressure promised relief.

Then he withdrew.

The absence shocked her, and she cried out. Twisting, she braced her hands on his chest and looked up. "What the hell…?"

Lowering his head, he kissed her like he wanted to memorize her taste. He gripped her hips and his consuming kiss bruised her lips. The fire and frustration in her core shifted, and she drew up her knees, searching for the pleasure they both craved.

Lifting her, he balanced her on the edge of the tub and stood. Water rained down his body.

Gripping the tub's edge, she grinned.

He wiped the steam and the sweat from his face, picked her up and kissed her hard.

If the last kiss had memorized her taste, this one branded her. She wrapped her legs around his waist and hoped he'd carry her to the bathroom vanity, grip her hips and slide into her heat. She would watch every thrust and match his passion.

"Say it again." He rubbed her core along his cock.

"You're cheating."

He grinned. "I like hearing the words."

She pressed her forehead against his, and something changed in the steam-filled air. Something changed in the way he gripped her ass and held her close. She raised her head and made eye contact. "I choose *you*."

"I believe you." Shifting his weight, he settled her in his arms, walked into the bedroom and lowered her to the bed. Dropping to his knees on the floor, he kissed the inner part of her thigh, spread her legs and lapped the water and desire from her skin. "You taste like heaven."

Reaching for him, she wanted to tangle her fingers into his hair.

He grabbed her wrists and held them against her sides. "You picked me." He spoke against her core and lapped at her heat. "I'm not an easy man." Releasing her hand, he sank his fingers into her and sucked her clit.

She bucked her hips for more.

Instead of shattering her world, he raised his head and pulled her forward to claim her mouth.

Tasting herself on his lips, she reached for his cock and gripped his length.

His shoulders bunched beneath her hands. Breaking the kiss, he pulled back, clenched his jaw and closed his eyes.

She stroked him again.

"Gisella, you'll undo me."

Increasing the pace, she grinned. "I have confidence in you." She also had confidence in herself. If she pushed his desire to the edge, he would stop teasing her with sinful kisses and give her the fulfillment she craved. Straddling him, she ground her heat along his muscled thigh.

"Fuck." Unseating her, he flipped her onto the bed, sucked her nipples into tight buds, and dipped his fingers into her heat. Before she could object to another teasing round of pleasure, he covered her body with his weight, pressed a kiss to her neck and drew a shaky breath. "I want to use you, and you deserve more."

His erection pressed against her stomach, and she flexed her hips. Wrapping her legs around his waist, she rubbed against his heat. "Use me."

He raised his head. "Do you want me to fuck you?"

She nodded.

"Tell me." He narrowed his gaze.

He stared at her with his beautiful, long-lashed eyes, and she raised her chin. "I want you to fuck me."

Groaning, he kissed her hard and moved his cock along her heated folds.

The moment she opened her mouth to urge him to continue, he filled her completely, flexed his hips and impaled her over and over again. Dropping her head back, she matched his fierce rhythm and cried out in pleasure.

If she expected slow and gentle, his thrusts shattered her illusions.

He pulled out until he was barely inside her. "Maybe I can't do romance."

She gripped his ass. "Screw romance."

Laughing, he thrust into her hard, but he watched her.

His control mattered. It let her ride the wave of passion carrying them both toward satisfaction. Maintaining eye contact, she lost herself in his gaze until the pressure built in her core and exploded. She cried out his name, closed her eyes and gripped him as he pulsed inside her.

He collapsed to her side, sweat-soaked and breathing hard.

She ran her fingers through his hair and smiled. They both needed a shower.

After a moment, he drew back and pressed a kiss to her shoulder. "I think they heard you."

Her cheeks warmed.

"Hell, even Linda heard you."

She swatted his chest and struggled to raise herself on one arm.

Smiling, he settled his arm over her waist and pinned her to the bed. "Not yet."

She tested his hold.

Sighing, he withdrew his hand and rolled to his back.

"Don't leave," she said.

"Where would I go?" Rolling to his side, he pulled her against his shoulder and stroked her hair.

Wrapped in his warmth, she could fall asleep, but she felt his arousal against her bottom, and she wanted more. She shifted her hips.

"Impatient woman," he said.

She smiled and felt him harden further.

"You need sleep."

She shifted her hips again.

"You're impossible."

Smiling, she looked over her shoulder. In the moonlight, his eyes took on the soft velvet of midnight moss. She could straddle him, wrap her lips around his cock and chase waves of mindless sensation, but in choosing him, she asked for more than a heap of exhausted limbs and labored breaths. "Will you dream of me?"

He tightened his grip and closed his eyes. "I've always dreamed of you."

Settling against his warmth, she doubted she would get a full night's sleep. If marrying him erased her peaceful slumber, she gladly chose her fate.

Chapter Eighteen

The next morning, Dante slipped from the bed.

Gisella propped her head on her elbow and watched him go.

By the time she slipped into the loungewear and robe Linda had procured, he'd pulled a cup of coffee from the on-demand coffee maker and made his way to the patio.

Ursula, Fr. Pietro, Martin and Lisette sat around half-eaten omelets and empty fruit bowls. Ursula's liquid black eyeliner fanned into cat eyes, and if she spiked her coffee, the alcohol had zero effect on her confidence.

Fr. Pietro shaded his eyes. "I should have worn sunscreen."

"Or stayed home," Dante said.

Lisette frowned. The expression never reached her forehead. "Are we having a wedding or not?"

Gisella stepped onto the patio. "We are."

He leaned over and kissed her cheek. "Good morning, beautiful."

"I wish you'd waited for me," she said.

"I've been awake since four."

"Well, in that case" — she settled next to her sister — "thanks for letting me sleep."

He handed her his coffee and let his fingers brush hers. "My pleasure."

The rich timbre of his voice and lingering touch suggested he told the truth. With his unfamiliar weight at her side, she'd drifted in and out of sleep, but her soft snores had little effect on his grip. He'd held her close. When she protested, he told her she had plenty of time in the morning to be fierce and determined.

As the sun rose over Miami, she'd awakened and found him cradling his laptop. She'd reached for him, but she'd glimpsed his laptop's screen and paused. Lost in thought, he rearranged his life like a gamer twisting a puzzle cube. Curling her fingers into a fist, she'd lowered it to the sheets and hoped their new life would be enough to ground him.

Sipping the dark roast on the patio, she tabled her uncertainties and sighed. "The day looks like it'll be beautiful."

Fr. Pietro shaded both eyes. "Do you have an extra pair of sunglasses?"

Staring, she tried to understand why the priest looked so out of place. Realization dawned, and she tilted his head. "You're not wearing your clerical collar."

Fr. Pietro cleared his throat. "For strictly personal reasons, I freely presented my resignation from the church this morning." He scooted his chair closer to Ursula. "I believe the bishop will accept it."

Gisella upended her coffee, grabbed a linen napkin and mopped up the mess. "Jezebel! Impressive!"

Ursula rattled the dregs of ice and coffee occupying her glass. "He made his choice."

Gisella turned toward Dante. "Tell her he made a good choice."

Pulling her into his lap, he settled his arm over her waist. "Did he? You Vitella women are trouble."

She slapped his chest.

Cocking his head, he adjusted her position.

The man could write a treatise on morning wood. Dropping her mouth toward his ear, she leaned close. "You like me."

He turned and nipped her earlobe. "I do."

Straightening, she remembered her audience, and her cheeks warmed.

Lisette looked toward the front door. "You have company."

"I do?" Following the woman's gaze, he found Linda carrying a grocery bag in each hand. Pressing a kiss against Gisella's temple, he stood, lowered her into the chair and strolled toward Linda. "Good morning."

"More pastries" — she lifted the bags — "that are dairy free, gluten free, soy free, refined sugar free or vegan. Take your pick"

"I'd prefer a slab of bacon and a buttered croissant." He took the bags. "But I appreciate how you spoil us."

"Alessio pays me, and I got your bacon, too."

Dante laughed.

Gisella eased into a smile. Doors opened and closed in parts of the penthouse she had yet to explore. Sleepy men padded through the kitchen in search of coffee, typed on their laptops or grabbed towels for post-workout showers. The atmosphere felt as easy as a troupe's morning call.

Depositing the pastry bags on the kitchen counter, Dante led Linda toward the patio crowd. "I have work I need to address, but this is Linda. She'll keep Alessio's crew in line. If you need anything while you're here, Linda can help you."

Pietro elbowed Gisella. "One day you'll be in charge."

She cleared her throat. "I know about as much about being a wife as I knew about scrambling eggs."

"Scrambling eggs is a piece..."

Dante leaned down and kissed her cheek. "Marry me?"

She pulled back and examined him. His face dominated her dreams, and she appreciated the strength of his restraint. So many of her relatives succumbed to vice's easy gains, but he amassed his savings through steady work, and she wanted to be by his side. "When?"

"One o'clock."

She nodded.

Smiling, he turned and left.

So soon? In a few hours, she would be a wife. Performance jitters raced up her spine. Deploying moves that kept her muscles warm and her mind off mistakes, she shook out her hands. "On one condition."

He turned.

"Come for a run with me?"

He checked his watch. "Give me thirty minutes."

"Deal." She had no doubt he could keep up, and carving out time for the two of them would soothe her nerves. "I'll call the hospital and check on Jandro and Aiden."

Dante's face fell.

"I know." She swallowed. "But I have to know."

He nodded.

"All right, who's hungry?" Linda asked.

Turning in her chair, Gisella let the room's inhabitants reclaim her focus. Each one came to her aid, and as soon as she finished her coffee, she intended to reward their loyalty.

Pushing back his chair, Martin seized his chance, approached Linda and bowed. "*Bella donna.*"

Linda blushed.

Gisella bit back a smile. She would stay for this show.

"Cheap trick." Lisette finished set down her glass and leaned closer. "What did he say?"

Judging by the tang of Lisette's breath, Lisette's glass held a Bloody Mary, and she'd gone light on the mix. "Oh, you know, 'hello'."

"I thought *ciao* meant hello."

Gisella shrugged and gestured toward Martin. "Linda, this is Martin. He keeps us in line. Can you give him a rundown of the penthouse?"

Martin offered his arm.

Linda accepted it.

Smiling, Gisella slouched in her chair and closed her eyes. Yesterday, she'd worried about paying a plumber's bill, but Dante had soothed her nerves. They could make this marriage work. She wouldn't have to live off ramen, but she would have to learn to manage a household. Taking notes from Linda and Martin would help. Opening her eyes, she considered following the pair.

Ursula folded her napkin and placed it on the table. "Did you have time to look at the dresses?" She stood and walked toward the rack. Someone had pushed it out of the way of foot traffic. "Which one tempts you?"

Gisella followed her sister's lead. "Let's start with you. Did you defrock a priest?"

Ursula shrugged. "Maybe he defrocked me."

"Ruthless."

Ursula smiled.

She rose, reached for the nearest dresses and skimmed her finger along the hangers. Most of the ones Lisette had culled from area boutiques screamed cocktail hussy. Gisella wasn't about to wear a white silk romper, and the cutout dresses and one-shoulder sheaths looked too casual. One day, her kids would ask for wedding pictures, and she wanted something to show them.

Pulling out the second-to-last dress, she smiled. A designer had added shimmering white sequins to an elegant lace dress with a flattering fit-and-flare silhouette. Stripped of the light embellishment, the dress looked fit for a garden party, but a plunging V-neck and a narrow waist gave it interest. "This one."

Lisette pulled the dress from her hands, checked the tags and shrugged. "I don't know why they sent that one. It's nearly knee-length. Pick something sexier." She wagged her eyebrows. "Give him a reason to stay."

"That's definitely the dress." Gisella pried it from Lisette's cold grasp and held it up to the morning sunlight. She could imagine wearing the dress with a neat white jacket and the nude ankle-strap heels she loved, but she wouldn't ask Linda to source the pieces from her father's house. Maybe Tia could bring them.

"Suit yourself." Lisette zeroed in on the bags of pastries and left.

Frowning, Gisella wondered why Tia hadn't decamped to the penthouse like everyone else. "Ursula, where's Tia?"

"Making granola?" Ursula shrugged. "Someone has to watch *Papà*."

"But Lisette's here."

Ursula laughed. "The moment she saw Alessio's crew, she trailed those men around *The Grace* like a bloodhound on a scent. Didn't you notice her quest for an upgrade?"

She only had eyes for Dante.

Thinking of him, she wondered if he had strong opinions on a veil. Her mother wore a beautiful, light veil that would match the dress. Tia could raid the attic, but finding and cleaning the piece would take her most of the day. Shaking off the sentimental thought, she decided to make do with windswept hair.

"I hoped *Papà* would see her behavior and call off the wedding."

Gisella tapped her chin and considered Lisette's ascent in *la famiglia*. Given the age difference between Gregorio and his intended bride, Lisette might play nurse longer than she played newlywed. "They each have their motivations."

Walking toward the bedroom, she shucked off the loungewear and the robe. Pulling the borrowed dress over her head, she faced the mirror. The dress gaped. Undeterred, she zipped the back zipper and smoothed her hands over the bodice. With a bra, it would fit. Turning in place, she watched the full skirt bell out and smiled.

"Beautiful," Dante said.

Gasping, she turned toward the sound of his voice.

257

He walked out of the closet and leaned on the doorframe.

Based on his admiring expression, she felt like the most beautiful woman in the world.

Rubbing his fingers together, he reached toward her, but he pulled back. "I can wait."

His control impressed her as much as his admiration. She unzipped the dress and turned her back toward him. "You're not supposed to be in here."

"I thought I had more time, but you make quick decisions."

He appeared in her life at the very moment she needed change, but she wanted to savor their beginning. Her mother's death, Jandro's injury and Aiden's accident reminded her how fleeting life could be. The roles mattered, but the people made the show. Holding the bodice flush against her chest, she looked over her shoulder and raised her chin. "I know quality when I see it, but you should get out."

He shook his head and approached. "I'd rather stay."

She lowered the dress an inch. "Do I get a choice?"

He trailed his fingers along her spine. "You always get a choice."

She smiled. "Forget what you've seen. I'll look better at one o'clock."

"I doubt it." Reaching around her torso, he pressed a small velvet box into her hand and stepped back.

"What is it?"

"Something I hope you'll keep," he said.

Rattling the box, she tried to guess its contents. The worn velvet suggested he'd had the box for a while, but she didn't peg him for a sentimental man. If the box contained an engagement ring, she didn't need one. She resisted opening it.

Turning, he walked out of the bedroom and eased the door toward the frame. It creaked, but before it latched, he paused. "Will you back out?"

"No." She looked up from the box and turned, clutching both the dress and the box to her chest. "Will you?"

He cocked his head. "You're already mine."

The dark, possessive statement sent a chill up her spine, but before she could craft a retort, he pulled the door shut.

Opening the box, she found two antique wedding bands and checked for engravings. The insides remained smooth, but the burnished gold reflected the morning light.

Slipping the smaller band on her ring finger, she marveled at the fit and wondered who'd worn it last. She liked to imagine a sweet couple growing old in two rocking chairs. The thought brought a grin to her face, and she released the dress. It pooled on the floor. Dante's rocking chair would rock until hell froze over, but she would be at his side.

Stepping out of the lace dress, she laid it on the bed, added the box containing two rings and slipped on her day clothes. If Dante could bring an heirloom to the ceremony, so could she. Lifting her phone from the bedside table, she dialed Tia. "I wish you were here."

"I'll be there at one."

Word traveled fast in her family. "Can you gather my white bolero jacket, my nude ankle-strap heels and my makeup?"

"You need sexy underwear."

What was it with the women in her life pushing her toward sex? If they knew how her relationship with Dante had begun, they might push her toward church. She might as well ask her aunts for marriage advice. *If you don't sleep with your husband, someone else will.* If anyone approached Dante for sex, she feared she would turn full mafia on them. "Really, Tia?"

"Super sexy underwear. You'll make a beautiful bride."

"*Non saprò mai cucinare come tu.*"

"You're strong, Gigi. I can send the driver with your things or you can come and get them. The place is a madhouse, but you could slip in through the back gate."

She puzzled over the practicalities. "Won't *Papà* notice?"

"Your father's...busy."

A siren wailed.

"Tia? Are you okay?" she asked.

"Right as rain." Tia ended the call.

Ursula walked into the bedroom. "Does the dress fit?"

"Like a glove." Gisella stared at the phone. "Tia just hung up on me."

"Funny. I saw her this morning, and she seemed fine." Ursula scooped the dress into her arms. "This thing weighs a ton. Are you sure?"

Her ballet costumes weighed more than that puny dress. "I can handle it. When did you go to the house?"

Ursula shrugged. "Martin wanted to join the party."

"You don't drive."

Ursula slipped the dress on a hanger. "Huh." Unclasping a diamond pendant, she extended her hand.

"What do you mean, *Huh?*"

"Do you want it or not?" Ursula asked.

The gem sparkled, but she refused to reach for the chain. *Papà* kept Mama's jewelry locked in a safe, but after her death, he let each girl pick out a piece. Gisella picked a slim gold watch. Ursula went for the bling. She'd always had good taste in jewelry, but her flashy taste stopped short of her clothes. "That's *your* necklace."

"Something old, something new, something borrowed and something blue," Ursula said.

"So far I'm raking in the heirlooms." She took the necklace, reached behind her and slipped the wedding rings onto the chain. Thinking of her mother's veil, she smiled. Ursula wouldn't be the only family member dropping by the family compound to retrieve mementos. "At least I picked the groom." She frowned. "I picked him, didn't I?"

"You picked each other." Ursula covered a yawn. "Me? I defrocked a priest."

She snorted. "Save it for the confessional."

Ursula grinned.

Someone in the living room turned on a televised newscast.

"Firefighters are responding to an outbuilding structure fire at the home of Gregorio Vitella. Initially, the reclusive billionaire and his extended family blocked first responders from entering the property. As the billowing smoke darkened, firefighters advised him to open the gates or risk losing the main residence. He relented, and the CBS4News chopper remains on the scene. Stay with us as the story unfolds."

Ursula shook her head. "Such a mess. Who knew a little fertilizer could be so combustible?"

She frowned. "Surely Tia didn't mess up…"

Ursula picked at her nails.

If she had to choose between her sister's dark side and her loving heart, she would refuse the choice. Ursula came as a package, and love ruled her machinations, but her sense of justice raised a few questions. "Actually, I don't want to know."

Rubbing the diamond pendant between her fingers, she exhaled and felt an inch closer toward her goals. She would go for a run, marry Dante and remake her life.

Following the television's sound, she found Lisette staring at the large flat screen. Mascara-blackened tears streamed down her face.

"How am I supposed to stage the ceremony in the backyard?" Lisette asked. "Look at the ruts!"

Unconcerned with her childhood home, Gisella watched the news broadcast for ambulances or signs of medical intervention. Ever since Lisette had arrived and chipped away at her mother's design choices, the building had felt less like a home, but she wouldn't abandon Gregorio. Once the county's first responders brought the fire under control, she could go about her day.

Martin cleared his throat. "Ahh, *Signorina* Gisella…"

She turned. "Did you lose your love interest?"

He blushed, and his ramrod posture pulled his height to an even six feet. "Ms. Linda is a classy lady."

She smiled at the display of loyalty. "Of course, but she won't mind if I borrow you for an hour. I need a favor."

Loosening his collar, he glanced at Lisette. "You asked me to look into your father's fiancée."

She thought upending her father's relationship would give her leverage to alter his business dealings and his retirement plan, but the more she learned about Lisette, the more she realized she'd gone off course. Lisette couldn't erase memories of her mother, and she couldn't remake her father. The more she learned about the woman, the more she understood paint colors and gilt mirror frames could change, but Lisette had little impact on her life. "What did you find?"

Martin glanced at the alcohol-infused, sobbing woman. "You were right. Some irregularities exist in the financial records."

Surprised he didn't pull out an Italian dictionary and enhance his report, she pulled him toward the bar. "No license? No insurance?"

"Worse." He wiped his brow. "She's using your father's identity to place winning bids on extremely valuable pieces of artwork."

"What artwork?"

"Your father received handwritten thank you letters from the auction house, but I fished them out of the trash."

"Martin, you nosy little busybody."

He worked his jaw. "None of the art pieces Lisette placed in the house match the thank you notes or the catalog descriptions referenced by the thank you notes. Lisette bid on your father's behalf, secreted away the real art and substituted trash."

She starred at the rocking woman and the billowing black smoke on the screen. "I wonder if he's her only victim."

"Umm…"

She turned and narrowed her gaze. "Spill it, Martin"

He lifted his chin like a sergeant at arms. "She has completed sales agreements for fifty-two artworks.

Based on my inquiries, her takes total more than two-hundred-and-seventy-five million dollars."

She slapped her chest. If Lisette had stockpiled pieces by Pablo Picasso, Edward Hopper and Henri Matisse, she had enough inventory to open one of Miami's best small art museums. "Where are the pieces?"

"Still at the auction houses," he said. "The sellers hold the works, but she has title and insurance on behalf of her clients. She can claim them at any time."

"Clever."

She glanced at the safe housing Dante's gun. The combination eluded her, but she understood the firearm's power. Antonio might pull the piece and threaten Lisette into a confession. Ursula might poison her, but Gisella refused to let her family dominate her. The two clever criminals could have each other. If Gregorio bailed on future alimony, Lisette's assets ensured she would never run out of vodka. "Lisette?"

Turning, the older woman hiccupped. "What?"

"It'll be okay. If you and *Papà* love each other, you can get through anything."

Lisette rubbed the snot from her nose.

She leaned closer. "I also know about your art collection."

Lisette widened her eyes and looked around the apartment.

Dropping to one knee, Gisella took her hand. "Take *Papà* to his island. Keep him busy. Keep him from harming people. I don't care if you bathe in caviar, but keep him out of this town. You understand me?"

Nodding, Lisette rubbed the heels of her hands over her eyes. "Crystal. I should have been nicer to you. I left one-star reviews of your ballets."

Speechless, Gisella pulled back. Screw being nice. "If I find out about any more irregularities, I'll destroy your art cache, and the burning outbuildings will be the least of your problems." She lowered her voice and channeled her family motto. "The forensics team will never find your body."

Lisette dropped her head on her arm and wailed.

Ursula approached. "What's wrong with her?"

"Drunk," Gisella said. "She can't hold her liquor."

Ursula wrapped an arm around her shoulder. "You're a terrible liar."

Lisette raised her head and wiped the tearstains beneath her eyes. "I really love your father," Lisette said. "He might be old school, but he appreciates refinement and sophistication. I just didn't know if I could trust him."

"Well, that's sweet." Ursula patted her head. "We all figured you wanted access to his bank accounts."

Gisella considered whether her sister knew more about the family business than she let on. Leaving her phone around the house had kept Gisella informed, but Ursula lingered in the shadows. The question was, had she avoided the stain?

Releasing her shoulders, Ursula turned, cupped Lisette's elbow, and pulled her into an awkward side embrace. "Imagine crying on a day like today. We're here to celebrate, aren't we?"

Swaying on her feet, Lisette flailed for support, wiped her nose on Ursula's shoulder, and wailed. "Everyone deserves to be loved! I just wanted a rich man to love me!"

"Well, I just want to rule."

Turning her back on the pair, Gisella rolled her tongue over her teeth and considered what she wanted.

Her parents loved her, but after her mother had died, Gregorio had cosseted her and focused on his cocaine empire. If she and her siblings reminded him too much of his wife, setting them apart failed to resurrect her. Gisella could forgive him many things, but she couldn't understand why he kept Antonio at his side. If it had to do with the size of Antonio's balls, she hoped her quick knee had shrunk them.

If she had children, she would protect them, but kids needed more than symbolic heroism. Since her mother's death, *Papà* treated her like an asset, and she was too inexperienced to know better. She might be a late bloomer, but she realized she was a decade late to her teenage rebellion.

Standing in a lavish penthouse, she wondered if she could break the cycle. Dante pulled passion from her body, made good on his promises and vowed to protect her. Did she love him? Everything she listed benefited her.

He also navigated his new life, looked out for people and meted out judgment using as little force as necessary. What else could she expect from love, honor and obey? Recalling his admiring bedroom expression, she grinned. Pleasure helped.

With Martin's help, she would slip home and collect the things she needed before the wedding. With her mother's veil over her hair, she would say her vows, lean close and whisper her love. If the man had any sense, he'd pull her in for a kiss and state his love in return. If he needed a little more time, she would give him a lifetime to catch up.

Chapter Nineteen

A few minutes after ten o'clock, Dante wrapped up a call in the office and listened to the muted commotion coming from the living room. When the team converged for a deal, he enjoyed hanging out with the other ADC associates, but he itched to boot them from the penthouse. His corporate experiences had turned him into something of a lone wolf, but Gisella attracted attention like moths to a flame. Going forward, he would learn to share her attentions, but he'd be damned if he celebrated his wedding night in a penthouse overflowing with cocksure loons.

The prospect of marrying Gisella and savoring her passion heated his blood. He initially thought the union would bring him fifteen million dollars closer his financial goals, but he couldn't put a price on her affection. Given enough time and soul-shattering caresses, he would earn her love.

Standing, he made his way through the hallways and stopped outside the master bedroom. "Gisella?"

Silence answered him.

"Gisella?" Easing open the door, he found the bed rumpled, her day clothes strewn on the floor and the empty box he'd given her resting on the duvet. Striding across the room, he checked for his grandparents' rings. Wherever she'd disappeared to, the rings followed, and the thought comforted him. Her mess did not. They'd obviously need to hire a housekeeper.

Smiling, he strode into the closet to pick out one of the three suits he'd brought to Miami. The bedroom door opened from the living room. Stepping out of the closet, he frowned to see Ursula walk into the bedroom with a cat's slinking curiosity. "Lose something?"

Ursula started. "What the fuck are you doing here?"

He cocked his head. "I could ask you the same."

"She's supposed to be with you."

Clearing his throat, he shrugged into his suit jacket. "And where are we supposed to be?"

"Swinging by the house for Mama's veil." Ursula whipped out her phone, picked a contact and lifted the device to her ear.

"Right." He adjusted his shoulders. Just after lunch, a city judge would officiate the ceremony and he'd whisk Gisella in a gallant blue speedboat to a Keys resort. "As soon as I'm dressed, I'll take her."

Dropping the phone into her pocket, she peered into the living room and frowned. "Martin's not here, either. Fuck. She's already gone."

Running his hand over his face, he replayed how much time had elapsed since he'd last seen his intended bride. If she had cold feet, a note would have sufficed. "And none of you idiots saw her leave? Where'd she go?"

"To my father's house." Ursula worked her jaw. "This is a cluster. Gisella said she'd meet Tia by the back gate, get the veil and bring her to the ceremony. I thought you'd be there."

He considered Ursula's truthfulness. He'd asked Gisella to marry him, but did she agree? His little spitfire could command a stage, but she barely understood her family's propensity for pain. The woman standing before him looked like her evil twin, but he hadn't been in town long enough to measure her truthfulness. "Liar."

She rolled her eyes.

His old, suppressed rage flared. How many times had his father mocked and belittled him? Striding forward, he grabbed Ursula by the arm, pushed her against the bedroom wall and cupped her neck.

Her eyes bulged, but she maintained eye contact.

The show of strength assured him, and the empty ring box gave him hope. Whatever compelled Gisella to leave without telling him, Ursula hadn't caved to external pressure, but internal threats could be just as deadly. He released his hand and let her find her footing. "If you've set her up, I'll kill you."

Ursula rubbed her throat. "Martin's with her, but you're the one who's supposed to protect her."

"And you?"

She cleared her throat. "I'm biding my time. As soon as *Papà* leaves, everything will be mine."

He had no doubt. Pushing past her, he flung open the door and counted the living room's occupants. Lisette clutched a drink and sobbed in front of the television set, Linda presided over the kitchen like a five-star chef and Pietro stared at his hands like he couldn't tell the left one from the right one. "Fuck!"

Alessio and his associates jumped to their feet.

"If we're not there by one, call the police." Grabbing his gun, he slid it into the holster, hailed the elevator and pulled out his phone. Typing out a text message, he asked for her location, told her he needed her and thought twice about the missive. If he wanted to declare himself, he would do it in person, and any man worthy of her love could find his woman.

The elevator doors opened, and he walked inside the conveyance. If taking the stairs had been quicker, he would have flown.

When the elevator doors opened on the ground floor, he pushed through a family of four encumbered with shopping bags, and he ripped Alessio's spare key from the valet stand. He would make it to the Vitella family compound before anything could happen to the woman he loved.

* * * *

Fire trucks blocked the street and jammed up traffic for a quarter mile surrounding Gregorio's house. Dante cursed. On a normal day, the traffic would have rankled him, but it might have ensnared Gisella, too. He checked his phone, but he hadn't missed any calls. Ursula's surprise and the missing rings encouraged him to proceed.

Slamming his hand against the dash, he told himself that Gisella was a competent woman who could handle her own damn family. With white knuckles, he recalled the pain he'd experienced handling his. Learning how little you mattered could scar a person. He would do everything possible to keep those scars from her silky skin.

In the tight car, his shoulder pained him. He itched to be free of the welded body, society's demands and his own damn mistakes. He wanted to shield Gisella and cradle her, but Gregorio proved that the woman demanded a different approach. What if she'd had second thoughts about walking out on her father? The man was a monster, but she loved him. Leaving her unattended after so many stressful encounters had been a fucking mistake. She could roll with the punches, but she was soft. Who would risk their safety for a veil?

A red convertible with a souped-up engine cut across the median. Horns blared, and traffic adjusted to fill the vehicle's wake as it roared up the pedestrian path.

Dante stared at the spectacle. The mid-morning sun shadowed the vehicle's occupants, but he would bet his life that Antonio drove the car and Gisella occupied the front seat.

Throwing Alessio's overpriced sports car into reverse, he backed into the vehicle behind him and made room in the traffic jam. Glass shattered, and a horn blared. Fuck if he cared. After he reclaimed his woman, he'd repay the bastard whose car he'd wrecked.

With room to maneuver, he put the sports car in drive, jumped the median and roared after Antonio and Gisella. Weaving through traffic, he kept his gaze on the red convertible and gripped the steering wheel. Antonio had a head start, but he drove like a fourteen-year-old boy racing video games.

Dante drove like a man.

In Antonio's path, pedestrians screamed and trashcans flew. A police car jerked to the left, hit a light pole and released a cloud of steam. Mel Gibson would be proud, but the 1990s hero's bottomless rage needed a woke spinal adjustment. "Amateur."

Dante slowed for a far-sighted pedestrian, punched the accelerator and raced through the intersection with the precision and the control necessary to navigate the art deco maze.

The tachometer climbed.

Leaning forward, he looked for an opportunity to cut off the asshole, draw his gun and reclaim his woman. What if he'd been wrong and she didn't want reclaiming?

The scenario stole his focus. They'd gone from zero to sixty so quickly that he'd reduced her dreams to the brief snippets of information she'd shared. She loved to dance, but she feared independence. Her ballet corps functioned like a family, but she maintained allegiance to her blood relatives. Fuck, if he still had a family, he'd cling to them, too. Did she even want kids?

Antonio jerked the wheel toward a bayside park.

A small five-person helicopter waited on the lawn. Its blades rotated, and a crowd of pedestrians clustered beyond their reach.

Slamming the convertible into park, Antonio jumped over the driver's side door, rounded the hood and yanked out Gisella.

If Antonio pulled Gisella onto the helicopter, Dante wouldn't have a chance of talking to her. He jerked the wheel and sent the sports car fishtailing toward Antonio's red, lacquered dream, but the pair moved clear of the vehicle.

She fought her brother's grip and scoured her nails along his cheek.

Dante would buy her a diamond big enough to take out the asshole's eyes. Leaving the keys in the ignition, he sprinted toward her and the waiting helicopter. "I'm coming."

Antonio yanked open the side door, shoved Gisella into the cabin and flipped him the bird. Climbing inside, he slammed the door in Dante's face.

He wasn't stupid enough to hang onto the helicopter's landing gear.

The helicopter rose into the air, tilted to the side, corrected and rose over the bay.

His stomach dropping, Dante bent and braced his hands on his knees. He looked up and saw Gisella's hand braced against the glass. He'd failed her.

"That your girl?" a boy asked.

He nodded and watched the draft rise. His associate, Jason, preached the dangers of single-pilot small aircraft. He insisted that Alessio and his crew fly with two pilots, but the tiny, sleek helicopter carrying Gisella had tilted on takeoff. The asshat flying it had better monitor the controls like his life depended on it. It did.

"She's headed to the campaign fundraiser on Billionaire Bunker. The helicopter's been ferrying people out there all day. I asked if I could hitch a ride, but the pilot laughed."

"I doubt he's coming back for me, either," Dante said.

"You could take the supply boat out to Indian Creek Village. My uncle makes the run at noon."

Raising his head, Dante stared across Biscayne Bay to the tiny private island. Its wealthy, high-profile residents included billionaire investors, supermodels and Latin singers, but apparently the rich had to eat, too.

If he approached the island by car, the guardhouse would halt his progress before he set foot on the island. He doubted the guard would accept a bribe, and he didn't want to pull his gun unless he absolutely had to use it. "Really?"

"It's gonna cost you," the kid said.

He raised his head. The helicopter carrying Antonio and Gisella looked like a black dot against the clouds. If it crashed, his heart would go with it. "That so? How much?"

Appraising Dante's watch and shoes, the kid smiled. "A grand."

"Big money." Dante stood and wiped the sweat from his forehead. Gisella had been right. This fucking city would eat him alive, but to claim her, he would fight its heat and crazy Italian mobsters. Stripping off his watch, he handed it to the kid. "Your uncle gets me to the island, and I'll pay you in cash."

The kid widened his gaze. "Cash?"

Pulling out his thick wallet, Dante slapped it against his palm. He respected the kid's hustle, but this wasn't the time for heart-to-heart talks and youth mentoring. "Cash. Now call your fucking uncle and tell him to bump up the supply run."

* * * *

Bouncing over the bay's waters, Dante watched the island grow nearer. Homes surrounded the village island's perimeter. Walls of glass and flowing infinity pools reflected the residents' waterfront views. Past the wealthy ring, an eighteen-hole golf course and a country club presided over the greens. He bet the helicopter would land at the club, but he had no idea which house to target.

"That one."

The kid pointed toward a lavish Mediterranean-style villa. Smiling, happy people milled around a pool and draped their jeweled arms over balcony railings. They came to one of Miami Beach's wealthiest, most secure private communities, but they came to party.

Dante nodded. "Tell your uncle to dock like normal. I'll make my way there. Wait for me. When I have her, I'll call you."

"What if she doesn't want to come back with you?" the kid asked.

"Then I'm ruined." Dante swallowed back his fear. She could have left of her own volition, but she took the rings, and she was strong enough to tell him she'd changed her mind. In his heart, she wouldn't have fled. "I'll need a ride to the airport. Without her, I'm gone."

"Sucker," the kid said.

"You have no idea." Hoping the wind-whipped approach preserved his suit, he jumped over the boat's side, landed on the dock and checked his gun. He had plenty of bullets, but he prayed he didn't need one.

Chapter Twenty

Stumbling from the helicopter, Gisella surveyed the greens. "Why the hell are we here?"

Antonio pushed her into motion. "Marco's here. I'm not wasting any more time. You're a liability."

"Fuck Marco."

Backhanding her, Antonio caught her hand and pulled her toward a waiting golf cart. "I told you to watch your language."

"What, like you watch yours?" The blow stung, but she maintained her balance and bided her time.

The helicopter's blades whipped hair into her face, but Miami was still America. People didn't let crimes occur in front of their eyes. She glared and strategized.

The legal courts wouldn't uphold a forced marriage to Marco or any other Italian asshole her family picked out. As soon as she escaped the island, she'd make her way back to Dante and sort out her family connections from the safety of his arms. She might be too old for emancipation, but kidnapping shouldn't be a family sport.

Antonio gripped her arm and dragged her toward a waiting car. "I told *Papà* he gave you too much leeway. Marco won't let you push him around like he's some fag on a leash. You want to be a woman? He'll teach you how to act. You want to be a man? Stop prancing around the stage and calling it art."

"You wouldn't know art unless you saw it above a urinal."

"Cute." Opening the rear passenger door, he shoved her into the car and walked around to the other side.

The helicopter alighted.

Somewhere between the Vitella house and Antonio's car, she'd dropped her purse and her phone. If Dante found her belongings, he might realize she had a problem. If she found a friend on the island, they might let her use their phone. Taking a deep breath, she stared out of the window at the million dollar houses and realized how little she cared if they burned to the ground. "Where are we going?"

"Mayor Frantz is hosting a fundraiser."

Frantz wanted to make Miami the new Silicon Valley. Big Tech and real estate developers poured cash into his coffers, crypto investors lobbied for deregulation and entrepreneurs proposed alleviating the city's traffic woes with a high-speed tunnel. With an agenda as big as his ego, Mayor Frantz turned a blind eye to a person's past and focused on the future.

With the Vitella coffers at stake, she couldn't count on his intervention.

Antonio draped his arm along his leg, and he tapped his fingers against his knee. Leaning forward, he adjusted the car's climate controls.

Nothing changed.

He slapped the driver's headrest. "Turn up the air!"

The driver turned. "Freon's low. Sorry, Mr. Antonio. I'll get it fixed."

"Fuck." Antonio rolled up his sleeves.

She stared at the long red track marks surrounding his veins. After injection, heroin quickly entered the brain. When users injected the same area without allowing it time to heal, the marks were more likely to occur. She thought the clever users injected between their toes, but Antonio wasn't a clever man. "Did you run out of coke?"

"Shut up," he said.

Closing her eyes, she tipped back her head and took his advice. Keeping *Papà* in town started as a sentimental pull, but she'd accepted Lisette and resigned herself to his departure. Now she wondered if she needed him to keep Antonio in check.

How much time did she have before *Papà's* empire imploded? She had to make plans for Tia, Martin, her aunts and the people who depended on her father's patronage. "I should have said something."

"About what?" Antonio asked.

"Our family's greed."

"Hah. You took everything you could get, too."

He was right, but she would get herself out of this mess and make amends.

The driver waved at a security guard and delivered her and Antonio to the estate's main entrance.

A curbside bar ensured attendees had a drink in their hand when they met Miami's debonair mayor and his charming, gilded wife. The pair stood by wrought-iron gates leading to a Mediterranean-inspired pool.

"I'm not dressed for a party," she said.

Amy Craig

"Tie your shirt in the front and stay quiet. You'll be fine."

She had zero intention of obeying him.

Antonio rolled down his shirtsleeves.

The driver opened the rear passenger door and stepped back.

Plucking his sunglasses off his face, she slid them onto her nose. "Any chance you'll take me back to the mainland?"

The driver averted his gaze.

She exhaled. "Here we go."

Antonio climbed out of the car and walked up to Mayor Frantz and First Lady Cathy. "Party looks good. Thanks for having us."

"We're glad you could attend." Mayor Frantz shook his hand. "Your father doing okay?"

"Electrical fire," Antonio said. "I'm sure they have it under control."

Cathy leaned close and pressed a kiss to Gisella's cheek. She wore a white kaftan and emeralds as big as robin eggs. "Don't you look chic."

"I don't want to be here."

Sighing, Cathy pulled back and tilted her head. "I know the feeling."

"Antonio basically kidnapped me."

Cathy laughed.

"No, really."

Beckoning a server, Cathy pulled two glasses from the server's tray. "This will cheer up your disposition."

She considered throwing the liquid in the woman's face. Instead, she downed the glass and strode toward the pool.

279

"Your father sponsored a cabana!" Cathy's lilting voice carried over the DJ's bass line. "Make yourself at home!"

Giving Miami's first lady her middle finger, she walked straight toward the house and wondered how quickly she could find a phone.

Antonio spun her around. "Where are you going?"

"To call a taxi."

He laughed, slung an arm around her shoulders and walked.

She ducked out of his embrace.

Marco stepped out of the shadows and gripped her arm. "Miss me?"

His strength shocked her. She considered dropping to her bottom, wrapping her arms around her knees, and making herself as immovable as a rock, but half the party's attendees would applaud her performance art. "I wouldn't phrase it that way."

Antonio laughed and took her other arm. "They don't call us Cocaine Cowboys for nothing. You're in my world now, sister."

She'd rather sweet talk Hades. Working with the youth ballet core and mentoring scholarship students felt like distant goals, and she wondered if she would leave the island alive. She wondered if Dante would know she loved him. "I refuse to play your games."

Marco shrugged a shoulder and pulled her toward a tented cabana. "As soon as I collect your fifteen-million-dollar dowry, you can sink to the bottom of the bay for all I care."

"I promised it to Jandro."

Marco released her arm. "Who the fuck is Jandro?"

Dante knew — and he cared.

When she didn't arrive for the wedding at one, she hoped he'd put together the pieces and trace her and Antonio to this selfish fantasyland. She thought restrained violence could be sexier than brute force, but she also thought she occupied a pedestal. Dante knew better.

From ground level, her companions looked like thugs and coked-out strippers. She pitied Dante for killing his father, but she understood his choice. When he fired his gun at Luca, he was clear-headed and logical, but Antonio was a bigger threat. If Dante brought his piece to the island, she would kill Antonio herself and let another crooked family satisfy the island's illicit needs

Chapter Twenty-One

Working his way through the palm trees, Dante watched estate guards greet vehicles and check a visitor list. Talking his way onto the estate would raise too many flags. Instead, he made his way back to the main road, stepped out of the shadows and held out his thumb.

A winsome redhead slowed her white luxury convertible. "Are you lost?"

He shifted on his feet, shaded his eyes, and burped. "Do I look lost?"

The redhead glanced at a brunette friend occupying the passenger seat. "Maybe he's drunk."

"Perfect." The brunette licked her lips. "Let's give him a ride."

"Where you going?" the redhead asked.

"Back to *Casa Grande*," he said.

The women laughed.

Sitting on the edge of the convertible, he made a show of swinging his leg over the side and dropping onto the luggage rack masquerading as a back seat. Leaning forward like a hood ornament, he pointed toward the estate's gates. "Drive on!"

The women giggled, approached the guard, and gave their names. "He's with us."

Dante cocked a finger pistol toward the guard and clicked his cheek. "Right-O."

The idiot admitted them through the gates.

Once inside the perimeter, Dante scanned the estate and looked for a means of escape. A small dock provided waterfront access, but barring a set of keys left near an ignition, he would need another way to leave the island with Gisella in tow.

"What's your name, *Gaucho*?" the redhead asked.

She might be a security team's worst nightmare, but she'd accepted his liquor-laced persona. He could make up a name or give her Dante. He'd assumed the nickname for so long that it felt like a second skin.

When he left home, Daniel Johnson was a scared young man, but Dante held court over millions of dollars, a ruthless reputation and a single-minded mission to matter. He would give up everything for Gisella. "Thanks for the ride, ladies." Turning, he walked into the crowd.

"Wait! I thought we had…"

The partygoers swallowed her claims. Taking a frozen drink from a passing server, he looked for anyone he recognized.

Mayor Frantz and his wife laughed by a poolside cabana. Their twin daughters posed for selfies by a bar they weren't old enough to access.

The old connection might come in handy, but he preferred not to make a scene. Sipping the drink, he judged the odds of that outcome at slim-to-none.

Instead of approaching the mayor and his wife, he looked for Gisella. Based on her expression in the sport's car, he doubted she'd come to the island willingly. If she had, he'd demand an explanation and the return of his grandparents' rings.

A heavyset man with an open-collared shirt and a thick gold chain around his neck stumbled out of the main house and made contact. "Fucking liberal!" He offered his hand. "Didn't think you had the balls to show up here."

Dante wanted to pull back from Marco, but he took the man's hand and slapped his back. "Small world."

"You're just in time for my wedding." Marco pulled a cigarette from a pack, lit it and exhaled. "Maybe yous could be a guest."

He wanted to take the smug asshole's cigarette and put it out in his eye. As his old violent impulses rose, he pushed down his reactions. Violence and passion summoned the same high but yielded different outcomes. The moment Dante and Gisella fucked, she belonged to him, and he would claim her. Marco postured, but Dante reserved his ire for Antonio.

"Maybe so. Who's the bride?"

"The boss's daughter."

On second thought, he'd happily kill this man. Instead of wiping Marco's ass with his oily smile, he drew a deep breath. "Congrats."

"Fuck, yeah." Marco exhaled. "You're not so bad."

He scanned the crowd for Gisella. "You have no idea."

Marco laughed.

Mayor Frantz's daughters walked by arm-in-arm.

"Sweet pieces of ass," Marco said. "Too bad they're coke heads."

"Come again?"

"Keeps 'em thin and stupid." Marco exhaled. "Antonio gives them the shit for free, and they rat on their dad."

Downing his drink, Dante connected the dots and drafted a diversion that would buy him time to escape with Gisella. As much as he loved her, she needed marriage's legitimacy to kick off the next phase in her life. If Marco thought he would claim the rite of marriage, well, fuck the asshole. "You don't say. So, where's your bride? I should offer my congratulations."

Marco glanced toward a cabana and frowned. "Good question."

The man had the subtlety of a street vendor. "Bashful bride?"

"I like 'em tight!"

He revised his plan a second time and decided to smash Marco's face into the pool decking. "Well, I look forward to the nuptials. Why don't you tell Antonio I'm here?"

Marco beamed and wandered off like a greaser captivated by a car show.

Dante marked his path, loosened his collar and turned toward the cabana hosting the mayor. A tall banana plant spilled into the walkway, and he stopped in the shade to empty all but one bullet from his gun. Dropping the rest into his pocket, he walked toward the cabana opening.

A burly security guard stepped out of the tent.

He brushed past him. "Fuck off." Stepping into the shadowed tent, he found Mayor Frantz, his wife and two political consultants mapping out the party's attendees. "Getting a jump on the next fundraising campaign?"

Frantz looked up, stood, and offered his hand. "Took you long enough to find me."

He and Frantz had finished their Harvard degrees at the same time, but their paths diverged. Until this moment, Dante cared little for the association, but he needed drama, and he needed it fast. "Your girls…"

"Cutest things this side of Florida." Frantz and Cathy beamed at each other. "Can you believe they're seventeen?"

He had zero time for memory lane. "I'm buying Cosmica Insurance Holdings from Gregorio Vitella."

Frantz frowned.

"You know him?"

Nodding, Frantz looked toward his wife. "Everybody knows him and his family."

"I'll be blunt," he said. "The company's a giant money laundering organization, but Gregorio's retiring, and I'll take it legit. In the meantime, you should know Antonio Vitella feeds your girls coke in exchange for information on you and your wife." Taking out his gun, he laid it on the table.

Frantz recoiled.

"It's untraceable," Dante said. "Do what you want."

Cathy picked up the double-action pistol and stormed from the cabana wearing three-inch heels.

"She knows Antonio?" Dante asked.

Frantz drew a deep breath. "Far too well. He used to be her dealer."

Beyond the cabana, a gun fired, and partygoers screamed. "Antonio Vitella, get your ass out here or I will find you." Cathy's primal demand cut through the noise. "Those are my babies!"

"Well." Dante cleared his throat. "I'll be in touch."

"Is it worth it?" Frantz asked. "Whatever set you off? This drama will make the news and set back my agenda. It'll upend your dealings with CIH and everything you've chased."

He cocked his head. "Are your daughters worth it?"

Frantz's face fell. "Of course they are."

"Well, there's your answer." Slipping from the canvas shade, he made his way through the terrified guests and focused on the cabana that had captured Marco's eye. Pulling back the canvas, he found the tent empty, but he hadn't expected the Vitella family to ride the turmoil like tourists on a duck cruise. "Fuck."

Turning, he looked for silhouettes he recognized.

Cathy claimed the DJ's booth and held the gun over her head. "Antonio! I know the police chief's shoe size. I want to see you now or I'll know your casket size!"

"Good luck." He turned and considered the large house. He doubted Frantz or the Vitella family owned the property, but they might have enough sway to take cover amid the mission-inspired walkways. Before he could choose an archway, he spied Marco crouched near a chaise longue.

The man looked both ways and bolted toward the garage.

Bingo. If the buffoon had a vehicle onsite, he doubted the valet had parked it in a garage bay. He followed Marco through the booze-whipped, stumbling chaos.

Detouring through a stand of palm trees, Marco slipped across a paver driveway and pounded the door. "You ready?"

Silence.

"Antonio?" Sweat dripped from Marco's forehead. "You there?"

A muffled noise came from the second floor.

Marco looked up.

Dante did, too.

Gisella made eye contact and slapped her palm against a window. Her hair hung loose, and tears reddened her eyes.

The violence rose in him. Wrapping his arm around the Marco's throat, he blocked the man's mouth and fought his struggles. A sudden and rapid drop in blood pressure rendered Marco unconscious.

Most people fainted and regained normal consciousness in a matter of minutes, but Dante refused to let the steroid-enhanced idiot bash his head on a curb. He removed his belt, strapped it around Marco's arms and chest, and dragged his moaning captive into the bushes. He wagered the man had few brain cells to spare.

Slipping open the door, he listened for activity.

Gisella cursed Antonio, Marco and every man in her family. *"Testa di cazzo!"*

As her future husband, he could think of sweeter endearments, but he would take what he could get. Bounding up the steps, he found a chair wedged beneath a door. "Gisella, sweetheart."

"Dante!" She pounded the door. "Dante! Get me the fuck out of here!"

"As you wish." Dislodging the chair, he threw his shoulder against the door and deformed the cheap wood. The door had the decency to splinter near the lock, and he pushed it open. Shaking off the pain of the impact, he strode into the room.

Gisella fell into his arms.

He wrapped his arms around her and held her close. Her body shook with an adrenal letdown, but she felt warm and secure in his arms. Her vitality soothed the violence itching for release, but her tears eroded his careful foundation.

"You came."

Pressing a kiss to her long, dark hair, he exhaled. "Of course I came." He ran his hands along her arms to check for injuries, and finding none, he relaxed his grip.

She pulled back. "What took you so long?"

"I opted for subtlety. Why is your brother such an ass?"

Looking over her shoulder, she peered down the stairway. "I don't know. He's still deferential toward *Papà*, but how long will that last? How does he treat people he barely knows? I'm so tired of playing two roles. I don't belong in my family's world, and I refuse to follow Mama's example."

"Well, let's set a new one." Lifting her chin, he claimed a second kiss, pulled back and cupped her face. He could keep an eye on the stairwell, cover her ass and set the record straight before anyone found them. "I don't care about your family, but I missed you. I'll always come for you. You mean everything."

"Do I?"

"You don't need a ring to know how much I love you." He swept her into his arms and walked down the stairs "You doubted me?"

Nestled against his chest, she sighed. "I don't know. I saw you, and I hoped you were here for me, but I wasn't sure."

"Foolish woman."

She laughed. "Am I foolish to love you?"

For close to a decade, he would have called her foolish, but sticking his toe into Miami's sandy, drug-drenched miasma affirmed how much he valued his life. He might carry a gun, but he only used it to protect the people he loved. "No, you're not foolish." He stepped outside before he said more.

"Let me up!" Marco wiggled in the bushes. He'd made it onto his knees, but his over-built torso destroyed his balance. Without free arms, he couldn't quite gain his feet. "Get me out of here, and we'll forget this ever happened."

Dante continued walking toward the estate's exit.

Upturned tables and spilled drinks littered the pool deck. Staff stood at the garden perimeter and scratched their heads. Without clear and present danger, the innocent looked bemused, the curious snapped pictures and the hungry helped themselves to the carving station. Patio lights swayed over sunlit paths, but the evening soiree ended before the sun went down.

With nothing better to do, he would drop into a lounge chair, nestle Gisella in his arms and enjoy a moment of solitude, but he had another agenda. "So, what do you want to do until one?"

She laughed and slid down his body. "Head back to the hotel and freshen up."

"I have a better idea," he said. "Let's get our own place."

Linking hands, she dug her free hand into her pocket and smiled. "Good call. I couldn't ask for a prettier day…"

Antonio clamored around a corner, lost his balance and scrambled to his feet.

A heartbeat later, Cathy rounded the same corner holding the pistol. "You little shit!"

Gisella recoiled.

Dante stepped in front of her.

Waving the pistol, Cathy backed Antonio into a stucco column and pointed the gun at his crotch. "You think I'll let you leave this island and pop up in my girls' future like an untreated venereal disease? You will stay here until the police arrive. If you move a muscle, you'll regret it, and the Vitella line will end with you."

"They're almost adults!" Antonio looked toward Gisella. "Gigi, tell her they made their choices."

She placed her hand in the center of Dante's back, but she stayed in his shadow. "Antonio, you're well past seventeen, too. You can handle your own shit."

Antonio doubled over and retched.

Sirens approached, and banana plants shook in the breeze, but nobody moved.

When Dante shot his father, he'd been nineteen. The line between adolescence and maturity could stretch over years, but once a person crossed it, they couldn't go back. He walked up to the heaving man and pinned his shoulder against the bright stucco.

Raising his chin, Antonio wiped the bank of his hand across his mouth. "What? You want a piece of me?"

"He's mine!" Cathy shouted.

He looked over his shoulder. "Wait your turn."

Gisella grabbed the older woman's arm and held fast.

"Pay attention." Ignoring the stench of fear and regret, Dante dropped his voice. "My research and experience have taught me that hundreds of millions of dollars require a network of crooked professionals willing to hide ill-gotten gains. I know the financial and legal professionals hiding your shit."

"They're loyal to me." Antonio spat.

Dante dodged the projectile. "Your lawyers in New York and Delaware and" — he leaned closer — "London know my name, and they know how deep my knowledge extends. You think they're experts at creating shell companies and secretive trusts? I'm an expert at finding them, and I pay handsomely for registration documents. If you think front men and proxies will hide your ass, you're wrong. So, run, little boy, and don't look back. If you threaten Gisella again, you'll have nothing." He unpinned Antonio's shoulder and stepped back.

Slipping past him, Gisella advanced on her brother and jammed her finger into Antonio's chest. "Cathy and Dante are the least of your problems. I'm done with the Vitella name! I don't care if honesty destroys my ballet career and my family. I won't stand by while you destroy lives. As soon as I get off this island…"

Marco burst through the foliage and stumbled onto the pool deck. Free of his leather restraints, he waved his arms, lost his balance and recovered on all four limbs. "Police!"

Pivoting, Cathy pointed the gun at him and pulled the trigger.

Nothing happened.

After regaining his footing, Marco waved his arms, slipped through the foursome and continued toward the exit. "Run!"

Antonio dove for Gisella and rolled into the carving station.

Cursing the moment of separation, Dante watched the tangle of arms and legs resolve into Gisella and her baby brother.

Plates and cutlery clattered to the floor. A bloodstained carving knife landed near the fighting pair, and Dante drew a deep breath. He could charge into the scramble, but he risked injuring her. Gritting his teeth and clenching his fists at his side, he waited.

Gisella's strength held Antonio at bay. Without the element of surprise, she struggled against his grip on her forearms, but she slammed her knee into his groin and scratched at his eyes. "Get your hands off me!"

Dante swore he would do all his household chores.

"Bitch!" Antonio kicked her legs out from under her, and she landed on her abdomen, her palms braced on the decking.

Antonio wiped the spit from his mouth and grabbed a fistful of her hair.

Seeing his opening, Dante charged forward.

She rolled to her back, reached for the carving knife, and slashed it against Antonio's forearm.

The sharp blade sank deep into tendons and flesh. Blood welled to the surface and Antonio screamed. Releasing her hair, he gripped her arm holding the blade.

Yanking free the knife, she cut deeper on the withdrawal and brandished it above her chest. "Don't talk to me ever again!"

Dante held back and admired the standoff. Gisella had cut Antonio's forearm muscles and flexor tendons. Stopping an attacker's most dangerous body part was the quickest and most efficient way to stop the attacker, but most people got symbolic and aimed for the heart. He could attest to the heart's resilience.

In another life, she might have overcome her aversion to trafficking laws and handled Gregorio's business like a pro, but he shook off the alternate image. The woman he loved would hate the mundane rigor of weighing and measuring product.

Pushing herself to standing, she faced her brother.

Antonio's blood dripped down his torso, and he stared at the wound like he doubted he could bleed.

It's just blood could comprise so many outcomes, but Antonio tore his sleeve to stem the flow. He would need surgery, but unless she took a second, poetic swipe, he would recover.

Her hand shook, and she lowered the knife.

The sirens stopped at the gates. Officers shouted commands.

"Gisella," Dante said.

Turning, she stared. "I couldn't stomach another abduction."

He nodded.

She dropped the knife and exhaled. "I'll stay to clean up the mess."

Walking slowly, he pulled her into his arms and stroked her back. Repercussions would follow, and he would do his best to shield her from the consequences. "It was self-defense."

She shook. "He's such a baby."

Antonio wailed. "Don't listen to her. She cut my artery. I'm dying!"

Cathy kicked him in the kneecap, and he collapsed. "Shut up!"

Dante winced, pulled off his suit jacket and threw it over Gisella's shoulders.

"Go." Cathy tossed him the unused gun. "I'll take care of his mess."

Catching the piece, he tucked it in his waistband, nodded his thanks and urged Gisella toward the manicured garden and open water. Free of the pool area, he stopped, turned her in his arms and measured her response. "I'm proud of you."

She swallowed. "You are?"

"I am." Tipping up her chin, he kissed her until her breath escaped in a soft caress. The living confirmation grounded him, but he needed more than pleasure before he understood the fallout. "I'll get you back to the mainland."

Pulling back, she nodded. "I need"—she swallowed—"some downtime."

"You'll have it." He wanted to tuck her against his side and keep her safe, but she'd proven her capability. Unraveling family dynamics left her muted, but he waited for her to tell him what she needed.

If she missed her gilded cage, he could give her shopping sprees, but he couldn't replace her family. "Antonio will have a hard time bouncing back from today. Cathy is pissed that he supplied her twins with drugs."

"Oh, she's wicked. Once you lose favor in this town, you're done." Gisella leaned against him. "Really, he's screwed. As soon as his friends find out I sliced him, they'll tear him apart."

Accepting her weight, he wondered how he would have survived the next fifty years without her. "Where would you like to go?"

She looked up. "I thought we were getting our own place."

He wanted another assuring kiss, but a tear marked her skin. Despite her bravado, battling her brother had impacted her, and he'd make sure the asshole kept his hands off her for good. "We are."

Blinking, she drew a deep breath. "I want you, Dante."

"You have me. I will spend the rest of my life protecting you. If that includes your family, fuck them. If it's me, I'll walk away. I'm not perfect."

She cupped his cheek. "You won't hurt me."

"I killed Luca." He closed his eyes. "I would kill for you."

"Only when he threatened me. Even then, you'd already claimed me."

"I knew you were mine" — swallowing, he opened his eyes — "but I didn't think I deserved you."

She turned into his chest. "You did. This high-octane life isn't for me. I buried myself in fairytale and fantasies, but my life was make-believe. I just want to dance and sleep in your arms. I don't care if you're poor."

He smiled and held her close. "I'm not poor."

"Or a West Coast hippie."

"Hardly."

"But I love you," she said.

He committed the moment to memory. "This is survivor's optimism talking. You had a scare, and you've gone from exhaustion to being in love with life."

"No." She pulled free. "I'm in love with *you*. You have so much to offer the world, and you're so tough, but you want to be with me. I can feel it. You want love, and family — and the little things that make life worthwhile."

He swallowed.

"We can be a real family. I meant what I said on the beach. I want to be with you."

For too much of his life, guns and power had equaled safety, but standing in the foliage, he'd never felt more vulnerable and more loved. "Choosing me isn't your only path. You have friends. You have your art. Jandro will recover."

"But I love you," she whispered. "The vulnerability hurts, but choosing you is my path. The moment I met you, I felt it."

"You told me to fuck myself."

She smiled. "We all have our love languages."

A helicopter buzzed over the estate.

He wanted to make her come apart in his arms, but if he indulged, they might end up on the evening news. He almost didn't care. She brought passion back into his life, and he savored it. He wanted to lift her ass and claim her, but she deserved more than a bushwhacked vow. He planned to give her everything.

She chewed her lip. "Dante?"

Looking away, he cleared his throat and focused on Antonio's sins. Idiots could fuck over the little guys, but the big guys would always eat them up. "Your brother's an asshole."

She pulled back. "I know."

"He preys on weak, vulnerable people. He doesn't deserve your pity."

Looking past his shoulder, she sighed. "I should have reported him to the police. I should have reported all of them. Defending myself?" She sighed. "It was a start."

"Cathy will press charges. His absence will create a power vacuum."

She linked their fingers. "I doubt it will last for long. Just get me out of here."

As soon as he pulled her away from his mess, he'd give her time to pick out the dress she wanted to wear and to plan the wedding of her dreams. If she wanted runners and roses, he'd make it happen. If she wanted cheap Chianti and food-truck tacos, they were hers. Right now, he needed space to protect her, and she needed freedom.

Tugging her toward the water, he explained how he'd arrived on the island. "I need you to blend into the crowd on the boat. The minute we step from cover, we're vulnerable. Don't let go of me."

"I won't," she said.

"Good." He wove through the lush landscaping, stopped at the estate's fence and pulled free.

"Dante, you said don't let go."

Cupping his hands, he nodded. "Step up. I'm right behind you."

Placing her foot in his hand, she pushed up, gripped the fence's edge, and lifted herself over the barrier.

"Beautiful." He would never forget the sight of her graceful ass vaulting over the fence. Grabbing a tree branch, he wedged it between two rocks, pushed up and joined her on the other side.

She held out her hand.

He took it.

A rocky bulkhead separated the island's estates from the lapping waves. Shading her eyes, she scanned the expanse of water. "Now what? Do we call the Coast Guard? I really don't know how to live in the real world."

"I know." Pulling out his phone, he called the little scamp who'd charged him a gold watch and a thousand dollars cash for a ten-minute boat ride. "We're headed your way. If you want your cash, you'd better be there."

"Haven't budged," the kid said.

Undoubtedly, a few security systems would catch their flight, but if anyone asked, the fundraising party had gotten way out of hand. He looked toward Gisella. The breeze whipped her long black hair over her face, but she'd never looked more beautiful. "So, should we look for a house out here?"

She laughed.

"You prefer inland?"

"I prefer you." She smiled.

He led her around the property corner and gestured toward the rusty, listing supply boat that charioted him to the island. "Your ride awaits."

The captain waved and pointed to his wrist.

He tried not to admire the flash of gold.

She tilted her head and considered the vessel. "Maybe we can call a water taxi. You said we're not poor."

Laughing, he pulled her hand to his lips. "With you at my side, I feel like a billionaire."

"I'm not sure that's a compliment." She returned the captain's gesture and smiled like she and Dante had spent the last hour discussing the weather. "Rich assholes are all a little unhinged."

He handed her up to the boat deck. "Does that include Alessio?"

She paused. "I don't know. Does it?"

"He's brutal, but he's effective." He swallowed. "So am I."

Cupping his cheek, she pulled her hand along his jaw and felt the mix of strength and softness she needed. "But I know you." Before he could react, she stepped over the siderail. "What if the boat sinks?"

Settling on a crate, he pulled her to his side and draped his arm around her shoulders. "We'll keep our heads above water, ride out the waves and make it to shore." Pulling her close, he closed his eyes and inhaled. "You know I've got you."

She smiled against his chest. "I know."

Chapter Twenty-Two

On the mainland, Dante held open the door to the sports car.

Taking the passenger seat, she bounced her heel, remembered Antonio's tic and stopped. "So, it's almost one."

"We'll reschedule the wedding." He put the car in reverse. "It's fine."

She gripped his thigh. "No, I want to get married...*now!*" The last word slipped out like a command, and she felt her cheeks warm. "I mean, where is everyone?"

"At the dock."

"Take me to the dock," she said.

Turning his head, he made eye contact. "Are you sure? I asked you to marry me, and you ran away."

"Hardly!"

He grinned. "At this point, I think I've asked you three or four times. How many times will it take?"

She wet her lips. "I guess you'll have to keep asking." He thought their marriage would be a business decision, but she wouldn't let that legacy haunt the relationship. No matter what kind of shit she stirred up, he had her back, and his steadiness gave her the freedom to soar. "Ask again."

"Gisella, will you marry me?"

He'd petitioned a judge to waive waiting period for a marriage license it, and she refused to make him wait a minute longer. "Of course."

Laughing, he put on his turn signal, switched lanes and roared up the coast.

Beneath a shaded pavilion, rows of chairs and white blooms signaled a wedding beside the dock. Ursula, Tia and the aunts held court over Miami Ballet Company dancers and staff. Dante's friends stood in a line like bouncers turned groomsmen. Pietro kept his back to the bay, and Linda held a white bouquet.

Unclasping the chain around her neck, she retrieved the wedding bands. "I'm not the kind of woman who takes off her ring and leaves it on her nightstand."

"Good." He held open his palm. "I hope you always take pleasure in wearing it."

"Is that a promise?"

He claimed a kiss, climbed out of the car, and opened the door.

"Such a gentleman."

"Hardly. You should know better."

"I do." Wiggling out of his jacket, she handed it back and knew she looked a fright, but she didn't care. Head high, she made eye contact with the assembled guests and accepted the bouquet from Linda.

"You look lovely."

"Liar." She swept her hair over one shoulder. "But thank you."

Linda laughed.

Martin turned on a CD player, and soft instrumental music fought the gull cries and rumbling traffic.

The air smelled of low tide, she had a gash on one knee and her mother's veil lay dormant in the attic, but she would never forget this day. For so much of her life, she balanced the things she wanted, needed and expected. Her ballet duffle, leather purse, and boutique purchases defined her life, but she came to this marriage with nothing but her strength.

And fifteen million dollars. She had no doubt Dante would extract it from *Papà*, but easy come, easy go. It passed through her hands like fine sand, and she refused to mourn it. With Dante, she would make a new life and hold onto it.

He offered her his arm.

She took it and walked with him up the small aisle. He told her suffering made him stronger, but it made her impatient. "Keep it short and sweet, Pietro."

Pietro nodded. "Dearly beloved..."

She raised an eyebrow.

"Only kidding," he said.

Ten minutes later, she wore Dante's ring and his kiss.

Ursula popped a champagne bottle and handed it to her.

Sipping from the bottle, she raised it high.

Martin ran up the aisle waving his hands. "That was for the boat!"

"What boat?"

Dante turned her and pointed her toward a sleek mahogany speedboat drifting on a line. "That one."

The vessel looked like the epitome of craftsmanship and engineering. A windshield defined the front of the cockpit, polished gauges lined the dash, and a glossy steeling wheel beckoned for a light touch. Below the waterline, mica-flecked navy paint reflected the bay's sparkle. Leather seats promised a comfortable ride, but she wasn't about to set foot on the deck. "Umm."

"Let's take it for a spin," he said.

"But it's so small."

Ursula cackled.

Ignoring her sister, Gisella leaned close to her husband. "I don't like the water."

"You don't have to get in the water." He lifted her hand, pressed a kiss to her knuckles, and pulled her into motion. "Trust me?"

"Dante…"

Releasing her, he lowered himself to the deck and raised his arms.

The speedboat shifted on a passing wake, but he looked steady. What harm could a few pictures cause? If he'd gone out of his way to procure the wedding gift, humoring him was the least she could do. Sitting on the edge of the seawall, she gingerly lowered her legs over the edge.

Gripping her waist, he lifted her and held her steady until she balanced. From the cockpit, the boat looked larger and steadier than she'd guessed.

She ran her hands over the sleek mahogany. *Papà* imported Cocobolo heartwood and exposed it to the elements. Someone had hand-selected this boat's dark wood for grain and color. They'd molded and shaped it into the hull's sleek lines. They cared. She exhaled. "Just a test drive."

He pressed the keys into her hand. "Why don't you keep it in the marina?"

She recoiled and dropped the keys. "I can't drive a boat! I don't even know how to drive a car."

Laughing, he scooped up the keys and started the engine. "I may have one hobby I forgot to mention. I'll teach you."

She shook her head and wondered if she could clamber back onto the dock. Looking over her shoulder, she caught Ursula's gaze and tossed her sister the bouquet.

Ursula frowned and let it fall into the water.

She rubbed her temples.

Before she could shout an admonishment, Dante pulled her in front of him, wrapped his arms around her and pressed a kiss to her back. "Trust me."

Pulling away from the dock, he wrapped a hand around her waist and hummed an old love song. "Do you want a life jacket?"

"Of course I want a life jacket!"

He laughed.

The engine's idle putter soothed her. Relaxing, she wiggled in his lap and enjoyed the soft breeze.

He reached behind the captain's seat and handed her a life jacket.

She appreciated the gesture and scrambled into the passenger seat to tighten it. Outside his frame, she missed the connection of feeling his chest, but she knew she could reclaim her spot.

He donned one as well.

His size dwarfed her, but she'd learned to appreciate his easy confidence and his leather loafers. At some point in the last few days, he'd stopped wearing socks, but the life jacket looked like concession. She would bet her last dollar he swam like a fish. "Does the boat have a name?"

"You name her." Clear of the buoy, he opened the throttle, and the boat roared to life.

"Dante!"

He grinned.

The wind slicked back his sun-streaked, wavy blond hair. On the open water, he looked thrilled to be in control, and he handled the craft with experienced ease. Instead of chastising him for keeping his hobby a secret, she reveled in it.

Cutting through the water, the boat picked up speed and left Miami behind them.

She could spend the rest of the afternoon soaking up the sun. She tucked her feet beneath her and watched the water ripple in the sunlight. He passed Virginia Key and rounded Crandon Park. Beyond the land, the Atlantic beckoned, but he sped south toward Cape Florida lighthouse. The Ritz-Carlton gleamed the island, but she wouldn't trade her seat for the world. "How far are we going?"

"Not too much farther!" He cut the engine and let the boat slow.

Shaking her head, she pulled off her life jacket and tossed it into the rear seats. "We should have brought the champagne."

"I had something else in mind." Standing, he dropped his life jacket and offered her his hand. "Let's swim."

She shook her head and wrapped her arms around her knees. "Oh, no, Dante, I don't swim."

He stripped off his shirt. "You're afraid of the water."

She swallowed. "My mother drowned."

"I know. I won't let you drown, Gisella."

Under the cover of darkness, she'd memorized the planes of his chest, but in the light, she savored the view. If she could abandon her fears of booze-soaked ambivalence and turning a blind eye, he could expand her worldview and let the salty waters wash away her sweat and her fears. "I believe you."

Stepping out of his slacks, he dropped them, tied a line around a rear cleat, and tossed the line in the water. A moment later, he dove in headfirst.

She hoped the water was cold enough to shrink his balls and compel him to climb back onto the boat, but the minute he emerged, she grinned. He treaded water like a champion. Worst case scenario, she could clamber back to the boat and hold on for dear life.

Grinning, she slipped off her clothes, dangled her feet over the edge and eased into his upraised arms. The cool water buoyed her, but his arms held her fast. She wrapped her arms around his neck and wondered if she could follow with her legs. If the handsome idiot wanted to swim in open water, he better be prepared to do the work.

"Not so bad, is it?"

She looked over her shoulder at the gleaming speedboat. "Can I keep the rope?"

He laughed and kissed her.

Holding onto his slippery skin, she abandoned her fears and savored his touch. This morning, she'd banked her frustration, but Antonio had pushed her too far. When maternal outrage had disrupted the billionaire's party, her pampered playboy brother cried, but she and Dante had come through the ordeal.

As she sank into his embrace, the kiss stole her breath. Each taste, test and scrape made her clamor for more. Beneath her hands, his skin radiated heat, and his strength kept them afloat. She wrapped her legs around his waist.

Drawing back, he made eye contact. "You're sure you're comfortable?"

"Every time I kiss you, I think it's the best kiss I've ever experienced. I wonder where you learned to kiss like a demon, then I don't want to know." She rubbed her cheek against him and bit his earlobe. Surrounded by water, she felt like the only woman in the world. "I could kiss you for hours, steal away in dark shadows and still want more. Every time we've been together, you've left me."

"I won't leave you again," he said.

"I know. You always come back, and each time, I want you more." She pulled back and met his gaze. "I can take it."

He drew a deep breath, cupped her ass and shifted her closer.

His arousal pressed against her folds, and she struggled not to take what she craved. "You're more than a convenience."

He shuddered. "Thank God."

"How many times do I have to tell you I love you?"

"Once will never be enough." Holding his palm against her back, he seemingly poured his passion into a kiss.

Melting beneath his touch, she tried to savor each sensation. The water lapped her breasts, his skin slid along her curves and his strength kept them afloat.

He slipped his hands under her thighs, gripped her smooth skin and shook his hair from his eyes. "I will always be there for you, but what I feel for you borders on desperation. Do you want a marriage of convenience or do you want me to love you?" he asked. "Love can hurt."

She pressed her hips against him. "I don't care if it hurts. Love me. Let me love you."

Pulling his hand along her thigh, he shifted her weight and stroked her clit. "And this? Do you want me here?"

Her breath caught. "Your priorities…"

"Are excellent."

She moved her hips and strained toward his heat. "In the beginning, I thought you were indifferent."

"You were wrong." He kissed her slowly, dragged his mouth down her neck and slipped his cock inside her heat. "Once I tasted you, I knew I would never let you go. The minute we came together, you were mine."

"Yes." Rocking against him, she stored away this memory like a treasured heirloom. After twenty-odd years of toxic masculinity and blind optimism, she'd faced reality, escaped her past and claimed a future.

He changed the angle.

"Oh." Pleasure built in her core, but she struggled to empty her mind and enjoy riding him. "Just so you know, you always deserved love…especially mine."

Closing his eyes, he grunted.

Worried that she exhausted him, she pulled back.

"No!" Squeezing her ass hard enough to leave bruises, he pumped into her and found his release. "Fuck!"

Laughing, she savored his pleasure, held onto his shoulders and uncoiled her legs from his waist. The sweet, slippery water had its merits, but she needed more than a sun-splashed dip before she could find her pleasure in its embrace. Given his promise, she would have ample chances.

He pulled her toward the boat, lifted her to the deck and pushed himself up next to her. "You destroy my self-control."

Laughing, she stretched out naked on the polished, sun-warmed mahogany. The breeze raised goosebumps on her skin, and the sun soaked into her bones. Turning her head, she admired her husband. He looked like a god. "When we get our own place, let's get a view of the water. I want to remember how it felt to be out here with you."

He trailed his hand along her sternum, dipped his mouth to her breast and rolled her clit between her fingers. "I'll make sure it's a good memory."

Savoring his touch, she believed he would.

Want to see more from this author? Here's a taster for you to enjoy!

The Devil in the Deep South
Amy Craig

Excerpt

"O beautiful for spacious skies…" Taylor Lenore sang along with the first-grade class occupying her bookstore. Rows of eager children filled the community space. Their seersucker shorts, ruffled cuffs and monogrammed collars reminded her of her idyllic childhood, and she loved Ronan's tiniest performers as much as she loved books.

The pudgy kid in the front row stuck his finger up his nose.

She stumbled over a verse but continued singing. Watching the kid made her nose itch, but she kept her hand pressed against her side, wrinkled away the sensation and exaggerated her participation. *"From sea to shining sea!"*

The kid sneezed and sent a green glob flying across the open space. The emission landed in front of the audience of grinning parents, doting grandparents and special guests.

Clapping, she rushed forward and placed her shoe over the snot. "Fabulous! Aren't they just the sweetest?"

The audience lowered their phones, clapped and nodded.

The children shuffled on the risers.

She scanned the crowded store, but everyone looked happy so she exhaled. After her engagement to Josh had fallen apart, returning to Ronan felt like a smart move, but she'd struggled to envision her future. Her mother Nancy wanted to coddle grandbabies and her father Jack wanted to protect her. She wanted to go to bed each night knowing she made a difference in her tiny corner of the world. Maybe she should let the kid wipe up his own snot. She glanced at her shoe and smiled. *We all have room to grow.*

Looking toward the pastry case, she sought out Plucky's encouragement. Her friend wore her shiny black hair cut in a chin-length bob. Long bangs swept over one eye like a brush of feathers tinged with blue. *I liked the pink tips better, but she never could settle.* Plucky's response to the performance would tell her whether the bookstore had displayed Ronan's germ-caked darlings to their full advantage.

Plucky grimaced.

They tried. Taylor swallowed and raised her eyebrows.

Plucky mimed gagging herself.

She slashed her hand across her throat. *I get the point. I tried to do a good thing!*

With a wink, Plucky turned back to the pastry case.

Clapping her hands together, Taylor turned back to the parents who were gathering their things. She inclined her hands toward the first-grade teacher's black curls. "I just want to say that Mrs. Jenkins did an amazing job teaching the kids. I never knew that song had so many verses." Avoiding her mother's gaze, she extended her hands toward the children. "Y'all are so impressive!"

Her mother, the elementary school librarian, stood near the nonfiction section. Plastic reading glasses hung from her neck, and a soft purple cardigan accented her bright-blue eyes. Risking a glance, Taylor saw her raise her chin. *She caught that fib about the song all right. I sang every verse at my first pageant.* Brushing her bangs out of her eyes, she ignored Nancy's reproach and focused on the stars of this show. "Kids, thank you so much for coming to our little bookstore and brightening our day."

Mrs. Jenkins squeezed the shoulders of two first-graders. "Thank you for having us. The auditorium intimidates some of our special friends, but everyone loves Ronan Reads."

She clasped her hand against her chest. If the elementary school wanted to utilize her space for a spring performance, who was she to turn away the free publicity? "Why, thank you!" She let the performance's spirit wash over her and exhaled. Nerves kept her on edge, but the little darlings charmed her. "Plucky has cupcakes for the kids and coffee for the adults. Everyone, please stay and visit."

The students leaned toward the sweets.

Mrs. Jenkins smiled. "Go, you little hellions! You earned it."

The orderly rows dissolved into chaos. Elbows flew, and several children stepped on their classmates' toes.

Holding the tray of cupcakes like a shield, Plucky skewed her mouth and turned her head to the side.

"Me first!" the pudgy kid yelled.

His suspender-strapped belly strained his shirt buttons, but he made his way across the room with admirable speed. A muscled little bruiser overtook him, snatched the first cupcake and shoved the icing into his mouth. Taylor covered a laugh.

"That one was mine!"

"Hog!"

The children crowded around Plucky.

"Charles Brannon hit me!" a girl cried.

"Did not!"

"C.B., mind your manners." Mrs. Jenkins's sing-song voice cut through the noise.

Charles Brannon mumbled an apology, but he gave his classmate side-eye.

Taylor sympathized with the girl. The first time she'd called that kid 'Charles', he'd shaken his head and turned his brown doe-eyes to his mother. "It's okay, Mama. She doesn't know me yet." The mixture of innocence and sincerity charmed Taylor, but she wondered if the little tyke would throw her under the bus for a slice of cake. Today's kids were so much worldlier than the kids from her dirt-tinged, polyester youth. *Good thing I didn't call the little tyke 'Charlie'.* Trusting Plucky to handle the first graders, she turned from the fray and keyed up the music.

Housed on the main floor of an old, three-story brick building, Ronan Reads offered everything from thrillers to obscure local publications. Online sales kept the balance sheet healthy, and a casual space in the middle of the store let customers read, nibble cookies or linger over free Wi-Fi.

She envisioned the bookstore as a gathering place and a hotspot for book releases. After a year of business, her dream felt naïve, and she struggled to keep the store afloat in the digital age. Sparrow County's population topped sixty thousand, but only a few thousand people lived within the city's limits, and even fewer of them cared for books. Bankers and health-care workers toiled away in the Historic District, but Thirsty Thursday remained an Atlanta gimmick. Given free time, Ronan's residents spent their hours praying, gossiping or binging television shows. Taylor could never pin down the right order.

Nancy walked up to her side. "How many verses does that song have, Taylor Lenore?"

She swallowed and met her mother's gaze. "Three?"

Nancy raised an eyebrow.

"Four?"

Nancy nodded.

She focused on the children's shrieks and laughter. Despite Nancy's public-facing job, she was an educator and an introvert who hid behind picture books and manners. Once strangers broke through her prim exterior, they found a loyal woman who loved her job. Taylor loved her, too, but she never had the luxury of distance. "I wanted to flatter the kids for a job well done."

"Do they look like they need your flattery?"

She considered the kids wreaking havoc in her store. Two boys finger-painted chocolate icing on the floor and a pair of girls chased each other with napkins. Their parents clustered around the coffee urn and exchanged pleasantries over cream and sugar. *They might not need my flattery, but I'm going to need a few hours to put the store back together.* "No, they're doing just fine without me."

"Those who flatter their neighbors are spreading nets for their feet," Nancy said, quoting the Bible.

After two-and-a-half decades of experience with Nancy's wisdom, Taylor wisely nodded. *I love Jesus, but the Bible doesn't get into detail about running a bookstore, balancing the bottom line and maintaining the goodwill of the online community.*

Nancy pushed her glasses up her nose and picked up a new release. She flipped through the first few pages. "You did good hosting the concert, but you don't need sweet talk to turn a profit."

Setting her phone on the table, she let a playlist direct the tracks. "Mama, I'm running a business."

Nancy looked up from the book. "Goodwill will come back to you in spades."

She frowned. "I don't recognize that verse."

"I made it up."

Exhaling, she met her mother's gaze. "Mama, please..."

"Is this book any good?" Nancy asked.

She considered the question. *Llama Serenade* was the story of a couple who abandoned their one-bedroom apartment in New York City for seventy-five acres in Flagstaff, Arizona. In poetic, reverent detail, Bunny and Brunswick Kissimmee explored their relationship with the llamas they raised, the land they owned and the clothing-optional hot tub parties they hosted in the desert. "I'm not sure 'new-age mecca' is quite your style."

"People have alienated themselves from the animals that feed them."

Her mother raised chickens but not the kind kids cuddled for backyard photo opportunities. "True."

Nancy turned to the back cover. "Whew. Twenty-four dollars. The authors think highly of themselves."

"Publishers set the price," Taylor said. "You know you get a twenty-percent discount."

"You're a good girl." Nancy tucked the book under her arm and walked toward the coffee urn.

Am I? She considered her mother's admonishment about flattery. Instead of waking to a cartoon alarm clock, she'd spent her first eighteen years opening her eyes to Nancy's steady inspiration. After she moved out for college, Nancy's inspiring messages came by text, but she often liked their comforting support, responded with an emoji and went about her day. *Now that I'm back, a little less maternal influence would be nice.* Remembering her bookstore audience, she shook off her personal issues. "Oh, Mama?"

Nancy turned.

Lifting her shoe, she revealed the green mess. "Would you do me a favor and get the sanitizing spray from the cleaning closet?"

Nancy stared at the glob and wrinkled her nose. "What is that?"

"Snot."

"Oh, my," Nancy said.

"Aren't children precious?"

Nancy smiled. "You were."

Her heart and her stance softened. "Thanks, Mama."

The door opened, and Ronan's city manager stepped into the bookshop. Jonathan O'Connor meant well and smelled pleasantly of cigar smoke, but he rarely ironed his shirts. A local dry cleaner offered him discounted services, but he'd shrugged off the offer. "If I wanted pressed shirts, I would have married a woman who liked to iron." Instead, he'd married a woman who spent most of her time getting her nails done, and they both seemed happy with their arrangement.

He was a decent enough manager for the city, but Ronan's citizens expected him to submit budgets, shake hands and cut ribbons. If they needed someone at the bargaining table, they redirected their figurehead and turned to their lawyers and the board of commissioners.

"Peaches!" Striding across the room, he stopped short and looked at the icing-smeared chaos running rampant through her bookstore. "What on earth is going on today?"

"School performance." The old nickname irked her, but her fourth-grade reign as Little Miss Georgia Peach Queen had delighted the town. "Did we forget to invite you?"

He frowned and patted his empty pocket. "No, no… It's just we have a special visitor."

"We?" she asked.

"Ronan."

"Ahh-h." In her experience, silence yielded answers.

"Christopher Durand is here." O'Connor checked his pants pockets. "All the way down from Atlanta."

She smiled. "I'm sorry, but who is Christopher Durand?"

"Owns Ocelot." Smacking his lips, O'Connor rolled his tongue across his teeth and patted his pants. "Heavy machinery and big bucks."

If he keeps digging in his pockets, I'll have to turn my back. "Sir, can I get you something?"

He looked up. "I ran out of nicotine gum. Do you sell that stuff?"

"Oh." Laughter slipped past her lips. Amid the screaming kids and chattering parents, the city manager's dependency reminded her why Ronan's residents banded together. When a family hit hard times, neighbors and church members stepped in to help. If O'Connor wanted to quit his cigar habit, she would help. "Is that all? I'm sure the pharmacy's open."

He shook his head and exhaled. "No time. Durand's on his way here from the chambers."

She frowned. "Why?"

"Dog and pony show touting Ronan's charm. He wants to build a new factory, and Ronan's in the running."

A little boy tugged O'Connor's pants. "Hiya, Mr. Manager."

He patted the boy's back. "Hiya, Smith. Where's your mama?"

"At work. My mamaw's here."

Making a face, O'Connor nodded and sent the boy back into the fray. "Hell of a day to have the kids over for snacks."

She crossed her arms. "Nobody told me the great Christopher Durand wanted to tour my bookstore. He doesn't like kids?"

"The kids aren't the problem." O'Connor lowered his voice and leaned in. "He's supposed to be incognito."

The rich, lingering cigar smoke used to intrigue her, but now she worried about his health. The man was active with the Kiwanis Club, the Salvation Army, the Historical Society and Uncle Brent's church, but his common sense went the way of his ironing board. "So, take him somewhere else for coffee and local-interest books."

O'Connor glanced at his watch and shook his head. "No time."

The door opened, and three adults stepped into the bookstore. She recognized the department directors in their power suits and high heels, but the man in jeans looked as inconspicuous as a cougar on a playground. A hat obscured most of Christopher Durand's face, but his bronzed cheeks and strong jawline cut a nomadic cowboy's striking, cinematic profile. Trying not to be rude, she looked away from him but risked a second glance. His weathered skin had bypassed Hollywood's warm glow, but if the sun's heat had hardened it to armor, he wore the look well.

Scanning the room, Durand looked at her.

She returned his stare, but his hat's shadow disguised his eyes' color. *Are they blue?* She watched his face for signs of emotion. Not a tic. "No time, indeed."

The girls chasing each other with napkins rounded a bookshelf and collided with Durand's legs.

Little Cecilia Williamson looked up, locked eyes with the man and screamed.

Every person in the bookstore turned and stared.

Durand frowned but stood resolute.

If the man wanted to go incognito, he picked a fine day to do it. Abandoning the slimy mess beneath her foot, Taylor strode up to the trio of adults, pulled the precocious girl against her legs and crossed her arms over the child's vibrating chest. "That's enough, Cece."

The girl looked up and quieted.

She smiled at Durand. "Welcome to Ronan Reads."

He removed his hat, placed it on the counter and inclined his head.

His eyes were as gray as a roiling thundercloud.

"Quite the welcoming committee," he said.

"Well"—she waved her hand toward the crowd— "we weren't expecting tourists."

"I'm not a tourist."

She tilted her head. "Who are you?"

"Peaches, this is Christopher"—the department director swallowed—"and we told him your store stocks local-interest books."

She kept her gaze locked on Durand. "Is that so?"

Cece's mother stepped up and reached for her daughter.

Taylor released the first grader and patted her shoulder, but she felt Durand's condemnation and refused to fold beneath his scrutiny. "Well, we aim to please, Mister…" She raised her eyebrows.

"Durand," he said.

At least he doesn't lie. "What types of books interest you, Mr. Durand?"

He rubbed his thumb along his lip. "I hardly know. Show me what you have."

His quiet concentration turned the request into a command. *Who doesn't know what type of books they like?* She opened her mouth to sass him, but the intensity of his stare sent a chill racing up her arms. Glancing over her shoulder, she considered her audience. Half of the first graders were barefoot, short one shoe or trailing laces. Their parents tilted their heads, offered slight smiles or whispered to their neighbors. Standing tall, she plotted a course through the crowd. "When in Ronan."

He cleared his throat. "I believe the phrase is 'When in Rome'."

"Hmm-m." She managed a smile. "I'll remember that fact."

Falling into step, he followed her through the crowd.

She strode past O'Connor. "You owe me."

The city manager nodded. "You're the best, Peaches."

Smiling, she found her gait, skirted the tables in the center of the store and led Durand to the local-interest books.

"Are you?" he asked.

She missed a step. "Excuse me?"

"Are you the best?"

Straightening her shoulders, she paused. "Ronan Reads is a community resource. We offer a variety of new and used titles, educator discounts, community events, bulk orders and book trades."

"I asked about you," he said.

Two children raced down the aisle.

Immune to her tension, the tumble-bumble first graders turned the corner and rolled through the store.

She wished she could slip away as easily, but she felt every inch of the stakes. Catching her reflection in the window, she saw the stiff-shouldered silhouette of a confident woman. *Or one who took too many dance classes and tried to live up to her parents' expectations.* Looking up, she met Christopher's gaze. His gray eyes intrigued her, but the sheen of steel-kissed flint looked too intense for life in Ronan. "I try my best."

He inclined his head.

If I had warning, I could have staged this tour better. She picked up a large-format book. "Ronan looks sleepy, but the city has a vibrant past and a promising future. General Dick gave one of the most important pre-war Secession speeches from Ronan's courthouse steps, and Georgia's largest Confederate training camp occupied the site of the new high school."

"You condone slavery?"

She bristled. "No! But the historic city reflected the state of the nation." She frowned. "The state of the South. One of the first paved sections of the Dixie Highway passed through Ronan, and our farmers pioneered advances in modern Southern agriculture."

"When was this? 1856?"

She swallowed. "1888."

He yawned and covered his mouth. "How modern."

She moved deeper into the shelves and reached for another book. "Textiles."

"Spare me." He scanned the crowd milling in the center of the store.

Devoid of front-row tickets, the parents and special guests had resumed their chatter.

Gripping the books against her chest, she tilted her head. "Why are you here?"

He shrugged. "The tour's part of the show. Local representatives lead me around town and show me the best and the brightest stars the town offers." He cleared his throat and looked at her. "Usually, they pick an up-and-coming lawyer with corporate ambitions."

She shelved the books. Freed from curt responses and a keen audience, his voice rippled like windswept grass. Amid her treasured books, their hushed conversation felt far too intimate. His rolled r's spoke of intense meetings held beneath a midday sun, but his cultured drawl left room for the horizon. Judging by his tailored shirt, speed and efficiency meant more to him than her idealistic notions. "Lucky you."

"Indeed." Reaching across her, he pulled both volumes from the shelves.

His woodsy aftershave and masculine warmth smelled better than the fresh-cut paper.

"I'll take these. Ring me up, please."

The please sounded like a caress. Needing space, she slid past him.

"Ronan intrigues me."

Turning, she tilted her head. "Why?"

He shifted the books to one hand, reached toward her and skimmed her upper arm.

"What are you doing?" She kept her voice to a whisper.

Holding up one finger, he smiled and held up his finger. "You're wearing chocolate."

Her cheeks warmed. "Thanks."

Pulling a handkerchief from his back pocket, he cleaned up the mess.

At least he didn't lick off the icing. Did I want *him to lick off the icing?* She swallowed. "Do you always carry a handkerchief?"

Folding the soiled cloth, he slipped it into his back pocket. "Are you always the center of attention?"

"No." Clearing her throat, she wondered what had possessed O'Connor to bring this man into her bookstore. *The devil himself would have been easier to ignore.* "You picked a special day to visit. Despite the chaos" — she glanced at two boys tousling on the story-time rug — "Ronan is a lovely town."

"I don't need lovely."

The admission stopped her from fleeing into the crowd. "What do you need?"

"Hard workers, reliable transportation and progressive tax policies."

She swallowed. "I can vouch for two out of the three."

He raised an eyebrow. "Can you?"

"The state empowered Ronan to levy property taxes on real and personal properties within its boundaries." She recalled a recent news article. "The state also empowered the city to extend its corporate limits by annexation. I promise you, when the roads get bad, the borders shift."

"Hmm-m." He glanced at O'Connor. "How often does that happen?"

She smiled. "Whenever the governing board deems it appropriate."

"And how would you run the town?"

The question caught her off guard. Scrambling for an answer, she wondered how long O'Connor would stay in his position. *Ronan's commissioners make that decision. If the town thought I was prepared and capable of filling the role, would I take on that challenge?* She shifted her weight. "Tell me, Mr. Durand, will your factory be inside or outside the city limits?"

"The factory doesn't exist yet, Peaches."

"It's Taylor."

He rubbed his lip. "And if I asked you to dinner, who would join me? Taylor, the savvy businesswoman, or Peaches, the town darling?"

She raised her chin. "Taylor."

"Give me your number, Taylor."

"No."

He frowned.

"I don't date overgrown boys who drive lifted, diesel-guzzling trucks."

He laughed. "The lady does me wrong."

She frowned.

He dipped his head. "I drive an electric truck."

Suppressing a smile, she scanned him from head to toe and tried not to show her approval. "I've heard the towing's a little" — she chewed her lip — "lackluster."

Laughing, he scanned the store but returned to her gaze. "I promise you that my truck hauls ass and tows like a fiend."

Heat bloomed in her core, but she raised her chin and scrambled to avoid a diplomatic disaster. "I prefer not to mix business with pleasure."

"But you enjoy pleasure?"

Her stomach flipped. "I'm sure I don't know what you mean."

He scratched his lip.

The wrinkles near his eyes deepened into laugh lines. No wonder the Atlanta newspapers published his charismatic smiles.

"No, I'm sure you don't," he said.

"You're welcome to follow Ronan Reads on social media." She brushed her hair out of her face. "Let us know what you think of the books."

Giving her a curt nod, he turned and preceded her through the crowd.

Social media? How lame am I? She charged ahead, rounded the sales counter and smiled.

Placing his books next to his hat, he pulled out his wallet and examined the crowd.

He's probably guarding his back against first graders. She scanned the books' bar codes, slid them across the counter and tried to repair her failed diplomacy. "The books are on the house."

"No." He pushed his credit card toward her. "I don't accept handouts."

"Oh, don't worry." She winked. "I'll bill the city manager."

His laughter drew curious looks.

"Goodbye, Taylor," he said.

She smiled. "Mr. Durand."

Shaking his head, he walked through the crowd, donned his hat and nodded to the department directors. "Thanks for the tour."

The stone-faced directors returned his nod.

O'Connor yawned, peeled himself away from his cronies and trailed the trio. Stopping in the doorway, he fixed his pants and walked into the sunlight.

Taylor exhaled.

Cutting through the crowd, Nancy came around the counter. "Who was that?"

Frowning, she tried to summarize the man. His weathered exterior and rigid command made sense for an executive who manufactured heavy machinery, but his laugh lines left her at odds. "He owns Ocelot."

Nancy arranged the pens in a cup. "What's Ocelot?"

She chewed her thumbnail, caught the uncouth habit and shrugged. "Chunks of metal that move dirt?"

"Oh," Nancy said. "*That* Ocelot."

Watching Christopher's silhouette cross the street, she shook her head and left herself a note to bill

O'Connor for the books. "That man doesn't belong in Ronan."

Nancy set aside the cup. "Who does?"

She surveyed the kids and their families. Some people wore dresses and pants from big box stores and some wore precious outfits from boutiques, but every child had a cupcake and a chance. In her small town, that chance mattered, and she refused to budge from her foundations. "I do."

Nancy patted her hand. "Of course you do."

Pulling free of her mother's tender touch, she found Plucky near the pastry case.

Plucky snapped her tongs.

Biting back a smile, Taylor reached for a roll of paper towels. "Give me a hand, Mama. I have a mess to clean up."

About the Author

Amy Craig lives in Baton Rouge, Louisiana USA with her family and a small menagerie of pets. She writes women's fiction and contemporary romances with intelligent and empathetic heroines. She can't always vouch for the men. She has worked as an engineer, project manager, and incompetent waitress. In her spare time, she plays tennis and expands her husband's honey-do list.

Amy loves to hear from readers. You can find her contact information, website details and author profile page at https://www.totallybound.com

Home of Erotic Romance

Sign up for our newsletter and find out about all our romance book releases, eBook sales and promotions, sneak peeks and FREE romance books!

www.ingramcontent.com/pod-product-compliance
Lightning Source LLC
Chambersburg PA
CBHW020219260626
47156CB00002B/450